Dedication

To Kathryn Marguerite Calder McNeill, 99 years young

Acknowledgements

Thank you to Jude Pittman and BWL Publishing Inc. for inviting me to write the Alberta story for the BWL Canadian Historical Mystery Series.

I appreciate the generous support of the Alberta Foundation for the Arts for my novel.

Many thanks to my astute editors: Nancy M. Bell, Erin Celovsky, and Rachel Small, and to my attentive and faithful manuscript readers: Will Arnold, Maryann Breukelman, Allan Coates, Shaun Hunter, and Marilyn Letts. Shaun's advice on Calgary's history and research sources, Marilyn's information about pharmaceuticals, and Dr. Pat Griffiths' knowledge of early nineteenth century medicine added accuracy and interest to my story. Any errors are mine.

I'm grateful to Gail Anderson-Dargatz for the idea to turn my short story "A Deadly

Flu" into a novel. Parts of *A Killer Whisky* were published in the short story anthology *Cold Canadian Crime* (Crime Writers of Canada, editor Taija Morgan, May 2022).

Lastly, my heartfelt thanks and love to Will, Dan, Matt, Anne, and Vivienne. You bring joy to this writing life.

A Killer Whisky
Canadian Historical Mysteries - Alberta
Susan Calder

Print ISBNs
Amazon print 9780228631989
Ingram Spark 9780228631996
Barnes & Noble 9780228632009
BWL Print 9780228632016

Copyright 2024 by Susan Calder
Editor Nancy M Bell
Cover art by Michelle Lee

Table of Contents

Chapter One
October 1918

Katharine's fingers slid over the piano keys. Her daughter strummed a toy banjo, and her son banged pots and pans. They drowned out her brother, John, on the alto saxophone. "Alexander's Ragtime Band" blared through the living room. Katharine turned to the next page of her sheet music. She struck a wrong note then a sour chord. The song stumbled to a merciful end.

She swivelled the piano stool to face John. "I haven't played that since before the war." She remembered the merry evening in this room with her husband and their friends. By the following month, all the men who had been there had enlisted. One had since died in the mud of Passchendaele.

"With a little practice, we'll be playing the dance halls," John said.

"Really, Uncle John?" Lillian's eyes lit up.

"Absolutely." John raised his saxophone. "What's our next tune?"

"Bedtime for Henry and Lillian," Katharine said.

"Why?" Henry bolted up from the floor. "We don't have school tomorrow."

"Uncle John will teach you."

John smirked at Henry. "I'm sharpening my ruler for when you misbehave."

Henry jumped onto the davenport and clapped his wooden spoon "drumsticks."

"You go change," Katharine told him. "Lillian and I will clean up."

He pointed the spoons at his sister. "There's a Hun. Pow."

"I'm not a Hun," Lillian said. "I'm an Ally."

"A dirty Hun. Pow, pow."

"An Ally." Lillian held her banjo to her chest in defence. "Tell him, Mama."

"We're all Allies," Katharine said. "Canadians."

"Huns. Pow, pow." Henry aimed a spoon at them both.

Lillian squealed and ducked between the davenport and piano.

"Pow."

"Stop it, Henry," Katharine said, firming up her tone. "If you don't get into your nightshirt now, Lillian and I will walk in while you're getting dressed."

Henry's lips pursed, but he leaped from the davenport, tossed the spoons to the floor in annoyance, and skulked out of the living room. Last week, he'd declared he was too old to dress in front of females. John said this was normal for a boy of eight, although John had shared a bedroom with Katharine and their sister at that age and any modesty had been entirely his older sisters'.

John sat on the upholstered chair and rolled up his right pant leg to remove his artificial limb. Lillian carried the banjo past the rocker chair to the toy box, which her father had built before he left. She'd been two then and had no memory of Eddie. Katharine glanced at his portrait on the sideboard. A stiff service dress cap sat on his head above his boyish face. Four years of war had surely changed him, but his letters alluded to no more than battle scars. *What scars?* she'd written back, knowing his next letter wouldn't address her concern. That was Eddie, brushing off hardships and pity.

Katharine gathered the pots and wooden spoons and told Lillian to brush her teeth.

"I brushed them this morning," Lillian said.

"Yes, but it's good to develop the habit now so you'll keep your adult teeth like Uncle John and me."

John looked up from pulling off his lower leg. "Our mama was tougher than yours, Lilly-pet."

That was true. "We didn't dare talk back to her," Katharine said.

"She whipped us when we did," John added.

"Not whipped," Katharine said. "But I had my share of taps with her wooden spoon."

"Closer to whacks in my case."

"Most of them well-deserved." She smiled at her baby brother, now placing his prosthetic on the coffee table. Her heart ached at the sight of his leg that ended below the knee and the scar on his left cheek. She nudged Lillian into the hall and toward the bathroom.

Katharine supervised her daughter's teeth brushing then left her to use the toilet and went to the kitchen to rinse the pots and spoons. She set them on the counter to dry and met Henry coming out of the bedroom dressed in his nightshirt and cap. While he brushed his teeth, she helped Lillian into her cap and flannel nightgown. Katharine opened the bedroom window an inch to let in fresh air.

"Can I play with my friends tomorrow?" Lillian asked, even though Katharine had explained several times that they all had to stay home to protect one another from the Spanish flu. "You're going to work," Lillian said.

"Dr. Upton's patients need me." In truth they'd survive without his receptionist, but Katharine's family needed her salary.

Henry breezed into the room and pulled down his covers.

"Prayers," Katharine said.

Henry groaned. Lillian sank to her knees and clasped her hands on the bed she shared with Katharine. Henry knelt by his bed across the room, his back to his sister. Both mumbled the bedtime prayer that had been Eddie's childhood ritual.

Now I lay me down to sleep,
I pray the Lord my Soul to keep.
If I should die before I 'wake,
I pray the Lord my Soul to take.

Katharine had argued the prayer was morbid, but Eddie said he'd glossed over the words' meaning his whole childhood. Now, the prayer's message was too real.

Lillian's voice rang strong and clear as she continued with her prayer. "God bless Mama, Pa, Henry, Uncle John." She listed several friends and crawled up to the bed. "Can we read a story?"

Their musical evening had run later than planned, but the gaiety had given Katharine a glimmer of hope that their lives would return to normal soon. The Central Powers were collapsing and the German army was in retreat, although today's newspaper warned it could be weeks before Germany surrendered.

"We have time for two poems," Katharine said. She picked up their book of children's verses and noticed the tape had come loose on the binding. "You each choose one."

"'Who Killed Cock Robin,'" Henry said.

"'Turtle Soup,'" Lillian said.

Katharine sat on the bed beside Lillian, leaning against her for warmth. Chilly autumn air flowed through the window. The book almost opened on its own to Henry's favourite rhyme, the most violent one in the book. Katharine read aloud, "'Who killed Cock Robin?'"

"'I, said the Sparrow, with my bow and arrow,'" Henry and Lillian recited, his tone boastful, hers defensive. "'I killed Cock Robin.'"

The chant went on, with no relief for poor Cock Robin.

Katharine turned the pages to the gentler "Turtle Soup" and read, "'Beautiful soup, so rich and green, Waiting in a hot tureen!'" Perhaps not so gentle from the turtle's perspective.

She finished the poem, deflected the children's pleas for her to read more, and tucked them each in with a kiss goodnight. "You behave for Uncle John tomorrow."

"He won't teach us anything," Henry said.

Katharine suspected her son was right. She left the door ajar and took the book to the living room for mending. John sat on the armchair finishing his saxophone-cleaning with a loving polish of the brass body. During the summer, he'd joined a band that played at a nightclub once a week.

She set the book on the coffee table. "Shall I put a record on the Victrola?"

"Not for me tonight," he said. "I need to turn in early to be up in the morning. What time do you leave?"

"Ten to nine." She put off getting the mending materials from the sideboard and sat on the davenport to meet him eye level. "John, I want you to do your best to complete the children's lessons tomorrow. You can't spend the day on music and recess."

"They're the only fun subjects." He flashed a grin.

"We don't want them falling behind their classmates."

She didn't worry about Lillian, who had barely started school, but Henry's minimal interest in academics could easily be derailed with this halt to his education. Katharine had decided to take them out of school on the advice of her employer, Dr. Upton. He'd written to Dr. Mahood, Calgary's medical health officer, to urge the closure of all places of public gathering to curb the spread of the deadly influenza.

John rose to carry the saxophone to its case. He hopped across the room, holding on to furniture with his free hand. As much as possible, he avoided wearing the uncomfortable limb that would make his daily activities so much easier.

She went to the sideboard beneath the front window and filled a tray with book cloth, glue, tape, a knife, and a ruler. The doorbell rang. She glanced at the mantel clock. It was past eight-thirty.

A telegram?

A second, longer ring. Her heart thumping, Katharine hurried to the hall and opened the front door. Cool air rushed in. A man stood on the dimly lit porch.

"It's Vincent," her neighbour's boarder said. "He can't breathe. You have a telephone? He needs a doctor."

"I'll call right away." Katharine moved to the telephone nook.

John entered the hallway. "Clarence?"

"I have to get back to them." Clarence turned and ran down the porch stairs.

Katharine called the telephone exchange while John closed the door.

"Vincent?" John said. "When I saw him last night, he was fine. Normal."

An operator answered. Katharine placed the call to Dr. Upton and tapped her foot, waiting. Vincent had contracted tuberculosis in the war. His lungs were weakened, susceptible to—

Dr. Upton came on the line. Katharine quickly explained what had happened.

"I'm leaving now." He hung up.

"I'll go help." John hopped into the living room.

But Katharine could get there faster. She grabbed her coat from the hall closet and a gauze mask from a hook on the hall chair. *Couldn't breathe* could mean the flu.

Henry appeared at the end of the hallway. "What's all the noise?"

Katharine looked into the living room, where John sat on the chair struggling to put on his prosthesis.

"John, I'm going," she said. "You stay here and explain to Henry."

"The army trained me in first aid."

True, but Dr. Upton had taught her artificial respiration.

Katharine rushed outside to the cold and dark. She checked for motorcars, which rarely came down this street, and ran diagonally across to the bungalow behind the short iron fence, its gate open. Up the sidewalk to the porch. *Don't waste time ringing the bell.* Katharine put on her mask and entered Vincent and Marguerite DeLuca's house.

Clarence stood in the hallway. "He's gone."

"No," a woman cried from the room to his left.

Katharine brushed past Clarence and into the living room. Marguerite sat on the floor, Vincent, her husband, lying in her arms, both in shadows. The room's sole light came from fireplace embers and a kerosene lamp on a table between two armchairs.

Marguerite looked up. "Where is the doctor?"

"He's on his way." Katharine threw off her coat and squatted beside them.

Vincent's eyes were glazed, his face slack, his nose bloodied. *The flu.* She jerked back from his body. *But he might be alive.* She felt his wrist, detected no pulse. Pressed her ear to his chest. Nothing, except her own heart pounding in her ears.

"*Partez.* Go if you cannot help." Marguerite clutched her husband's head.

"Dr. Upton taught me a technique. It's a last attempt. I can't guarantee—"

"Do it." Marguerite's voice was shrill. "Do anything."

Katharine touched Vincent's shoulder then gently manoeuvred him off Marguerite's lap and onto the carpet, face down.

Marguerite knelt over his head as though in prayer. Dr. Upton had outlined the procedure to Katharine, but she hadn't practiced on a human being. She bent Vincent's arms and placed his hands under his chin, turned his head sideways, and checked his mouth for obstructions. The orderly procedure seemed to calm her down. In her peripheral view, she noticed Clarence edge closer.

On her knees, she angled toward Vincent, positioned her hands like a butterfly, and pressed her palms to his middle back. One, two, three. Pause.

"What are you doing?" Marguerite rasped.

Katharine continued the rhythmic compressions. Dr. Upton had said the Shafer method rarely revived a person whose heart had stopped, but it would keep the oxygen flowing to the brain until a doctor arrived with an oxygen cylinder.

"*Ça ne sert à rien.*"

No response from Vincent's body, but experts insisted the method could work for hours. Katharine pressed deeper into his back.

"Vous êtes en train de le tuer!"

A click and rustling from the house entrance.

"Where is he?" Dr. Upton burst into the living room carrying his medical bag and wearing a mask that steamed his spectacles.

Katharine started to stand, but Marguerite pushed her sideways and shouted something in French. Katharine banged into Clarence, who grabbed her arms.

"You waste my last minute with him." Marguerite sank to the floor.

Dr. Upton placed his cape and muskrat-fur hat on an armchair, crouched next to Vincent, and rolled him onto his back. Marguerite cradled her husband's head once more.

"I need more light," Dr. Upton said.

Clarence drew away from Katharine and turned on two electric lamps, which sat on décor tables in the front corners of the room with a card table between them. Vincent and Marguerite had moved in a year ago. Dr. Upton played card games with them on Saturday evenings and John visited here regularly for after dinner drinks, but Katharine hadn't grown close enough to the couple to be invited in. The room also contained two armchairs, two hardback chairs, a secretary desk, and a sideboard. There were no ornaments or pictures on the mantel or walls. She'd have expected a woman from France to decorate in a style more flamboyant than stark.

While Dr. Upton listened to Vincent's chest with his stethoscope, Katharine motioned Clarence into the hallway to give the doctor and Marguerite privacy. They stopped past a closed door, which probably led to the front bedroom. The house seemed to be the mirror image of Katharine's.

Clarence shook his head. "One minute he's drinking whisky, the next he's gasping for breath."

"Was it that quick?" Katharine whispered. Sounds carried through the walls of these newer homes.

His Adam's apple bobbed. Over six feet tall, Clarence was a gangly man. John had said he was twenty-eight, a couple of years younger than Katharine.

"Actually, fifteen or twenty minutes." Clarence kept his voice low. "Marguerite heard him from the kitchen and dashed in with a glass of water. When Vincent stood to reach for it, he coughed and fell forward to the floor. I jumped up but couldn't stop his crash."

"Was he hurt in the fall?"

"Who could tell from his gasps and wheezing?"

Marguerite's cries flowed into the hall. Her words sounded French, but Katharine didn't know the language.

"Marguerite loosened his clothing," Clarence said. "Tried to make him comfortable. She knows a little about urgent care from her work in a field hospital in France, albeit as a cook."

That was where she'd met Vincent, a patient recuperating from tuberculosis.

"She ordered me to get the smelling salts." Clarence spoke through the rising cries from the living room. "I didn't know where they were. She called me an idiot then ran to get them herself. They made Vincent stir, briefly. I caught a whiff." His nose wrinkled. "Vile odour. How do you women stand it?"

The salts sent oxygen to the brain, but less effectively than Dr. Upton's portable oxygen.

"Next she ordered me to your house," Clarence said. "You know the rest."

Marguerite's wail pierced the wall. Katharine went through the archway to the living room, Clarence behind her. Dr. Upton rose and approached them. He shook his head.

Marguerite sat on the floor, Vincent's head on her lap. She leaned forward, her dishevelled hair concealing her face.

"Let's give her these last moments alone with him." Dr. Upton coaxed them back to the hall and toward the rear of the house.

"You're both wearing masks," Clarence said, his eyes growing wide. "Is it the Spanish flu?"

Dr. Upton squinted up at him. "We must consider this."

Clarence grimaced. "If Vincent got it, odds are I've already caught it from him. Bloody hell. A damn mask won't help me now."

"It wouldn't hurt." Katharine turned from him to Dr. Upton. "Clarence told me Vincent's breathing attack came on relatively suddenly."

"He was normal at dinner," Clarence said. "No doubt he coughed a few times, but that's so usual I hardly notice. Would his history of consumption increase his chance of death from the flu?"

"It would," Dr. Upton said. "There was blood from his nose, a tell-tale sign of this flu. His face was flushed and hot to the touch."

Fever.

"His skin looked dark to me," Dr. Upton added.

Another sign. But the room had been dark at first. "Anyone would look dark in that lighting," Katharine said. And Vincent had an olive complexion.

Clarence nodded. "They scrimp on electricity."

"Nevertheless," Dr. Upton said. "Given the blood and sudden onset, we must suspect Spanish influenza. I will report it to the health department." He looked at Clarence. "You, sir, will stay home from work."

Clarence started. "They'll dock my pay. I have no fever or cough or headache or runny nose." He sniffed and didn't sound congested.

"The incubation period is thought to be two days prior to symptoms," Dr. Upton said. "You have a duty to protect your fellow workers."

"And streetcar passengers," Katharine added. Clarence worked at the Ogden Shops, southeast of Calgary, at least a forty-minute ride from here.

"Mrs. Sterling," Dr. Upton said. "Would you telephone the morgue to pick up the body?"

She nodded. The front door clicked, and John walked in.

Katharine met him at the entrance. "Why are you here? You left the children—"

"I finally got Henry back to bed. Don't worry. They're both asleep."

"John?" Marguerite called from the living room.

He brushed past Katharine, and Marguerite leaped up from the living room floor. She lunged into John, who wrapped his arms around her. His back trembled, as though it absorbed her tears.

Dr. Upton drew up beside Katharine. His eyes narrowed at the pair. Katharine had sometimes noted a tenderness in Dr. Upton's voice when he'd spoken of Marguerite and wondered if the middle-aged bachelor was sweet on her.

Now, Katharine's stomach twinged at the sight of John holding Marguerite, stroking back a loose hair as she mumbled into his chest. Katharine tucked some straggled hairs into her tight bun. The past few months, John had spent many evenings in this house talking, drinking, and even playing his saxophone. One night, Vincent and Marguerite had gone to his club. While describing these occasions, John had portrayed Marguerite as an incidental presence, less significant than Clarence.

Marguerite and John separated. He took off his coat and dropped it on Dr. Upton's hat and cape, while Marguerite glared at Katharine. John looked down at Vincent, who lay supine on the floor. Marguerite's glare intensified.

Was the widow blaming her? Katharine bit her lip. *I did my best. It was more than you managed. He was beyond saving.* But was she being defensive? Could a person skilled in the method have saved him? All she'd brought to the task was a little theory without any experience.

"I need a smoke." Clarence got his coat from the closet, went out the front door, and closed it behind him.

Marguerite wove past Katharine and disappeared into the room across from the living room.

Katharine wasn't needed here anymore, and her children were alone in the house.

She faced Dr. Upton. "Should I stay home from work tomorrow?"

"Did Vincent breathe on you?" His gauze mask moved in and out with his words.

"I suspect he was dead by the time I arrived, but the others might be contagious." This included John. He'd been here the previous evening, and tonight, he'd hugged a weeping Marguerite. "It's also possible it wasn't the flu. Vincent might have struck his nose when he fell, and his dark colouring could be his natural shade in the dim lighting. But the sudden, violent cough and rapid progress to death is harder to dismiss."

Dr. Upton nodded. "I'll get their full accounts and write up my assessment while we wait for the hearse to arrive."

John hobbled toward them. "Poor chap. Completely unfair. Vincent survives the bloody war and now this."

Katharine had once naively believed life was fair. "John, we have to leave now. The children."

"I'll stay, for Marguerite." He looked around. "Where is she?"

Katharine looked at the closed door. "Her bedroom, I presume. Perhaps she wants to be alone."

"Vincent deserves company now, even if he's stone dead." John returned to his spot overlooking Vincent.

Katharine picked up her coat from the floor and stood beside John for a last glance at Vincent, his black hair mussed from his final ordeal, dried blood on his nose and beard. Dr. Upton must have closed his eyes, out of respect.

"Was it the Spanish flu?" John asked.

"Very likely, so please take care and assume Marguerite and Clarence are infected. Don't stand close or touch the same surfaces, open a few windows, and wear your mask."

He kept one in his pocket and tended to wear it when he went out, mainly, she suspected, to hide his scarred left cheek. Odd that he hadn't put it on now when it would be most prudent. She hoped Marguerite would send him home the minute the hearse arrived.

At the front door, Katharine thanked Dr. Upton for his prompt attendance.

"Doing my job," he said. "I think you can do your job tomorrow, unless you or your brother develop symptoms. We can't withdraw our medical attention at the least exposure."

She nodded, although their patients would survive without her clerical attention. Outside on the porch, she paused to say goodbye to Clarence and wish him the best.

"The best is long past any of us in this miserable world." He drew on his cigarette.

She appreciated his despair. Vincent's life had ended, and Marguerite's had changed in ways none of them could fathom yet. "Yes," Katharine said, "but when the war and this worldwide sickness are over—"

"Nothing will be the same." He dropped the cigarette butt and mashed it on the porch.

John had told her Clarence was a cynic who opposed Canada's participation in the Great War. This had resulted in spirited arguments between Vincent and John—honourably discharged veterans—and him. John thought Clarence had enjoyed the confrontation. Katharine suspected John had too.

A dog barked and trotted up the stairs. "There's the mangy creature." Clarence leaned down to scratch its fur. "At least it might provide comfort to Marguerite."

Katharine hadn't known they had a dog.

Back inside her warm home, Katharine hung up her coat, telephoned the morgue, and quickstepped to the rear bedroom to check on Henry and Lillian. They lay on their beds, lumps under the covers, curled on their sides, both facing into the room and each other. Surely their futures made this miserable world worthwhile. Katharine's tension melted away. All she wanted was to hug her children tight while she waited for John to return.

Lillian rolled toward the wall. Katharine lay down beside her and wrapped her arm around the small body. She drifted and then bolted awake, chilled by the air gusting in. The room was still pitch dark.

Katharine slowly got out of bed. Lillian stirred and rolled onto her face, her bottom pushing the covers upward. Katharine tiptoed into the hall. John's bedroom door was ajar. She peeked into the room. No John on the bed. In the dark living room, she peered at the mantel clock. Ten minutes past one. She'd slept over three hours.

Outside the front window, the dimly lit street was deserted. Dr. Upton's car was gone. Presumably the hearse had come and gone, and John had stayed to comfort the new widow. Katharine shivered, her easy sleep over.

Chapter Two

When the children were settled at the kitchen table with their porridge, Katharine padded down the hall to see if John was on his way home. She opened the door to a blast of cold morning air. There was no John emerging from Marguerite's house or crossing the street and no chance now that Katharine would get to work on time. She cursed his irresponsibility then cursed herself because Marguerite's need was greater.

Katharine slunk inside and followed the sound of the children's laughter to the kitchen, where Henry and Lillian tossed pieces of bread into each other's porridge bowls.

"You'll have to eat that soggy muck." Katharine hated her sharp tone. "Finish it all up so we can go tell Dr. Upton I won't be at work today."

"When's Uncle John coming back?" Lillian asked.

That was an excellent question. Katharine rubbed her head, which was dull from fitful sleep. She'd told them about Vincent's death and that John was helping the widow.

Lillian gazed up, her hazel eyes wide. "Is Mr. DeLuca in Heaven?"

"Yes." Katharine recalled her childhood image of Heaven. Meadows and sky in primary colours; puffy clouds and grasses dotted with flowers and gambolling lambs. Since the war began, Heaven had become shadowy spirits floating through darkness.

Apparently satisfied with the simple answer, Lillian dug her spoon into her bowl and scooped up a mess of bread and porridge. The front door clicked.

Katharine darted to the hall as John walked in. "You're home," she said with a mix of relief and annoyance.

"Why wouldn't I be?" John carried a bulging brown bag. "You told me ten to nine. I've given you a few minutes to spare." Without removing his coat, he limped into the living room, dropped into the armchair, and set the bag on the coffee table with a clunk. He raised his pant leg and untied the laces of the thigh corset that held his artificial limb in place.

She glanced at the mantel clock. Two or three minutes to spare for a multitude of questions. "If you're tired, I'll stay home. Dr. Upton will understand."

He yanked off the limb. "Ahhh, that's better." He placed it on the coffee table next to the bag. "I'm used to sleepless nights and will be fine after I've had some breakfast. I didn't want to put Marguerite out by having her make it for me when she wasn't hungry."

"Poor woman." Katharine sat on the davenport. Her work could wait. "How's she doing?"

"As well as could be expected." John rubbed his knobbly stump. He didn't usually wear the limb for twelve hours at a time, and vanity would have prevented him from removing it at Marguerite's. "I told her she could come over this morning to phone Vincent's parents. She saw no point in ruining their good night's sleep."

Katharine nodded. For parents, this would be the worst news possible. Her gaze landed on the paper bag. "What's in there?"

"Vincent's last bottle of whisky."

She recalled Clarence saying Vincent had been drinking before his cough began.

John chortled. "After the hearse and the doctor left, Marguerite flew into a rage, blaming everyone and everything for Vincent's death, including the whisky—and you, in fact, for pounding his lungs until they burst."

Katharine flinched at the recollection of Marguerite's accusing glare, but was it possible the inept pounding had killed him?

"Clarence and I calmed her down," John continued. "Later, when I was throwing out a broken glass, I noticed the bottle in her garbage pail. Why waste perfectly good whisky?" he said with a shrug. "Marguerite prefers wine, and Clarence is a teetotaller."

"So, she gave you the bottle?"

"In a manner of speaking. I confiscated it secretly to avoid riling her up."

Footsteps sounded in the hall. Lillian ran into the room and leaped onto John. "Uncle John, you're back."

"Why does everyone think I'm leaving?" He looked at Katharine. "You best get going."

Henry lumbered in and rummaged through the toy box.

"You're sure, John?" Katharine asked.

He squeezed Lillian. "These monsters will look after me, starting with breakfast."

"There's porridge on the stove. I'll be home for lunch." How much damage could they do in three hours? "If you need me for anything, send Henry to the office."

"Go, go." John waved her away and slithered Lillian off his lap. "Fetch me my extra leg."

Lillian ran to get his crutch, which rested against the sewing machine. Usually, he scorned assistance and got around the house using his hands on surfaces. He had to be tired.

Katharine kissed Lillian goodbye. "You be good for Uncle John and do what he says. You too, Henry."

As she went to give him a kiss, Henry pulled a rifle out of the toy box. "Bang, bang." He aimed the toy at Lillian and chased her through the archway. Her shrieks and their footsteps echoed down the hall.

"You're really sure, John?" Katharine asked.

"Yes," he snapped. "Let me contribute to this household."

She'd wanted that since he moved in this past spring, but so far, he'd done little household work and the pittance he earned from playing with his band didn't cover his personal expenses. "If you have time," she said, "you can make vegetable soup. There's broth in the refrigerator and root vegetables in the cellar."

"Women's work?" he said, his tone teasing. "I'll do it, but schoolwork comes first."

Yesterday she'd have said that. Today she'd be happy if they made it through the morning without showing signs of the flu. She realized John hadn't shown any. Not yet. A morsel of good news.

He propped the crutch under his armpit and shuffled into the hall. Katharine glanced at the bag on the coffee table. If the children knocked the whisky bottle over and it broke or spilled, the room would reek for days.

She pulled the squat container out of the bag. It was about half-full of the amber liquid. John didn't drink in the daytime, to her knowledge, but she clearly didn't know everything about him. Yesterday he'd hugged Marguerite as though she were more than a casual friend and spent the night consoling her at her home. He'd referred to a broken glass. Had she hurled it in her rage? Perhaps both he and Clarence had been needed last night to help settle Marguerite.

Katharine would question her brother further in the evening.

To keep the bottle away from him and the children, she stashed it in the sideboard beside her knitting basket. John would never look there. Eddie's portrait looked out from the top of the sideboard. She wished he were home to handle this situation.

No sounds flowed down the hall from the kitchen. Best to leave well enough alone. Katharine put on her hat and coat and exchanged the used mask in her pocket for a fresh one.

Outside, the wind blew fiercely from the west. A dark Chinook cloud blanketed the sky. Katharine headed east to Centre Street, four houses down. She paused at the corner in front of Fielding and Sons Drug Store. A Closed sign hung on its door. Vincent had been the store manager, and Marguerite assisted him in the mornings. He'd never enter that building again. Would Marguerite continue working without him?

Katharine rounded the corner and entered the medical office, which was adjacent to the drug store. Dr. Upton stood behind the reception desk, his back to her. Mrs. Allan sat beside a man in the waiting area who sniffled and coughed. Katharine dug her mask from her pocket and put it on.

Dr. Upton turned around, and his eyebrows rose above his spectacles. "Mrs. Sterling, thank heavens you've arrived. I can't locate Mrs. Allan's folder."

"It's in the second-to-bottom drawer."

"Why? Don't you file alphabetically?"

Katharine joined him behind the desk. "I do, but she hasn't been here in over a year. I reserve the top drawers for recent patients." This way she wouldn't have to squat every time Mrs. Young or Mrs. Zelinski brought in one of their children. Katharine bent to pull out Mrs. Allan's file.

"Good idea to mask up." Dr. Upton kept his voice low. "We're both at risk after last night."

"Do you think it was ...?"

A new patient walked in, his face blotched red. From fever? Katharine told him to take a seat, then she and Dr. Upton went into his office. She hung her coat and hat on the coat tree and checked that her bun was in place.

Dr. Upton stroked his handlebar moustache. "My best guess is that Vincent died of Spanish influenza. I'm convinced there are more cases in the city than most of my colleagues believe."

"I'll start requesting patients to wear masks." Katharine collected a handful of them from the box on Dr. Upton's supply shelf. She'd place them in the basket on the reception desk.

"I recall now that Vincent sniffled and blew his nose several times during our whist card game Saturday night," Dr. Upton continued. "Most disturbingly, Marguerite was fatigued. She didn't play her usual lively game and suggested we finish early. Last night, she admitted her fatigue persists but denied any other symptoms. It makes me wonder, though, if she caught a mild case, which she passed along to Vincent. She told me that on Thursday she served a customer with a severe cough. The incubation period would fit.”

Katharine remembered the closed drug store. “Does Mr. Fielding know about Vincent?”

Dr. Upton nodded. “I phoned him at home before I left for work. Naturally, he was shocked.”

“While the store is closed, I’ll refer patients to other drug stores.”

“Fielding said he might open the store himself. You can check when there’s a lull between patients.” He flapped the file folder. “Now, I must attend to Mrs. Allan.”

Katharine returned to the waiting room and found that a woman with three children had arrived while she was gone. They sat crammed between the coughing and feverish-looking men. Why not make use of the waiting area’s third wall to keep patients who might be contagious separate from the rest? She carried Mrs. Allan’s vacated chair to the wall on the other side of the door, asked the cougher to the desk to create a file for him, and handed him a mask.

For the next hour, Katharine recorded information for new and returning patients, typed receipts, and processed payments. At last, a lull arrived. Two regular patients she trusted remained in the waiting area. One said she'd noticed an Open sign at Fieldings' store. Katharine asked them to tell Dr. Upton she'd gone next door for a few minutes. She didn't bother with her coat and hat for the short walk.

Mr. Fielding served a customer at the store's central counter. His office was downtown, in his company's flagship store, but he visited the Tuxedo Park branch once or twice a week and his wife replaced Marguerite in the afternoons.

Katharine moved up to the counter when Mr. Fielding's customer left.

"Terrible business with Vincent," Mr. Fielding said. "I still can't believe it. As you know, we play whist Saturday nights. He seemed in perfect health this Saturday, aside from his habitual cough and possibly a sniffle. Upton says you did your best to help."

"It wasn't enough."

"Some things are beyond our control." He pressed his hands together in a gesture of prayer, perhaps thinking of his three sons in Europe. The two eldest had attended the Ontario College of Pharmacy with Vincent and enlisted the summer after their graduation. The younger of the two, Vincent's close friend, was missing in action.

"Will you keep the store open for the rest of the day?"

He nodded. "My downtown manager can cover the main branch until the weekend. After that … Do you know if Marguerite plans to return?"

"I expect she hasn't thought that far ahead."

"Quite right. I'll visit her during my lunch hour to offer my condolences," he said. "And assuming my business partner agrees, I'll offer her free rent while she considers her next step. I'll also ask my partner—excuse me a minute." He sidled over to serve a new customer.

Katharine had forgotten that Mr. Fielding owned Vincent and Marguerite's home. His real estate partnership had wisely bought land in Tuxedo Park before the streetcar extension up Centre Street and hired a developer to build half the homes in this neighbourhood. The business sold most of the houses to people, like Eddie and Katharine, but kept some for rental income.

While Mr. Fielding served his customer, Katharine scanned the side cabinets, which displayed products that Marguerite had introduced to the basic pharmaceutical business. Women's cosmetics and toilet waters, soda drinks, cameras and film, Chinese medicines. Marguerite bought the exotic herbs from a Chinese farmer who lived this side of Nose Hill. She'd urged Katharine to give his vegetables a try. The bok choy that Marguerite had carried home looked similar to spinach.

Mr. Fielding rang up the sale and returned to Katharine. "Where were we?"

"You plan to ask your partner ...?"

"Right." He cleared his throat. "You're familiar with the Hicks Block?"

Katharine nodded. She'd taken her children to the library and Methodist Sunday school on the ground floor of the building, which was a ten-minute walk from her house.

"Our firm owns the building. I'll suggest to my partner that we let the vacant apartment upstairs to Marguerite's boarder for the same rent he pays her now."

"Does Clarence want to leave her place?"

Mr. Fielding's brow puckered. "It would be unseemly for him to stay with her alone."

"Many widows take in boarders. In fact, they tend to need the extra money."

"Yes, but when they're young and attractive, there's bound to be gossip."

Katharine couldn't dispute Marguerite's appeal to men. She had thick hair, flawless skin, high cheekbones, and an hourglass figure. Katharine also couldn't delay longer, and another customer was approaching the counter. She said a quick goodbye and left. During her walk back, Katharine wondered if Marguerite and Clarence worried about gossip. While Katharine didn't know them well, neither one struck her as the sort to care much what others thought. Clarence's objection to the war would reap scorn from almost everyone and, she had to admit, his views had prejudiced her against him. She'd be curious to hear his reasons.

Back at the medical office, she found that three more patients had arrived in her absence. She registered them and the next arrivals until eleven thirty, when she turned the door sign over to Closed. As the last morning patient walked out, Dr. Upton asked Katharine how John was feeling.

"He's well, as of the time I left," she said. "Henry would have come to fetch me if John had developed symptoms. Serious ones, at any rate."

"Did he stay all night at Marguerite's?"

"Yes." Her face warmed and Dr. Upton's grew red, perhaps betraying his own interest in Marguerite. "If I find he's too tired at lunch, I won't be able to come in this afternoon."

"Understandably," Dr. Upton said. "I plan to catnap after eating. Call if you need to stay home." He pivoted and went into his office to eat the lunch he brought every day—cheese, bread, and pickled onions with cold beef or ham, depending on his recent roast. If he ever married, a wife might vary his diet, but he'd remarked more than once that food was an inconvenient necessity. This didn't keep him from being portly.

Outside, Katharine rounded the corner to her street. The Chinook wind blew against her all the way home, but not enough to dissipate the oppressive cloud. She walked in the door to savoury aromas wafting from the kitchen, where Henry and Lillian sat at the table eating soup and bread.

John stood by the stove wearing Katharine's apron. "We had cooking class this morning. Everyone chopped vegetables and tossed spices into the broth."

"You let them use knives?" Katharine said.

"Blunt ones." He looked at the children. "Lilly-pet, is that a sliced-off finger I see in your soup?"

Lillian giggled. Since both children's fingers looked intact, Katharine agreed cooking was a useful skill. John ladled a bowl of soup for her. He wore his artificial limb, which he needed for balance while chopping and carrying pots.

"I could get used to this service," Katharine teased, partly to encourage him to wear the limb more often. "Have you already eaten?"

"I'll wait for Marguerite," he said. "I invited her for lunch, to save her cooking. She had a bundle of tasks this morning."

Katharine wasn't eager to share a meal with someone who'd blamed her for killing her husband. During a break between patients Dr. Upton had assured her that death by inept pounding was unlikely. Katharine tasted the soup. Too much salt, and the chunks of carrots, turnips, and potatoes were too large for single bites. "What else did Uncle John teach you besides cooking?" she asked.

Lillian's face brightened. "Sums. Six plus four equals ten."

"Good for you," Katharine said, genuinely impressed. Academics might be sprinkled into their learning after all.

"May I please be excused?" Henry asked.

"Me too," Lillian said.

Both bowls were half-full. "Finish your soup first," Katharine said.

They devoured the rest of their meal and tore out of the kitchen. John removed the apron, which had protected his pressed shirt and trousers. His typical home attire was casual, approaching slovenly.

"Did Marguerite talk to Vincent's parents this morning?" she asked.

He grimaced. "Yes, and it wasn't pleasant. They want to bury him in Crowsnest Pass, near them, so they can tend his grave. Marguerite resented the implication that she'd neglect him."

"They probably didn't mean that." Katharine too would want a deceased son close to her, despite a wife's first claim, and understood how Vincent's parents might blurt out this sentiment in their initial grief.

John leaned against the counter. He'd be weary from standing. "They think she'll return to France when the war is over."

Katharine ate some soup to hide any expression of hope that this would occur. Before John and Marguerite's embrace last night, Katharine would have been indifferent to the widow's plans. The doorbell rang.

"That's her." John disappeared into the hall.

Katharine joined him at the entrance, as did Henry and Lillian. Marguerite's wide-brimmed hat with netting shaded her upper face. She carefully removed the hat, set it on the hall chair, and took off her coat. John hung it in the closet. Her mauve dress, cinched at the waistline, followed the lines of her hips and legs to her ankles. Did her tasks for today include shopping for mourning clothes? Regardless, mauve was relatively subdued.

Marguerite leaned toward Henry and Lillian. "Such a lovely boy and girl. I've noticed you on the street, playing a game with a ball and sticks."

"With our friends before the flu." Henry's expression turned glum.

Marguerite's face trembled, but she steadied her gaze and asked if she could freshen up.

"You know the way." John waved her toward the bathroom.

Katharine considered putting on a mask as a hint Marguerite should do the same, but they would have to take them off for eating. Had John wiped the phone after the widow's use? Evidently, he didn't mind her seeing the crooked scar that ran from his cheekbone to the edge of his mouth as much as he did her noticing his missing leg.

In the kitchen, Katharine cleared the children's dishes from the table while John set places for Marguerite and him. Katharine filled their bowls and topped hers up to warm the soup, recalling the French were known for their superb cuisine. She hoped they were liberal with salt. Marguerite returned and took her place across from Katharine, who hesitated to say grace. Was it the custom in France? Marguerite dipped her spoon into the soup, so Katharine began eating. It was easier than talking.

"How were your meetings with the lawyer and bank?" John broke the silence.

"Busy." Marguerite paused to chew a chunk and swallow. "Vincent left everything to me, as he'd said he would. There's more money than I expected, enough to provide for me until spring."

"That's great news." John beamed, insensitively, Katharine thought, given that this news had resulted from a death.

Marguerite stirred her soup. "When I got off the streetcar, I saw the drug store was open. Mr. Fielding was there. I asked him for Vincent's job, but Mr. Fielding insists the manager must have a diploma, even though I know as much as Vincent about medicines."

"That's unfair," John said.

Marguerite nodded. "Mr. Fielding himself has no degree."

"Times have changed," Katharine said. Mr. Fielding had started work in pioneer days, when anyone who wanted could open a drug store and call himself a pharmacist. "I hear the University of Alberta, in Edmonton, offers a diploma course after a three-year apprenticeship. You've already completed a year."

"They increase the one-year diploma to a two-year licentiate course," Marguerite said. "It would cost too much to go to school there for two years with no salary from work."

John tore off a chunk of bread. "This is about you being a woman. Fielding's putting up stumbling blocks."

"His downtown manager is female," Katharine said. The shortage of men had forced him to hire her. "She has a diploma from the U of A."

Marguerite glowered at her. "Work is far from my *priorité*."

"Of course." Katharine spooned up some soup to hide her flush. She'd been trying to offer encouragement. "Mr. Fielding told me he planned to visit you during lunch to discuss your rental."

Marguerite sniffed. "He offered me free rent, but I don't want his *charité*. I told him I would pay and keep Clarence as my lodger. He likes my food." She touched her spoon but didn't eat. "I've decided to let Vincent be buried in Crowsnest Pass. If I have to move to Edmonton or *France*, there would be no one here for him except a cousin he dislikes."

"He has a cousin in Calgary?" Katharine asked.

"Could I telephone Vincent's parents again?" Marguerite said, ignoring her question. Her face looked pale. She needed nourishment.

"Certainly," Katharine said. "But eat first, before your soup gets cold."

"I want to settle this." Marguerite rose and swept out of the room.

"Who is this cousin of Vincent?" Katharine asked John.

He shrugged and ate some soup.

She shifted the subject. "I told Dr. Upton I'd stay home this afternoon if you're tired."

"Honestly, I've been too busy to feel tired. This afternoon, I thought the children and I would do dinner cooking class. What were you planning to make?"

"Stew. I could write out the recipe."

John scraped his spoon over the bowl to get the last bits. "It's fortunate I like salt, but I'll tell Lillian to be less generous with it the next time." He stood as Marguerite returned to the kitchen.

"For once, I made Vincent's mother happy," she said. "Tomorrow, I'll take the train to Crowsnest Pass and must make arrangements. Please excuse me from your table."

"You haven't finished your soup," Katharine said.

She looked down at the bowl. "Thank you. It was a little salty."

Katharine knew she shouldn't take that personally, but she did.

"Let me know how I can help," John said to Marguerite. They left the room.

Rather than see her visitor out, Katharine finished her lunch so she could return to work on time. With luck, the widow would extend her stay with Vincent's family in Crowsnest Pass for a week or more. Katharine didn't dislike Marguerite, but she hadn't warmed to her either during their encounters in the drug store, Marguerite's appointments at the medical office, and their brief talks on the street. Yet, Dr. Upton's patients invariably described her as friendly, helpful, and as knowledgeable about medicines as Vincent. Marguerite's boast that she could do his job might be true, but Katharine sided with Mr. Fielding about the need for credentials.

John re-entered the kitchen. "I'll wash up."

"I accept your offer." She flashed a smile.

While he loaded the dishes into the sink, she checked that they had all the ingredients for her meatless stew and wrote down the recipe.

"I told Marguerite I'll bring over some stew," John said. "Clarence will expect his dinner."

"Did he go to work?"

"Yes. He felt well this morning."

No one who'd been in contact with Vincent the previous evening was showing symptoms. By tomorrow night, the end of the flu incubation period, they'd all know if they had escaped.

Chapter Three

Detective Bertram Tanner strode into Calgary Police Headquarters, his steps lighter than they'd been this morning.

"How was your walk?" Julia, the receptionist, asked.

"Reflective."

"I often think while walking too."

It was too soon to tell his colleagues he might be leaving the police force. "How was your lunch hour?"

"Busy," she said. "I tracked down balloons for my son's birthday celebration tonight."

"Which son?"

"The oldest. He's ten years old. We decided to limit the party to family due to the flu. He's disappointed his friends can't come, but it will be lively with all of us there."

Julia, a war widow with three children, lived with her parents—the police chief and his wife.

"I phoned my mother after lunch," Julia said. "She went to every confectionary in town and managed to find all the children's favourite sweets despite the sugar shortage."

The chief's wife was a ball of energy. A leader in the local suffragette and Prohibition movements, she claimed personal credit for Alberta women gaining the vote and the province going dry in 1916.

Bertram went into his office, closed the door, and draped his coat and hat on the coat tree. What work could he do this afternoon? Reports of the Spanish flu's arrival on a train from Eastern Canada were keeping people away from the pool rooms and dance halls. Calgary hadn't had a brawl or knifing in a week. Even the criminals seemed to be staying home.

He took out an old file, a robbery scheduled for trial next week. A man broke into a house in the Sunalta neighbourhood and stole $2.75. Disturbed by a noise, he fled through a window but foolishly returned an hour later. Caught red-handed by three residents, the robber could be sentenced to up to a year of hard labour. Bertram tried to organize his trial notes, but his thoughts kept shifting to his plan to leave the police force when the war ended and soldiers came home to replace him on the job. After fifteen minutes, he set the robbery file aside and decided to take a methodical approach to his lunch hour reflections about leaving.

He took out a clean sheet of paper, drew a vertical line down the middle, and titled each side "pro" and "con."

The first positive was that his parents would be thrilled when he phoned them to say that by spring, at the latest, he'd move back to Beiseker and fulfill his father's dream of his only son taking over his grocery store.

At thirty-eight, Bertram was no longer bewitched by city charms.

He wrote *simpler, quiet life* as positive number two. Number three was a question—*safer from the flu in the countryside?* Number four was *look after parents.*

While his father had fully recovered from his heart attack last winter, the experience had made Bertram aware that his parents were aging and would increasingly need help. It would be unfair to leave the entire burden to his three sisters, who had all stayed in the Beiseker area. Bertram foresaw hours spent hunting with his father and nephews, numerous birthday parties, daily dealings with people who weren't criminals. *Family connection* and *better people* were reasons five and six.

Seven. The most important. Beiseker was a mere two-hour drive to Calgary and the graves of Nellie and their son. Bertram could still visit them on Sundays, as he did now. Yet he'd be farther geographically from them—farther from his lonely home with its constant painful reminders. That was reason number eight.

The negatives? A year ago, he'd have said his work. But since the death of his wife and son last November, he didn't give a pat of cow manure about catching criminals and bringing them to justice. He shuffled by rote through cases like the home robbery. What was the point of this job without heart? He liked his colleagues, most of them at any rate, but his friends had all been couple friends. Now, he was the outsider, the third hand in their card games, Nellie the glaringly missing fourth– especially when the friends invited female players to fill her place. He hated their efforts to convince him to move on.

Bertram left the negatives column blank and dragged his attention back to the robbery file. Someone knocked on the door.

Julia poked her head in. "The chief wants to see you in his office."

Bertram gladly set the file aside. He nodded at constables and clerks on his way to Chief Wilson's office. The front was glass so the chief could survey the activity at headquarters. He'd been in his position ten years, and no one used his surname anymore. Even his daughter referred to him as "chief" in the context of police work.

Bertram took a seat across the desk from the chief, who explained that the Alberta Provincial Police was organizing a raid on a club in East Calgary that was purportedly serving liquor. With a virus running through the unit, the provincial police had requested Calgary Police Service provide a few officers.

"They don't think it's the flu," the chief said. "But, in this atmosphere of fear, their men who are coughing and sneezing can't go into the club to pass as customers. That will be your role this Saturday night. An ordinary, middle-aged man out for a card game and musical entertainment and not averse to an illegal drink. I thought of you because of your prior undercover work, and our beat constables are more likely to be recognized than a detective. I also recall a rowdy poker game from our younger days." His eyes twinkled.

Bertram smirked. He'd cleaned out the chief that day. "My poker's rusty but passable."

"You'll go in with a couple of their men, ascertain the club is selling liquor, then one of you will leave to advise the men prepared to raid. You can work out the details with them. I trust you're interested and available?"

"I have no pressing work," Bertram said. "But my contacts at city hall predict Calgary will follow the lead of eastern cities and close public meeting places this weekend."

"If that happens, the expectation is the owner will flout the city ordinance as willfully as he's flouted Prohibition."

"I'll prepare with the unit then. Anything more?"

"All for now. You'll keep me apprised of the plans?"

Bertram nodded. This job was more interesting than preparing for a trial that would be postponed if the courthouse closed. But the prospect of a raid didn't excite him, as it would have in the past. A decision to leave the police force was right.

* * *

Katharine's afternoon at the medical office flew by thanks to the steady flow of patients. She didn't realize how exhausted she was until Dr. Upton emerged from the examination room with the last patient of the day. While Katharine processed the woman's payment, the doctor went back into his office to get his medical bag, cape, hat, and walking stick. He returned as the patient departed.

"I've been thinking about your brother." He set his medical bag on Katharine's desk. "I want you to take an oxygen cylinder tonight."

Work had taken her mind off her potential need for this. "What if you're called to an emergency?"

"I'll keep my other one with an oxygen mask, but the tube is effective when used correctly." He opened the bag, took out a cloth sack, and pulled out the cylinder kit. "It's simple," he said. "Make sure the tube is secured to the cylinder, insert the tube into the patient's mouth as comfortably as possible so he won't spit it out, flick the release and then the oxygen switch." He pointed to each one—red for release, blue for oxygen.

Katharine mentally went through the steps. "I don't suppose I could practice on you?"

He shuddered. "I have a strong gag reflex. Lord help the person who has to use this device to resuscitate me."

"Then don't call me tonight," she joked and held up the cylinder. "Seriously, if there's no better choice, I want you to phone, and I'll bring this and do what I can."

"Let's hope it's not needed for any of us," he said. "Show your brother how to use it in case you succumb. I trust Marguerite or her boarder would come to you for help as they did for Vincent."

She put the cylinder in her handbag, which was large enough for small grocery items. "You might train a neighbour on using the cylinder so he can come to your aid if the flu attacks you."

"Good thought." He stroked the curl of his moustache. "Attack. In many ways, medicine is war on an enemy that isn't visible to our current eyes."

She'd enjoy pursuing that idea if she weren't weary and eager to get home.

Outside, they walked together around the corner. Fielding and Sons was still open. With more time, Katharine might have gone in and talked to Mrs. Fielding. A pleasant woman, she'd started assisting in the store when the war began but was less knowledgeable about the medicines than Marguerite, who had worked there less than a year. Marguerite would have to apprentice two more years before pursuing a licentiate degree but would earn money during that time. In Marguerite's place, Katharine would've latched onto that plan.

Dr. Upton wished her a good night and turned into the lane behind the drug store and medical office, where he parked his motorcar. Katharine continued to her home, the Chinook wind in her face. The blue arch to the west had grown wide enough to let the sun peek from the edge of the cloud.

On her way up her sidewalk, she tensed with her fear of finding a letter from Eddie's commanding officer advising her that he was missing or wounded or taken prisoner or dead. A telegram could arrive any minute of the day or night. She didn't know if that potential shock or this daily anticipation was worse.

Aromas of stew greeted her when she stepped inside. Before removing her coat, she leafed through the mail on the telephone counter. Nothing from the army or from Eddie. Relief mingled with the disappointment of not hearing from him in over two months. She left her handbag with the oxygen cylinder on the oak hall-chair. After the children were in bed, she'd explain the procedure to John.

In the kitchen, John stirred the potato and parsnip stew simmering in the Dutch oven. He wore her apron again, as well as his prosthesis, and carried the three-quart pot to the stove.

"Where are Henry and Lillian?" Katharine asked.

"Playing in the yard."

She looked out the back window. They squatted in the sandbox, which Eddie had made when Henry was two. Father and son had spent hours building castles and roadways, and later, Lillian joined Henry in the construction work with equal enthusiasm.

John scooped some stew from the Dutch oven into the three-quart pot. "I'll take this to Marguerite's and finish the cooking there, so it's warm when we eat. She invited me to dinner when she stopped by earlier to phone Vincent's parents. Her train trip to Crowsnest Pass is all set." He placed the lid on the pot.

She decided not to nag him about minimizing contact with Marguerite. After tonight, the woman would be away for a few days, fortunately. "What time does she leave?"

He took off the apron and smoothed his shirt, a fresh one since lunch. "Early in the morning so Clarence can help carry her bags on his way to work. He'll drop her off at the station, where she'll meet Vincent's cousin who'll travel with her."

"The cousin Vincent dislikes?"

John nodded. "I forgot to ask Marguerite why. All I know about the cousin is she's older than Vincent and lives downtown." He gripped the handle of the pot. "Can you open the front door for me so I don't tip this sideways?"

The pot swayed with his gait as he carried the stew down the hall to the entrance. Katharine opened the door and watched him walk down the stairs and across the street. The pot banged his thigh, but nothing appeared to spill.

While the children were still occupied with the sandbox, Katharine changed into her combination underwear, enjoying the warmth to her arms and legs, and put on her housedress and "John's" apron. She sliced bread, the last of the loaf. Moments later, Henry and Lillian bolted inside from the back door.

"I can't wait to try your delicious meal," Katharine said and told them to wash up.

"Where's Uncle John?" Lillian asked, when she returned with dripping hands.

Katharine explained he was eating at Mrs. DeLuca's house to keep her company.

"She taught us penmanship today," Henry said.

"She did?"

"Uncle John said she's a better writer than him."

Marguerite had evidently spent more than a few minutes at the house after her phone call. So much for minimizing opportunities to spread the flu. The children settled at the table. Katharine filled three bowls with stew and asked Henry to say grace. Naturally, he chose the shortest prayer and mumbled and raced through it.

"God is great, God is good. Let us thank him for our food. Amen."

As the children dug into their meal, Katharine asked how long penmanship class had lasted.

"I wrote the alphabet," Lillian said. "*A, B, C, D—*"

"She left before you finished," Henry said.

"I finished by myself."

A short class, Katharine gathered. "This stew is very good." Not salty. In fact, she'd have liked to sprinkle on a little more salt but didn't want to discourage them from cooking.

After dinner, she cleaned up and let the children play in the living room until bedtime. Would John be spending a second night at Marguerite's house? Surely she wouldn't want him there when she had to pack and get up early in the morning.

Katharine coaxed the children through their bedtime ritual and tucked them in. Still no John at eight o'clock. She mended *A Child's Garden of Verses* and was collecting materials for the masks she planned to make for patients when the front door clicked open.

She met John at the entrance. "You're home," she said, conscious of repeating her words of this morning.

He hung up his coat. "I stayed to help Marguerite prepare for her trip. She spent ages selecting which of Vincent's personal items to take to his family and ended up with two full suitcases to bring. Good thing Clarence will be with her to lug them on the streetcar. The plan is for me to meet her at the station when she gets back Saturday afternoon. Now it's off with this bloody leg." He hobbled to the armchair in the living room.

Katharine sat on the matching rocker that angled toward John. He pulled off his limb and breathed a sigh. It was good that he was wearing it more often, good that he was helping a person in need, and good that Marguerite would be gone tomorrow.

"Will there be a service for Vincent in Crowsnest Pass?" Katharine asked.

"His parents said the priest was available Friday. She left it to them to make plans." He looked at the coffee table. "What happened to the whisky I brought back this morning?"

Katharine glanced over her shoulder, at the sideboard. "I put it away for later."

"Later is right now. Let's raise a toast to Vincent since we'll miss his service."

That seemed an appropriate use for Vincent's last bottle. Katharine hated the burning taste of whisky, but she'd enjoy a sherry to relax her into sleep. While he massaged his stump, she got the bottle of whisky from the sideboard and the sherry and two glasses from the kitchen. On her way back, she noticed her handbag on the hall chair. John's instruction on oxygen use could wait until after the toast.

Seated again, she poured their respective drinks. They clinked their glasses of liquid, both golden, hers tinged with red.

"To Vincent," John said. "May he rest in peace."

The fireplace crackled seemingly in agreement. Katharine sipped the sherry that Dr. Upton had prescribed for her monthly "female pain." She rarely used it for that but found a drink soothing during moments when the burden of handling a household alone overwhelmed her.

John downed his whisky in a prolonged guzzle. He set his glass on the coffee table and got up to put on a record. "It's a Long Way to Tipperary" flowed from the Victrola.

He returned to his chair. "A war song seems appropriate. That's where Vincent's ending began." He reached for the bottle.

"Save it for another night," she said.

"A second one won't kill me." He refilled his glass, quaffed the drink as quickly as the first, and plunked his glass on the table.

"I'll enjoy mine slowly." She drained her glass of sherry, savouring the rich flavour.

The British army song drew to a close. John changed the record to the jaunty, "Pack Up Your Troubles in Your Old Kit-Bag, and Smile, Smile, Smile." He coughed, went back to his chair, and coughed again.

His coughing turned to spasms. She set down her glass next to John's. He clutched his neck and wheezed.

Katharine leaped up. "John!" She pushed his hands aside, loosened his collar, moved him forward, chest downward. "Is this better?"

Cough

She moved him backward.

"Better?"

Cough, cough

Sideways.

His face went red. He was choking.

God, no.

The oxygen.

She ran into the hall.

Chapter Four

Dr. Upton's instructions raced through Katharine's mind. *Secure the tube tightly to the cylinder. Insert tube into mouth, as comfortably as possible.* Panic drained away with her practical, mechanical steps. *Red for release.* She pressed the button then the blue one and heard a faint whoosh. *Was that sound oxygen?* She held the cylinder and tube, inhumanly calm, and glanced at Eddie's portrait on the sideboard. *Was it like this for soldiers in the war? Did they become machines to complete frightening yet necessary tasks?*

John stirred. He blinked. Katharine's heartbeat skipped, back to human.

The whoosh ended; the cylinder drained, emptied.

He opened his eyes, redness fading from his face. She slowly pulled out the tube.

"What happened?" he rasped. "All of a sudden, I couldn't breathe."

Alive.

She longed to hug him, hold him tight, but he still wheezed. Spasms could erupt again.

"I felt myself drowning in my own lungs."

That was death by Spanish flu, which could progress rapidly from nothing to violent coughs. She sat on the davenport, their empty glasses and the whisky and sherry bottles on the coffee table between them.

"Was that the flu?" John's voice and breathing sounded normal. "The experience was eerily like Vincent's seemed to be."

Except the conclusion, when the oxygen stopped John's symptoms as quickly as they had started. For both men, the severe coughing had begun not long after an evening drink, and the drink had come from the same bottle. "Can whisky go bad in the production process?"

"Whisky is never bad." John grinned feebly. "But I can't say I'm eager for another glass this soon."

She stared at the bottle. "I don't trust that whisky." An idea hit. "I could have Hamish analyze it."

"Who?"

"Dr. Upton's friend, who works in the hospital laboratory. When patients come in with food poisoning, they sometimes bring the food they believed caused it. Dr. Upton has me take it to Hamish for analysis. Food poisoning is their shared hobby."

John snickered. "A strange hobby."

"They both believe numerous lives would be saved if we understood the principles of poisoned food," she said.

"They're actually working together on a study they hope to eventually publish."

"Whisky isn't food."

"Drinks, like milk, can spoil too and cause illness or bad reactions."

He shook his head. "Whisky can sit on a counter for decades without going bad. It improves with age."

"My understanding is whisky goes through a complicated manufacturing process."

"Fermenting, adding water, distilling," John said. "I've never made moonshine so don't know the details."

"Water can carry bacteria," she reflected out loud. "A foreign substance could get introduced at any stage of the process. It might be poisonous on its own or when mixed with the whisky."

"Vincent and I had no ill effects from it on Monday night."

"True. Could it have deteriorated to that deadly point in a single day? I doubt it."

The Victrola ground round and round. She'd been too preoccupied to notice when the song had ended.

Another thought struck her. Poisoning could also occur after manufacturing. Could Marguerite have accidentally squirted cleaning fluid into the bottle while polishing their sideboard? Or dropped something into it on purpose? She worked in a drug store, which sold pills and syrups, many with no taste or smell.

These were wild thoughts. Katharine tried to shake them away but couldn't. "John, did you tell me that Clarence doesn't drink liquor?"

"I've never seen him with a glass in all my times at their house. Why?"

"Does Marguerite drink whisky?"

"Like I said, she favours wine. That's why she threw out the bottle."

She'd blamed the whisky for her husband's death. Would she have said that in front of John if she'd added a drug? Katharine felt a twinge of guilt for her suspicions.

"Come to think of it," John said. "Marguerite joined us in a glass some evenings when I'd visit during the summer, maybe even last month." He squinted at her. "But what does that have to do with Vincent dying?"

Perhaps Marguerite had been setting herself up as a non-drinker of whisky so that Clarence and Vincent wouldn't question her abstaining last night. But this was speculation—and cruel if she was innocent.

Realization crossed John's face, and his nostrils flared. "Are you insinuating Marguerite poisoned this bottle after our Monday drinks? That's impossible." He crossed his arms. "She'd never do that."

Katharine's gaze didn't waver.

"They were happily married and even if they weren't ..." He glared at the bottle. "She was smart to throw this out. I'll respect her wish and get rid of it."

Katharine struggled to find an argument to convince him. "There's no harm in having Hamish examine it. If he says the whisky's good, I'll bring it back and we'll drink another toast to Vincent."

"No," John said. "This belongs in the trash."

Why rile him up? The important thing was that John had survived. "All right."

"I'll have a glass of sherry instead." He picked up the sherry bottle.

"Don't pour it into your glass. I'll get a fresh one from the kitchen."

She carried the glass and whisky bottle into the hall and paused at her closed bedroom door; the children had slept through the event. Should she and John stay in the living room all night so she could watch over him? No, he'd insist that he take the chair and she sleep on the comfortable davenport. She should be the one to stay awake. Instead, she'd suggest they leave their bedroom doors ajar so she'd hear him if he called or had a coughing spasm.

Did John have the flu? This was more likely than Marguerite contaminating her husband's whisky. Katharine would have to stay home tomorrow to protect Dr. Upton and his patients.

But two men had come down with similar symptoms after drinking from this bottle in her hand. She couldn't brush away the coincidence and didn't need John's permission to have the whisky analyzed.

Katharine tiptoed into the bedroom. Her children were lumps under their bedcovers. She opened her dresser drawer and slipped the bottle beneath her clothes.

* * *

In the morning, Katharine slipped out of the bedroom in darkness and carried her clothing to the bathroom so as not to wake the children while she got dressed. On the way, she stopped to look into John's bedroom. His bedcovers moved up and down with his breathing. Relief washed through her. The clock in the kitchen said 5:35 a.m. She had time to make bread before the children were up.

Warm in her underwear and housedress, she sipped tea while she waited for the yeast to foam in water. If Marguerite remained in Calgary, Katharine wouldn't be able to tolerate seeing her every day and wondering if she'd murdered Vincent. Especially if romance developed between John and Marguerite. She wouldn't be the first lonely widow to turn to an attentive man. If Marguerite had killed her husband, why not a lover when she grew tired of or cross with him? The deeper John became involved, the harder it would be for Katharine to accuse his beloved of a horrible crime.

She added corn syrup, salt, oil, and flour that was largely oats to the foamy water. "Reserve the wheat for our soldiers," the advertisements declared. Katharine longed for the return of real bread.

There needed to be justice. Katharine owed this to Vincent, an innocent man. Moreover, Hamish's laboratory analysis would most likely exonerate Marguerite, which might be a relief to John. His insistence on throwing out a bottle of whisky that might be good suggested that he too had suspicions—ones he was prepared to overlook.

There wasn't a single reason not to take the bottle to Hamish, Katharine concluded, as she rolled and pressed and kneaded the dough. She placed the pans in the oven to the sounds of the children getting up. Before making porridge, she checked on John again. He still slept with apparent ease.

Over breakfast she told Henry and Lillian that John had taken ill the previous night. "He's better now but will need his sleep this morning, so I'll stay home to supervise your lessons."

Henry's groan confirmed that yesterday's academics had been light.

They finished eating and cleared the table. Katharine suggested the children work on their penmanship while she washed up and phoned Dr. Upton to say she wouldn't be in.

"But I wrote all my letters," Lillian said. "*A, B, C—*"

"You need to write them again and again," Katharine said. "Practice makes perfect."

She called the office at the time Dr. Upton usually got to work. While waiting for him to answer, she discovered that by standing against the opposite wall she could see John's lower body on the bed. The covers shifted. Dr. Upton came on the line, and she described the harrowing experience.

"Good Lord," he said. "I thought I was being overly cautious."

"I'm glad you were. I'll return the cylinder when John gets up, but I won't linger at the office in case I'm contagious."

"Quite right. Take the rest of the day off." He paused. "A stream of patients has walked in. I have to deal with them."

She hung up, called the telephone exchange, and asked to be connected to the Calgary General Hospital. In John's bedroom, the covers moved near his legs. The hospital switchboard operator replied and put her through to Hamish McBride's laboratory. When he answered, she asked if she could bring him a liquid sample for analysis.

"Certainly." He rolled the *r* with his Scottish brogue. "We aren't busy today, aside from the flu unit. Everyone with nonessential complaints avoids the hospital like the plague and wisely so. It's the best place in Calgary to get sick."

John's lower body now lay still under the covers. She'd let him sleep as long as he wanted. "Would around two o'clock be fine?"

"Perfect. I'll look forward to seeing your charming face."

This would give her time to serve lunch and assess John's ability to be left alone with the children. Strictly speaking, she shouldn't ride the streetcar to the hospital with possible contagion in her home, but she'd sit as far from others as she could.

In the kitchen, she found the children drawing pictures rather than letters on their slates. Rather good likenesses of ogres and trolls. She decided Marguerite had covered penmanship yesterday and suggested they practice reading in the living room.

"I only know my letters," Lillian said.

"You'll listen to Henry read, and we'll both teach you how to sound out words."

How did one teach children to read? She sat on the davenport, a child on each side. Henry stumbled and droned through the story in his third-grade reader. She told him to pause in places, so they could show Lillian how the consonants and vowels blended to form a word. Katharine repeated words, to reinforce the sounds, but she doubted Lillian grasped the concept or, with the disruptions, that either child followed the story's plot.

After less than an hour of reading, all of them were ready for something else. Sums,

Katharine supposed, although she understood now why John had substituted cooking and playtime for academics. Blue sky outside the front window beckoned, but she trooped the children to the kitchen to work at the table. The aroma of baking bread saturated the room.

A half hour later, John emerged from his bedroom dressed in loose pants and a shirt with a hole in the elbow. No one to impress today.

"The bread smell woke me up," he said.

"Can we play outside?" Henry asked.

Katharine wouldn't mind a break from sums, which she'd enjoyed as a child but didn't need to relearn. "Your hard work has earned you recess before lunch."

"Yay!" They bolted from the table.

John put the kettle on for tea. "I'll wait to eat your war bread. I've grown used to the taste."

"You look well today."

He nodded. "Makes me think this flu is overrated."

"Only because Dr. Upton gave me the antidote."

The kettle whistled. To prevent John from pouring while standing on one foot, Katharine filled both of their teacups. She shoved the school materials aside and set his cup on the table.

John took his usual chair facing the side window. "You're not going to work today?"

"I'll go in this afternoon unless I develop symptoms," she lied. Why resurrect their argument about the whisky?

"They say once you've had the Spanish flu, you're immune," he said. "Now I'm free."

"To do what?"

"Among other things, play my sax with abandon at the club Saturday night."

Katharine nodded. If Hamish said the whisky was good and John probably had the flu, she wouldn't have to worry about him catching it from club staff or patrons. Another reason to have the bottle checked.

* * *

Katharine set the cannister on her reception desk. Dr. Upton was in his office with a patient. Others filled the waiting room. She longed to get them organized for their appointments but had to treat herself as possibly contagious, and Hamish awaited.

The streetcar ride reminded her of how much she enjoyed her rare travels out of Tuxedo Park. Tucked behind her mask, alone at her window seat, she loved looking at the passing view. As the streetcar cruised down the hill toward downtown, the numbers of people, carriages, and motorcars increased. Since it was sunny, she got off one stop early and walked the extra distance to the General Hospital. Hamish McBride's job involved creating medicines for patient treatments, although he also used his laboratory on evenings and weekends for his personal projects. She didn't know if this was with or without the hospital's approval. Dr. Upton had told her that Hamish was developing a rheumatism tonic that he hoped to manufacture and sell to the public.

The hospital receptionist recognized her from a visit three months ago. Katharine assured her she knew the way to the basement lab. She'd hate working in the windowless space, but Hamish paid no more attention to sunshine than Dr. Upton did to the food he ate. On her way down the stairs, she wondered how she'd got on a first-name basis with Hamish, who was roughly Dr. Upton's age. Her boss always called her Mrs. Sterling.

She knocked on the lab door. Hamish answered, dressed in a lab coat and protective glasses, and greeted her with his usual effusion. "Katharine, wonderful to have you drop by. What can I do for you and George?"

"Dr. Upton didn't send me this time."

Hamish removed his glasses, placed them on a table next to some beakers, and grabbed a mask from a wall hook. "Since you're wearing one, I'll join you. I keep these for going around the hospital." His blue eyes crinkled. "We look like a pair of bandits. My wife says I came to Alberta to find the wild west, and now, it's here."

"We should stand apart too."

He backed up to a table covered with weigh scales, as well as mortars and pestles of various sizes. In the room's far corner, his assistant attended to their laboratory mice. As Katharine described the events of the past two days, Hamish's frown lines deepened.

"Is it moonshine?" he asked.

"I've assumed the whisky was produced and imported legally. The bottle has a label."

"Let me see," Hamish said. "Labels can be fabricated."

She took the bottle out of her handbag and passed it to him. "Is moonshine subject to natural contamination?"

"Yes. It's a danger." Hamish peered at the label. "I'm pleased to see they've spelled *whisky* correctly. The Irish and Americans insert a frivolous *e*, although the Yanks can't make up their minds and sometimes follow the proper Scottish way."

"Does the label look fake?"

"It's a Canadian brand I don't recognize." He tried to peel the label off. "A good sign—it adheres well. Made in Ontario, although labels on legal bottles sometimes falsify details. The colour's a beautiful amber. Another good sign."

These might be bad signs—moonshine would be more prone to accidental rather than intended contamination.

"I'll risk a sniff." Hamish opened the bottle, lowered his mask, and inhaled the contents. "Ah. The water of life." His bushy eyebrows moved up and down. "The word *whisky* comes from the Gaelic *uisge breatha,* which means 'water of life.'" He sniffed again. "I detect smoky and spicey flavours. Nutmeg, cinnamon, toffee. Probably corn based, assuming it truly is Canadian, but rye driven. Would you like a whiff?"

She shook her head. "I wouldn't be able to tell the difference. The aroma is good?"

"Superb for the probable price," he said. "I'd recognize the brand if it were expensive." He held up the bottle. "I'll study this after I get through my hospital work. Can I phone you at home if I find something later today?"

"Please do." After pleasantries and goodbyes, she left the hospital and rode the streetcar back to her neighbourhood, where she stopped at the butcher's and bought a ham on sale for twenty-four cents a pound. They would have meat tonight.

She entered her house to the sound of John's saxophone and the banging of pots. The post had arrived with no significant mail.

John stood beside the piano. He stopped playing when he spotted her in the living room archway. "Music class," he said. "We're learning the C major scale."

Lillian spun the piano stool. "*C, D, E—*"

Henry's "drums" drowned out the rest of her chant.

"You're home early," John said.

"Dr. Upton feels I deserve a break after the recent events." Each lie led to another. She'd be glad when the lying stopped.

In the bedroom, she took off her work clothes and corset and put on her long underwear and gingham dress. Did John feel equally relieved when he removed his artificial limb? As she entered the hall, the children ran by her into the kitchen.

"Time for cooking class?" she said.

"Uncle John says he'll play catch outside," Henry said.

John emerged from the living room wearing his leg. "I could use the fresh air."

Evidently cooking class had lost its allure. Katharine prepared the ham and peeled and chopped vegetables hoping Hamish would call soon with an all-clear result.

After dinner, she suggested another evening of music. This time, she played "Alexander's Ragtime Band" with every key hit correctly, but the joy was gone, perhaps because she now associated the tune with Vincent's last day on earth.

She and the children slogged through their bedtime ritual. Teeth brushing, dressing in nightclothes, prayers, pleas for an extra story or poem. Though tired enough to crawl into bed with Lillian, Katharine tucked the children in and joined John in the living room.

He stood by the sideboard. "Where did you put Vincent's whisky? I didn't see it in the garbage pail."

"You looked?"

"Seems I didn't trust you, with good reason."

She was too weary to think of a lie. "I took it to Hamish McBride at the hospital."

"Why?" His eyebrows raised.

"To allay our suspicions."

"*Your* suspicions. I told you not to do this."

"I disagreed, upon reflection."

"It was my bottle and wasn't your place to decide what to do with it."

He brushed past her, holding onto the sideboard and the archway on his way to the hall. She followed him to his bedroom door, which he slammed in her face.

She paced to the kitchen, back to the hall—no sounds from behind his door—into the living room. Surely his anger at Katharine's need to know the truth about the whisky was evidence he suspected Marguerite of doing wrong. How could he hope to form a friendship with Marguerite, perhaps love her, if he had these doubts about her character? Katharine had done him a favour, regardless of Hamish's verdict.

The thought calmed her down enough to sit and make masks while she waited for word from Hamish—or John. At nine o'clock, she gave up on them both. She'd risen early and needed sleep for her busy day tomorrow catching up on patient files. As she collected the sewing materials to put away, the telephone rang.

"Katharine?" The Scottish brogue.

She tensed. "Yes."

"I've run your whisky through every test and found something unusual."

Her heart thumped. She glanced at John's door. Still closed, no sounds.

"An ingredient with a chemical structure resembling opium," Hamish said.

"Resembling?"

"That's as precise as I can often get."

She lowered her voice to a whisper. "Do you mean morphine or heroin?"

"Possibly," he said. "But opium poppy derivatives have a taste too bitter for even whisky to mask. My best guess is laudanum."

A tincture of opium flavoured with spices and sometimes honey to make it palatable. Dr. Upton had prescribed laudanum to Vincent for his chronic cough. An overdose could kill a man.

"That whisky was certainly poisoned," Hamish said. "When I fed wee drops to my laboratory mice, they expired of apparent respiratory distress. As you know, opium and alcohol both depress the respiratory system. Together they can be lethal."

How many times had she told patients who left Dr. Upton's office with morphine or heroin prescriptions not to drink liquor? "Should we bring this to the police?"

"That's for you to decide," Hamish said. "These are your neighbours, and I avoid the police when I can. My 'wild west outlaw' nature, my wife would say. Speaking of which, my dear wife will kill me if I don't leave for home right now. Can you come by tomorrow to discuss this?"

This would mean lying to John again and lying to Dr. Upton tomorrow. She also needed to go to work after missing a day, but she couldn't stop when she'd taken her suspicions this far. "What time?"

"Nine-thirty?"

What would she do with Hamish's information? Now she understood why John wanted to throw the bottle out. It might have been better not to know, but it was too late for that.

Chapter Five

Someone knocked on Detective Bertram Tanner's open door.

Julia stood in the doorframe. "A woman's here claiming a case of suspicious death. Do you have time to see her?"

Bertram nodded and shoved aside the case file he'd been perusing. Julia handed him the initial report she'd prepared and left to get the woman.

He skimmed the details. *Mrs. Katarzyna Sterling.* Julia had typed *Katharine* in brackets. *Age thirty. Residence Tuxedo Park.* A fairly new neighbourhood north of the Bow River, it was one of the suburbs that had burst into existence with Calgary's prewar real-estate boom. Bertram hadn't been to Tuxedo Park but had heard it was working class.

Julia reappeared with the woman, introduced her to Bertram, and departed. Mrs. Sterling's mask prompted him to take one out of his desk drawer. The chief had advised the staff to wear them for indoor meetings, but so far no one had complied, including the chief.

"Please take a seat, Mrs. Sterling." Bertram waved at the chair across from his desk.

She sat and touched her mask. "I believe we're far enough apart. If you don't mind, I find it easier to talk without one."

Bertram agreed—and masks concealed suspects' and witnesses' facial expressions. Easier to tell if they were lying or concealing information. He left his mask on the desk.

Her mask had concealed an oval face and a chin that jutted up in confidence. She wore a felt hat with a rolled brim decorated with a simple green ribbon. He found feathers, plumes and bows on female hats fussy adornments. Her chestnut hair was pulled back in a bun behind her neck. She clutched a large handbag on her lap.

He eased into the conversation with pleasantries. "I noticed your Christian name. Is your background Ukrainian?" Several families from that part of the world had settled near Beiseker.

"Polish," she said. "From Manitoba. My husband and I moved here in 1911."

As did many others that boom year. Bertram placed his palms on his desk and shifted to business. "I understand you wish to report a suspicious death?"

"Yes." Her green dress had a wide collar, which he gathered was the fashion. Her direct gaze struck him as open and honest, not challenging. The form stated that she worked as a doctor's receptionist.

"I don't know where to begin," she said, but instantly began by telling him about a knock on her door Tuesday evening.

Bertram jotted notes while she described the events with minimal digressions. He judged her a competent woman and was impressed with her attempt at artificial respiration—it would be a useful skill for police officers—and her later success at reviving her brother.

"He was fortunate you were present," Bertram said, when she paused for a breath.

"It helped that, unlike Vincent, John's lungs weren't compromised by tuberculosis—you might call it consumption."

She related her suspicions following her brother's brush with death and told him about her connection to the hospital technician Hamish McBride; his analysis of the whisky; and his conclusion that an opiate, probably laudanum, had entered the whisky after Monday evening, when both men drank from the bottle with no ill effects.

"Vincent had a prescription for laudanum," she said, "but it's a common medicine found in most households."

Including Bertram's, prescribed for his depression. Laudanum had helped him sleep, but he'd stopped taking it from fear of growing dependent. "You mentioned that your neighbour, the deceased, was a pharmacist," he said. "He'd be aware of laudanum's potential dangers, especially when mixed with alcohol."

She nodded. "His wife, Marguerite, assisted him at the drug store and would be

81

equally aware." She paused. "I'm not accusing her."

But she just had, and the spouse was always the first suspect in domestic cases. "Did Mrs. DeLuca benefit financially from her husband's death?"

"She inherits all that he had, which, she told us, is more than she'd expected. I don't know if he had a life-insurance policy. She only works mornings, though, and earns far less than he did as a full-time certified pharmacist. My guess is she loses a great deal financially from his death."

Bertram agreed it looked to be so on the surface. "Would Mr. DeLuca have reason to take his own life?"

Mrs. Sterling jolted upright, as though this hadn't occurred to her. "He had a chronic health condition," she said, her tone reflective. "I found him reserved, perhaps saddened by his experience of the war. As a pharmacist, he had the knowledge. If Marguerite had told him she'd lost her taste for whisky, Vincent would know he'd be the only one drinking from the bottle that night. I think his boarder, the other resident in their home, is a teetotaller."

Bertram liked how she reasoned this through. He had no doubts that her account was credible and essentially correct.

"But why would he take his own life in this fashion?" she asked.

He kept his stare neutral, leaving her to continue her thought.

"To make it appear a natural death by Spanish flu? Bad as that is for loved ones left behind, it would be less disturbing. Vincent and Marguerite were both raised Catholic. The Church views taking one's life a mortal sin." Her brow furrowed. "I'm saddened by his death but would be satisfied with this conclusion."

Bertram glanced down to hide his thoughts. *Unfortunately, we can't choose our conclusions.* "I'd like to see this bottle. Does Mr. McBride still have possession of it?"

"He returned it to me." She reached into her handbag, took out a bulging paper bag, and pulled out a bottle.

Bertram got a handkerchief from his desk drawer, although a fingerprint analysis would almost certainly be useless, given that several people had handled the bottle. Still, he protected the glass with the handkerchief while he studied the label.

"Produced in Ontario," she said. "Hamish believes it was legally manufactured."

"We'll have our expert test the contents and container."

"Of course, but unless his laboratory equipment is superior to the hospital's, I doubt he'll discover more than Hamish did."

She had a confidence he liked, and a pretty smile. Her account implied no husband was living with her. Was he deceased or away at war?

"Will you let me know your expert's results?" she asked.

"I will," he said. "If this leads to interviewing your neighbours, I won't mention your name, but will they guess you brought this our attention?"

"I wrestled with my deed and decided to accept the consequences. But if Vincent did end his own life, would Marguerite be better off unaware? That would have been his wish."

Bertram's Protestant church forgave suicide, officially at least. Since the death of Nellie and their baby, he'd thought about killing himself numerous times. But the act would leave his parents devastated, and that understanding, one low, awful night, had held him back from putting a bullet in his head. A pharmacist's natural method would be a medicine, which was better than a gun for disguising suicide. Loved ones were best left ignorant of a child's or spouse's depth of misery. "Do you have more to add?"

"I'm sure I've forgotten some details."

Everyone did, unintentionally and on purpose. What was Mrs. Sterling leaving out? She'd mentioned her brother had spent the night comforting the widow. Were they having an affair? Did she realize this made him a suspect?

"You've given me enough for now," Bertram said. "We might require a more formal interview later." He hoped they would.

Hope? Had he felt this since Nellie's and Robert's deaths?

"A thought just occurred to me," Mrs. Sterling said. "Mrs. DeLuca will be with her late husband's family in Crowsnest Pass until tomorrow afternoon, when my brother will meet her at the train station downtown. Her boarder should be home tonight, if you want to speak to him without her present."

A sharp idea. "What is his name?"

"Clarence ... his surname escapes me. My brother is friendlier with their household than I."

Indeed. Bertram used the handkerchief to pick up the bottle and repack it in the paper bag. "I'll walk you to the reception area. Thank you for taking the time to come in."

"Thank you for listening." She smiled again. "I'm sure I went on too long."

"Not at all," he said, and meant it. "I'll telephone you when I get our expert's report, which should be no later than Monday." He liked knowing they'd speak another time.

In the reception area, he bade her farewell and asked Julia to type up the details written on the bottle label. While he trusted Mrs. Sterling, he should confirm the existence of her expert. "Please telephone the Calgary General Hospital and ask if a Mr. Hamish McBride works in their laboratory. You don't want to speak to him, though."

"Will do," Julia said. "I'll set up a file for the case."

"Thanks. You can get the initial report form from my office while I confirm with the chief about sending the bottle to our lab."

Through the glass wall, he saw the chief at his desk eating a sandwich. The chief noticed Bertram approaching and motioned him in. Seated on the visitor's chair, Betram recounted Mrs. Sterling's report.

"Death by whisky?" The chief chuckled. "My wife would say liquor is its own poison."

"I think it's worth having our expert analyze the bottle and contents."

"Go ahead. Give him a chance to play with his fancy new equipment the taxpayers bought him."

"Since timeliness is essential, I'd like to start interviews tonight."

"Before our lab report?" the chief said. "That's premature."

"One key witness is available this evening without the prime suspect present."

"Could this woman who came in have a vendetta against her neighbour?"

"That's possible," Bertram had to admit. "But I can afford to jump a gun or two when I'm not busy with other work."

"True. If this flu shuts down all of our citizens' boisterous activities, you and I will be out of work." The chief picked up his sandwich. "Go on and do what you think best."

Bertram returned to the reception area. He was still certain about his decision to leave police work, but the whisky case had caught his interest for reasons he'd mull later. If the case didn't fizzle, it might prove a fitting finale to his career.

"Hamish McBride exists at the General Hospital," Julia said. "The receptionist called him an eccentric genius."

McBride wasn't only credible—he might be fun.

Fun? Another word Bertram hadn't associated with his work or himself for almost a year.

* * *

Katharine left the office with Dr. Upton, exhausted from her morning trip downtown followed by her afternoon spent cleaning up the piles of scribbled notes that had accumulated during her day and a half away from work—patient details to type and place in files or use to create new files as well as receipts to record. She suspected a couple of patients had slipped out without paying.

Between her catch-up work and the steady flow of patients, she hadn't found an appropriate time to tell Dr. Upton she'd taken the whisky to Hamish and the police.

They rounded the corner. Dr. Upton stared ahead. "Looks like a game going on."

"That's John with his back to us." He stood in the middle of the street behind Lillian and Henry, who kicked a ball to a group of children about twenty feet down the road.

87

"Good to see he's feeling better." Dr. Upton waved goodbye and turned into the lane.

During breakfast and lunch, John had acted as though their argument the previous night hadn't happened. Katharine went along, glad to avoid telling him about Hamish's phone call and her plan for today.

Her next-door neighbour Irene Murphy was outside raking her front yard. The opposing kickball team of five children belonged to Irene and her boarder, Gladys Lysenko. Both were war widows. Gladys worked downtown, while Irene minded the children, an arrangement that enabled both women to live comfortably.

Katharine passed her own house and stopped in front of Irene, who rested her hands on her rake.

"John told me about Vincent," Irene said. "How shocking and sad for him and Marguerite. I hadn't got to know them as well as I should have, but I'll make an effort with her now that we have this in common, both with lost husbands." Her eyes darkened.

A cheer erupted on the street. John tottered on his right foot. With his left, he kicked the ball to the five opponents, who scrambled for a kick.

"What's that game called?" Katharine asked.

"Kickball," Irene said. "They made it up. Don't ask me the rules, but I insisted they stay in their family groupings and don't cross the no-man's land between them."

"That sounds reasonably safe."

Irene looked beyond Katharine's shoulder. "Who's that coming down the street?"

Katharine turned around. A woman approached. "Gladys?"

"It doesn't look like her walk."

The woman carried a handbag and valise and was shorter than Gladys. Katharine had also never seen Gladys wear a skirt several inches above her ankles. The woman studied each house on her way and stopped at the border of Katharine's and Irene's yards. The woman's dark hair was cut short and crimped into waves, a style worn by several of Dr. Upton's younger patients.

"Do you know where Vincent DeLuca lives?" she asked Katharine and Irene. "I've misplaced his address, but the drug store owner told me he lives on this street."

"Are you a friend?" Katharine said.

"His cousin, Pina."

He had a second cousin in Calgary? "Have you heard what happened?"

"You mean that he died?" Pina said. "I've just come from his funeral in the Pass."

"Marguerite went there with his cousin."

"That was me," she said. "I took an early train home. I'd had enough of listening to relatives wail and turn Vincent into a saint. I don't know how Marguerite can stand it."

When John had referred to Vincent's older cousin, Katharine had pictured a woman in her forties or fifties. Pina didn't look older than thirty-five, which would be ten years older than Vincent. "Is Marguerite still in Crowsnest Pass?"

Pina nodded. "Until tomorrow. She said I could stay at her place tonight to avoid my evil landlady." She smirked. "Another reason I left early was to talk to her boss about the apartment he has to rent before someone else grabs it. I caught him as he was leaving the drug store. He said he's saving the place for Marguerite's boarder, but she told me nothing about this. I'll clear that up with Clarence."

"I haven't noticed him come home yet," Irene said.

"Marguerite gave me a key," Pina said. "Which is their house?"

Katharine pointed diagonally across the street. "It's the one with the short iron fence. Do you know Clarence?"

Pina nodded. "What are your names, by the way? We'll become neighbours if I get the apartment."

"I'm Katharine, and she's Irene. Is Clarence expecting you?"

"No, but he won't mind my staying overnight."

That arrangement wasn't Katharine's business, but Pina might have overlooked the presumed cause of Vincent's death. "Clarence might be contagious with the flu.

Keep your distance and don't stay if he shows the least symptom."

"I'll be prudent." Pina thanked them for the directions. She veered behind Irene's and Gladys' children and continued to Marguerite's gate.

"Prudent doesn't seem her style," Irene said, her tone amused. "Morals have changed since the war."

Katharine glanced at Irene's shadowed face. She was Irish Catholic and devout, Katharine gathered, based on Irene's regular churchgoing and past comments.

On the street, John's gaze followed Pina to Marguerite's front porch. The ball rolled past him. Pina searched through her handbag for several minutes, evidently found the key, and disappeared into the house.

"Perhaps not the most organized person," Irene said.

"I should get inside to organize dinner."

"When this is over, let's have tea sometime," Irene said. "Between the war and managing my household, I've let our friendship drift."

"My fault, more than yours, with my work and John moving in."

"I enjoyed his saxophone music through the window this summer," Irene said. "Do you still play the piano?"

"When I find the time."

"I remember that evening at your house as my last joyful time before the war stole our former lives."

Irene's husband lay among the dead and buried near Passchendaele. As Katharine walked the short distance to her house, she reflected that part of the friendship's drift had occurred because she was always conscious that her husband had survived while Irene's hadn't. *Survived so far*, she corrected herself. If a letter from Eddie had arrived today, John would have left the game to tell her.

Footsteps pounded on the stairs behind her. John joined her on the porch.

"You abandoned kickball?" she asked as they went inside.

"I claimed a bathroom break. Who was that you sent to Marguerite's house?"

Katharine explained about Pina and hung up her coat and hat.

"Marguerite says she's Giuseppina to her relatives and Pina in Calgary," John said. "Vincent's family views her as the black sheep."

"A modern woman?"

"She smokes and never wears corsets." John winked and walked down the hall.

He and Marguerite had discussed such intimate matters? Even Katharine avoided talk of corsets with him.

She marched to her bedroom, stripped off her petticoat and corset, and couldn't deny she loved the easier breathing. John's teasing wink was a good sign he held no grudge against her for last night's argument.

* * *

Bertram exited the streetcar at Mrs. Sterling's street and crossed to the west side of Centre Street, dodging a buggy and motorcar. As he'd expected, Dr. G. W. Upton Family Medicine was closed for the evening. So was Fielding and Sons next door. The drug store's door was angled to the corner, which gave the building more style than most of the suburban structures Bertram had viewed on his ride to Tuxedo Park.

He walked down Mrs. Sterling's street and tipped his fedora against the blinding sun to the southwest. It would be dusk now on standard time. He appreciated the extra hour of evening light that enabled him to read these street numbers and would support continuing daylight savings time after the war, mainly because it would reduce crime. The police had no doubts about the correlation between evening darkness and robberies and brawls, but the newspapers insisted the government's emergency measure to reduce fuel and electricity costs during the war was temporary.

At Mrs. Sterling's house, Bertram paused to study the bungalow with a central door flanked by two windows, the common design on this street. In the course of his work, he'd visited enough of these boxy homes to predict the floor plan. The larger window on his right-hand side would look into the living room and the other window a bedroom, with a kitchen, bathroom, and second bedroom at the back. Bertram preferred his rambling, if less functional, downtown home, although he liked the quiet here. Car engines and horse-and-carriage clops frequently woke him at night.

To recreate Katharine Sterling's action of three evenings ago, he crossed her street diagonally to the DeLucas' home. A knee-high iron fence enclosed the front yard, which was overgrown with dead plants. They'd likely bloomed beautifully in summer. He rang the doorbell and mentally rehearsed his introduction to Clarence, the boarder. A woman opened the door.

Bertram repressed his surprise. "Mrs. DeLuca?"

"*Miss* DeLuca. Oh. You mean my cousin's wife, Marguerite. She's away for the night. Are you a friend of hers?"

Miss DeLuca had cropped, wavy hair and wore a skirt that revealed her lower legs, a style he'd noticed lately on women. A male voice that might be singing bellowed behind her, presumably from a Victrola.

"In fact, I'm here to see Clarence," Bertram said.

"He's in the bath."

To hide his further surprise, he took out his badge. "I'm Detective Bertram Tanner.

I'd like to speak with him about Mr. DeLuca's passing."

Her arched eyebrows shot up. "Why are the police involved? He died of the flu."

Bertram had promised himself to do his best to avoid implicating Mrs. Sterling. "A routine investigation." He held his breath and prayed she accepted his reply.

She glanced at the badge. "I suppose you can come in if you can stand the singing."

Relieved, he entered and realized the voice flowed from behind the door directly down the hall, which likely led to the bathroom in this home that was similar to Mrs. Sterling's. The singing was loud and out of tune. He didn't recognize the song.

"Marguerite hates his singing in the tub," Miss DeLuca said. "He's taking advantage of her absence and used her hot water last night as well. Otherwise, Clarence is harmless."

Or he might be guilty of a terrible crime. Bertram intended to glean which was true.

* * *

The rigorous outdoor play before dinner had tired the children enough for Katharine to progress them quickly through their bedtime routine. She contemplated telling John tonight that she'd taken the whisky bottle to the police even if he didn't bring the subject up. If the police expert found nothing wrong with the whisky and Detective Tanner chose not to pursue the case, she might keep her deed from John indefinitely.

But as she tucked the children in, she decided John had to know now. If the detective had taken her advice to interview Clarence tonight, John was bound to find out from Clarence or Marguerite and feel Katharine had betrayed him. Worry about this would prey on her all weekend. Best to reveal her deceptions and get his anger over with.

She left the bedroom and followed the saxophone tones to the living room. John sat sideways on the davenport, his legs extended, the instrument propped on his lap. As she sat in the armchair, he leaned toward the coffee table and crossed out something written on a sheet of paper.

"What are you doing?" she asked.

"Trying to compose a song."

"I didn't know you wrote music."

"I don't, it would seem." He placed the sax on the coffee table. "Let's put some real music on the Victrola."

"John," she said. "I haven't been completely truthful this past day."

"Is this confession time?" His glib tone contrasted the quiver in his face. He shifted to a straight sitting position, one foot on the floor, his pant leg dangling from his stump.

"Hamish called after you went to bed last night."

"I heard the ring and wondered if it was him."

But he hadn't asked her about the call. Sometimes she didn't understand why he kept certain things to himself, but she had been equally guilty of this lately. "Hamish said he'd completed his research and asked me to come to the hospital today." She summarized Hamish's findings. "He returned the bottle and left me to do what I thought was right."

"I hope you tossed the bloody bottle in the Bow River."

She fixed her gaze on John. "I took it to the police."

He jerked back. "Why? This will do no one any good."

"If the police confirm no wrongdoing, our suspicions will be allayed."

"Your suspicions. Not mine. I have none." He crossed his arms.

He might have had none initially, but she'd planted them now. "John, if you want to become more than friends with Marguerite ..."

His hands dropped to his thighs. "Is that what it's about? You're afraid I'll leap into the arms of a murderess?"

That was essentially right.

He looked wide-eyed, innocent. "All I've done is help a neighbour, the widow of my deceased friend, like any decent human being."

He seemed to believe this. Perhaps it was true, but proximity led people to slip into romance.

John picked up the saxophone, resumed his sideways position on the davenport, and blew notes that appeared to be random. She watched the mutilated half of his lower face puff out and in.

It was almost a year now since his attempt at taking his own life. November 1st. She still cringed at the memory. Her father had called to tell her John had placed a hunting rifle under his chin. Evidently, the weapon had slipped and blown through his cheek. Her mother had been too distraught to come on the phone line.

If the police eventually determined Vincent's death a suicide, he would be long buried in a Catholic cemetery. His family lived far away and wouldn't need to know he should not have been buried in consecrated ground. Marguerite would be saddened to learn of her husband's desperation, assuming this was news to her, but she didn't appear to be religious. Katharine had never seen her and Vincent leaving or returning from church.

John stopped playing and returned the saxophone to the coffee table. "Did your detective indicate what he plans to do with your information?"

"He said he'd have a police expert analyze the whisky, but I don't know if he'll do more than that."

John scowled. "Let's hope the case falls into the police wasteland." He picked up his saxophone again.

Even if the police expert determined the whisky was nothing more than a naturally developed poison, she hoped Detective Tanner wouldn't drop the case. During their brief meeting, he'd impressed her as an intelligent man willing to consider any reasonable argument, however out of the ordinary.

John's saxophone scales segued to Debussy's *"Rhapsodie mauresque"* for saxophone and piano. An invitation for a duet with Katharine? Instead, she went to the front window. Detective Tanner could be on his way to interview Clarence right now.

No motorcars drove down her street. Nobody strolled through the dusky evening light. Still, the detective might have followed through on her suggestion. Perhaps she'd just missed him.

Chapter Six

Seated in the living room, Bertram listened to Pina—she had insisted Bertram call her by her nickname, and he agreed Miss DeLuca was too formal for her—ramble about her trip to Crowsnest Pass. Vincent's father and her father were brothers, who had immigrated to there to work in the coal mines, like many Italians.

Pina's depiction of grieving relatives brought Bertram back to the blurred days following the deaths of Nellie and their son. Nellie's mother's red eyes and her father's stooped shoulders had reflected their inward tears. No doubt Bertram had looked equally wretched as he nodded at visitors' platitudes. *She was a beautiful person. It was God's will. They're both in a better place.* He'd wanted to throttle them all. Worse had been the doctors' and nurses' clinical remarks. *At her age, childbirth was a high risk. Had the child lived, there was a likelihood of brain damage. He'd have been a burden for life.*

Bertram balled his fists on his lap. The mourning of Vincent DeLuca sounded similar, although louder and Italian. According to Pina, his mother had wept and wailed. His father had cursed the war that had weakened his son's lungs and spread the flu with the movement of troops around the world.

"'There would be no problems if everyone stayed home.'" Pina quoted Vincent's father. "He forgets that he left home for Canada."

In contrast, Pina said, Marguerite had been largely silent behind her veil. Cousins and aunts had loaned her their surplus mourning attire. "My family lives for funerals and weddings." Her scowl implied she viewed both occasions as equally unpleasant.

She crossed one leg over the other, causing her green dress to ride up her calf. Their armchairs faced the front window, Bertram's chair next to the crackling fireplace. A card table stood in front of the window, a pile of papers on top, a cabinet underneath.

Bertram realized the singing had stopped. He'd give Clarence time to dress before sending Pina to fetch him. She'd advised Clarence of his visitor through the closed bathroom door.

"They all hate Marguerite," Pina continued, "even the ones who'd never set eyes on her before the funeral. Vincent only brought her to the Pass once to meet the family." She leaned toward Bertram, conspiratorially, her dark eyes bright. "Before the war, Vincent was seeing a nice Italian girl in the Pass. He'd visit her from Calgary and take her out for drives in a friend's motorcar. She waited for him for three years of war, so you can imagine the shock when Vincent appeared with Marguerite. He hadn't told the family he'd married overseas."

A common story, but sad for the woman left behind.

"She came to the funeral on the arm of the motorcar friend to show she'd moved on."

"Good for her," Bertram said. Good that she'd either moved on or didn't want people's pity. Or both.

Pina said that whenever a relative caught her alone at the funeral, they'd comment on Marguerite's coldness. Most interpreted it as proof she didn't care about Vincent. One cousin said she'd understand if Marguerite were English, but the French wore their hearts on their sleeves. "Half of them think she married Vincent to get away from wartime conditions in France," Pina said. "The other half are convinced she'll go back to France as soon as the Germans stop torpedoing our ships."

"What do you think?"

"I don't know." She shook her head. "Marguerite and I hardly talked on the train ride to the Pass. I asked her to leave early with me, but she wanted to stay. Duty, I guess. I preferred riding home without her. Not talking was awkward."

Bertram could see that silence might be difficult for Pina.

Footsteps sounded in the hall. Clarence appeared in the doorframe, his hair slicked back from his bath. He wore a sweater and baggy trousers. Bertram rose to greet him.

Clarence extended his hand and withdrew it. "I keep forgetting. No contact, although had Vincent passed the damn flu on to me, I'd have shown symptoms by now."

"So would Marguerite," Pina said. "I heard on the streetcar that the city has ordered the closure of dance halls, theatres, and everything fun in Calgary."

Clarence nodded. "It's about time the health department acted to prevent the spread of this disease."

But Clarence hadn't put on a mask, and Bertram wouldn't encourage it. People were more open without them.

Clarence apologized to Bertram for keeping him waiting. "I love singing, but the church and the bath are the sole places that tolerate my voice. The churches have also been ordered closed, and I rarely frequent them anyway." He looked at Bertram. "Pina said you're a policeman. You aren't in uniform."

Bertram took out his badge and introduced himself. "Detectives wear civilian clothing. We investigate rather than enforce the law." No need to add that their suits enabled them to blend in and put suspects and witnesses at ease in hopes they'd reveal more.

"What are you investigating?" Clarence asked.

Rather than answer, Bertram turned to Pina. "Would you allow us privacy?"

"I'm sure the detective would appreciate a cup of tea," Clarence told her. "I would too. Marguerite keeps it in the cupboard above the side counter."

Pina frowned at him but left the room. Clarence sat on the wooden chair against the interior wall, which had floral wallpaper and displayed not a single picture. Nor were there any pictures on the other walls or on the fireplace mantel. Nothing personal in this room.

Bertram returned to the armchair near the fireplace and took out his notebook. "I like to start with particulars. What is your full name?"

"Clarence Aloysius Oxenham."

"How do you spell that?"

He spelled each name and didn't object to Bertram taking notes. "I'd prefer to be simple Clarence. The others are cumbersome."

"Your age?"

"Twenty-eight last month."

Bertram would have guessed he was several years older. Clarence's blotched skin might be ruddiness from his bath. He sat straight in his chair, didn't fidget, and answered primly, like a student to a teacher.

"What is your occupation?"

"Painter at the Ogden Shops."

Bertram nodded. The Canadian Pacific Railway repair yard was the city's single largest employer. He was curious to know what Clarence painted, but this wasn't likely to be relevant. "How long have you worked there?"

"Going on three years," he said. "Prior to that, I spent seven years at the Angus Shops in Montreal until the railway offered me this opportunity."

Bertram made point-form notes. "How long have you lodged with Mr. and Mrs. DeLuca?"

"Eight months. I used to live downtown but found the rents expensive. Ogden was almost as bad. Residents know employees want to live near work and jack up their rates."

"Why did you choose Tuxedo Park?"

"Pina," he said. "She's my bank teller downtown. We got to talking, and I asked if she knew of any decent, inexpensive accommodation. It happened her cousin was thinking of renting a room, which led to this." He gestured around the living room. "It's about as far in this city as I can get from the Shops, which isn't necessarily a disadvantage. When I leave work, I like leaving the job behind. Don't you, Detective?"

Bertram bristled at the deft lob. In the past, his work on a hot case stayed with him obsessively, day and night. He'd loved the passion of his work.

"What's keeping Pina?" Clarence glanced over his shoulder at the living room arch and returned to Bertram. "Is this about Katharine Sterling?"

Bertram startled too quickly to hide his surprise.

"Did Marguerite report her?" Clarence asked. "It's the sort of mad thing she would do. After Vincent died, Marguerite blamed Katharine for pounding his lungs to death. I'm sure by then he was a lost cause and nothing anyone did could have made him worse."

Bertram recovered his composure enough to recall Mrs. Sterling's attempt at artificial respiration. He decided not to question Clarence on her methods to avoid mentioning her.

"After the doctor left with the morgue car," Clarence said, "Marguerite ranted against him too, saying he'd taken too long to arrive. It's human nature to lash out in anger and blame everyone but ourselves."

Footsteps clacked in the hall.

"Here she is now with our tea," Clarence said.

Pina entered the room holding a tray with a tea service. "It took me forever to light the stove. I've grown used to my landlady doing all the cooking."

"And yet you want to move." Clarence smirked.

"She has other problems."

"Such as house rules." Clarence's eyes crinkled. "Curfews. No suitors in the boarding house. No smoking in rooms, even with the window open."

"She has a nose like a hawk." Pina carried the tray to the card table. "Can you move these papers?"

Clarence went to the table and picked up the papers. "These are Vincent's word-cross puzzles. He worked on them every evening."

"I didn't know he liked puzzles," Pina said.

"They were his main hobby," Clarence said. "He subscribed to newspapers from the United States that featured word-cross but found most of their puzzles too simple. That started him designing his own. He sent them to the newspaper editors, but none bought them. The *Calgary Herald* wasn't interested either." Clarence stashed the papers in the cabinet under the card table.

Pina set the tray on the table and told Clarence to help himself to tea. "How do you take yours, Detective Tanner?"

"One milk, one sugar, please," Bertram said.

Pina brought him a full teacup, spilling a few drops on the Oriental carpet, which was faded but an attractive blue and red with octagon shapes. Clarence watched her stride back to the card table, admiringly, Bertram thought. He found Clarence spoke to Pina with a tone of familiarity. She'd explained to Bertram that she was spending the night here to line up more congenial accommodation in the neighbourhood.

"How did Vincent get interested in word-cross?" Pina asked.

Clarence brushed Pina's arm as he stirred his tea. He carried the cup to his chair. "It started with the war, in a sense. He did puzzles to pass the time and discovered he had a knack for them. An officer encouraged him to practice working on codes and apply for a transfer to intelligence, mainly to escape the bloodshed in the trenches. But the army turned his application down because he was born in Italy."

"Isn't Italy on our side?" Bertram asked.

"They weren't originally, so, he said, the Allies don't quite trust them."

"That isn't fair." Pina filled a third teacup.

"Perhaps that was Vincent's excuse for not getting the job," Clarence said. "He caught tuberculosis shortly afterward."

Pina headed for the vacant armchair.

"Would you mind taking your tea in the kitchen?" Bertram asked her. "It's best I speak with Clarence alone."

"Why?" Pina halted. "Vincent's my cousin. I deserve to know what happened. Marguerite told me nothing about that night."

"She can stay as far as I'm concerned," Clarence said. "I have no secrets and still don't know why you're investigating, Detective."

Pina sat on the chair. Bertram decided not to object. Forcing her away was less important than getting Clarence's information. Bertram asked him to describe the events of Tuesday evening, hoping to succeed once more at deflecting the question of "why?"

Clarence took a sip of tea. "I was sitting on this chair, Vincent in your chair, Detective, where we sat most nights after dinner. We'd read the newspaper and discuss the war, flu, incompetent governments while Marguerite cleaned up and did the dishes."

"Women's work." Pina sniffed.

Bertram glared at her. "If you're going to stay, you'll have to be quiet, or I will remove you from the room."

"I'll gladly help him." Clarence chortled.

Pina stuck her tongue out at him.

Clarence's expression turned sombre. "Marguerite took longer than usual. Our conversation lingered long enough for Vincent to get his evening whisky from the sideboard." He glanced at the back of the room.

Bertram set his teacup on the table between Pina and him. They both twisted around to view the sideboard, which lined the back wall along with a secretary desk.

"They kept the bottle on top of the sideboard," Clarence said. "As well as glasses for whisky and wine."

Now nothing stood on the sideboard. Mrs. Sterling had said that Marguerite had hurled a glass in anger that night.

While Bertram and Pina drank tea, Clarence recounted the events he'd described to Mrs. Sterling, which she'd passed along to Bertram. Nothing Clarence said contradicted her report, as far as Bertram could recall.

Bertram exchanged his empty teacup for his notebook and pen and scribbled notes to catch up on his recording. Pina remained thankfully quiet. Clarence reached the point in the story where Mrs. Sterling's brother, John Wozniak, appeared at the house.

"John and Vincent became friends this summer," Clarence said. "He'd come over a couple of times a week for a drink."

"Did they usually drink whisky?" Bertram asked.

"Always," Clarence said. "Vincent developed a taste for spirits in the war. Rum and gin reminded him of the trenches."

"Did you ever join them for a drink?"

"Never." He shook his head. "I don't touch liquor of any kind."

"That's your misfortune," Pina said.

"I'm not against it on principle," Clarence said. "People are free to choose their own poisons. Later, after the doctor and the hearse left, and once Marguerite had gone through blaming Katharine and the doctor, she turned her ire on the whisky. She grew hysterical, grabbed the wine glasses from the sideboard, and hurled them at John and me. Nearly clipped my ear." Clarence chuckled.

Mrs. Sterling had indicated a sole glass was thrown. Most likely John had told her this to understate the extent of Marguerite's anger.

"Perhaps there's something to letting your anger out, though." Clarence sounded reflective. "She became perfectly reasonable after that, enough that I felt free to go to bed. I had to get up early the next day for work. I did take John aside and tell him to wake me if he needed help. He didn't."

When he went into the kitchen the next morning, Clarence added, he had found them both seated at the table, drinking tea. Marguerite insisted on making Clarence's breakfast and lunch to take to work. John said his sister needed him at home and left. Marguerite then discussed her plans for the day, which included phoning her in-laws and seeing her lawyer and banker.

Clarence paused to sip his tea. "Brr. This has grown cold with all my talking." He looked wide-eyed at Bertram. "Your turn, Detective. Why are you investigating what appears to be a routine death by influenza? The doctor was virtually certain of this. Has he changed his mind?"

Pina stared at Bertram too. Something howled from the rear of the house.

"What's that?" Pina set down her teacup.

"Probably the dog in the backyard," Clarence said. "It runs free most of the time and shows up here for food."

"Vincent has a dog?" Pina got up.

"It's Marguerite's pet, a feral stray. She let it in last week, and now, we can't get rid of it."

"I'll go see if it wants food." Pina disappeared down the hall.

Clarence rose and hovered over Bertram. "Now where were we, Detective?"

Bertram couldn't press his luck and evasion skills any longer. He stuffed his notebook and pen in his pocket. "I'm on my way out and will leave you to feed the dog." He moved toward the front entrance, and Clarence followed.

"I expect I'll learn what this is about in due course," Clarence said, as Bertram put on his hat, coat, and gloves. "Marguerite and Vincent have been good to me. I hope my talking to you helps them in some way."

"It has." This might not be true.

Bertram thanked Clarence for his time and walked out to the cool night air. Across the quiet street, he stopped in front of Katharine Sterling's home. Light shimmered from her living room window. It wasn't too late to talk to her brother, but she might not have told him she'd taken her suspicions to the police. Bertram wouldn't put her in an uncomfortable position.

He left her house behind and continued to Centre Street. This afternoon, his police contacts had confirmed the distillery in Ontario was a legitimate business that exported whisky to the Alberta government store. The contacts weren't aware of any illegal activities. The distillery hadn't answered Bertram's phone calls. He'd try them again in the morning and request sales records from the government store to customers, which might include this drug store he passed now. Most critically, the lab report on the bottle of whisky should be in tomorrow or Monday. If their expert's analysis found any shred of suspicion, the case would be on its way. Bertram sauntered to the streetcar stop.

Chapter Seven

Dr. Upton paused at the reception desk before he called in his last patient of the day. "I'll close up if you need to go home."

Katharine checked her wristwatch: ten past one. "John won't have to leave for another hour."

"Let us hope Marguerite returns safely." He lowered his voice. "Careless of Vincent's cousin to let her travel alone in her state."

"She's calmed since you saw her Tuesday night."

His lips pressed together, as though he doubted Marguerite's recovery. He motioned the patient toward his examination room.

Katharine returned to typing up Mr. Lawson's appointment details. Every Saturday he came in for his prescription of rum, the only medicine that relieved his back pain caused by constant heavy lifting at his warehouse job. The bottle lasted him a week. Mrs. Lawson and the children were also regular patients. A cheerful woman and a lively brood, Katharine saw no evidence her husband's drinking did them harm.

These two hours past her usual Saturday noon departure would clear her backlog of work, despite the high number of drop-in patients that had prompted Dr. Upton to stay overtime. A woman walked into the office. Katharine started to tell her they were closed, but then recognized Pina DeLuca.

Pina stopped in the middle of the room. "Mr. Fielding says he'll rent me the apartment subject to your recommendation."

Katharine leaned back. "But we only met yesterday."

"He values your judgment."

Pina had abandoned Marguerite in Crowsnest Pass and spent the night with a man, but would that necessarily make her a bad tenant?

"He says he'll keep the drug store open for you to stop in on your way home from work," Pina said. "I have to dash to get the streetcar, so I can give notice and pack and arrange for a car. Thanks for your help." She whirled and left the office without waiting for Katharine's response.

Katharine wouldn't lie for Pina, but presumably Pina had a job, and she was the cousin of Mr. Fielding's late, trusted store manager.

Dr. Upton and his patient emerged from the examination room. Katharine processed the woman's payment while Dr. Upton went to get his overclothes and medical bag.

When he returned, Katharine steeled herself to make a just demand of her employer. "I have a request," she said.

"Could you pay me for my additional time today?"

Dr. Upton looked at her almost cleared desk. "For completing your regular work?"

"I wasn't paid for the day and a half I missed, which was a considerable savings for you."

He snorted. "I lost money while you were away. Two patients grew tired of waiting and walked out, and one I treated escaped without paying."

More than one, she estimated from his records, but this should indicate her value.

"Mrs. Sterling," he said in a cajoling tone. "You're talking about eighty cents."

Those pennies would buy groceries for her family. Dr. Upton, in his fine tailored suit, had no dependents and ate meat every day. But his giving her the oxygen cylinder had probably saved John's life, which was worth far more than a year of potatoes. She brushed off her disappointment and prepared to back down.

"I'll agree," Dr. Upton said, "given the circumstances."

She exhaled in relief and surprise. He didn't part easily with money.

"You appear to show no symptoms," he said, shifting the subject. "No headache, sore throat, fatigue?"

"I'm well so far." More evidence that Vincent and John weren't victims of the flu, which reminded her she'd yet to tell Dr. Upton about her trips to see Hamish

McBride and the police. She'd been too busy with work this morning, and now, she had to talk to Mr. Fielding before getting home to relieve John. Dr. Upton's discovery of her actions would have to wait until Monday.

He wrapped up his work and left before Katharine. She finished with plenty of time for a drug store stop. Mr. Fielding served a lone customer at the counter. The man left with a paper bag that bulged around a bottle of gin. Dr. Upton had told her of doctors who accepted money in exchange for writing liquor prescriptions for no medicinal purpose, but he prescribed spirits only when he genuinely believed they were the best treatment for a particular case. Some patients, including Mr. Lawson, viewed the medicine's intoxicating features as a side benefit.

When the customer left, Katharine stepped up to the counter. "Pina DeLuca said you want to speak to me about the Hicks Block apartment."

"Right," Mr. Fielding said. "My business partner is eager to let it to anyone who will pay the rent. I discussed this with my wife last night. She thinks it would be good for Marguerite to have a relative living nearby. While it would be proper for Clarence to take the apartment and the women to share the house, my wife argued that two women usually clash in the kitchen."

Katharine hadn't thought of Pina as having in interest in domestic tasks, but

Italians, like the French, were known for their pride in cooking.

"Miss DeLuca pointed out that she'll be safer from the flu in an apartment than in her boarding house. Her landlady insists on meeting with her women's groups, and her roommates socialize with friends."

That argument made sense, assuming Pina remained isolated in her apartment.

"She'd like to move in tomorrow, when she can borrow a friend's motorcar," Mr. Fielding said. "What happened to the Sabbath as a day of rest?"

"That ended with the war."

"Hasn't everything?" His eyelids flickered.

Katharine remembered his son missing overseas. She had stopped asking him every time they met if there was news. He'd tell her if there were news, good or bad.

"I was able to reach the manager of the bank, where Miss DeLuca is employed as a teller," he said. "While the new health order permits banks to remain open, he's wisely decided to close on Monday, but she'll receive a salary for the duration. Generous terms."

Mr. Fielding's forehead creased. His drug stores were deemed essential and not included in the health order. He didn't have to consider paying staff despite no income coming in. Of course, banks would continue to earn from investments on the money they held for clientele. This might have made it easier for them to be generous with staff.

"The bank manager confirmed her employment and seemed to know her well," Mr. Fielding said. "His impression was she paid rent and bills on time. Miss DeLuca asked me to wait until dinnertime to call her current landlady for a reference, so she'll have time to give notice. I sensed the woman won't be sad to see her go." He stifled a chuckle. "My concern, of course, is for the tenants in the neighbouring Hicks Block apartments."

"The librarian told me she lives upstairs."

"Yes. The two other units are occupied by schoolteachers, one with children. I wouldn't want them disturbed by loud music or the unsuitable friends Miss DeLuca might bring in. She promised me she'd be quiet, but in business you learn to read people."

Katharine's reading of Pina was probably similar to his, but to mention her overnight stay with Clarence would be gossip, and Katharine could only assume Pina favoured loud music. It would be fair to both landlord and tenant to stick to the facts. "I hadn't heard of Pina DeLuca before Vincent died and met her briefly for the first time yesterday."

"The same for me. Despite our many evenings of whist, Vincent never mentioned relatives in Calgary. Does he have other ones?"

"Not that I'm aware."

"Do you know Marguerite's future plans?"

"No. I expect they're up in the air right now."

"Naturally," he said. "Before her trip, she told me she planned to return to work on Monday. I doubted she'd be ready but didn't want to discourage her. Now, Upton says she might have a mild case of the flu, and I recall she was fatigued at whist a week ago."

"Dr. Upton told me this too."

"I can't have her infecting customers."

"She might be past the contagious stage—if his theory is correct."

"Might." Mr. Fielding sniffed. "Theory. This flu is too new for us to understand its properties. It's equally possible she caught the flu from Vincent and has no symptoms aside from fatigue, or she caught it on the train or from a relative at the funeral. Italians are prone to hugging and kissing."

Katharine glanced behind him at the cabinets filled with bottles of pills, powders, and liquids, many containing opiates. If Hamish was correct, Vincent hadn't died from the flu and Marguerite's prior fatigue was incidental. Or she'd feigned it and added the detail of serving a contagious customer to set up the flu as her husband's cause of death. That would be subtle and clever.

"My wife and I owe Marguerite a visit to express our sympathy," Mr. Fielding said. "I understand she returns by train today?"

"That's right."

"We'll go tomorrow and advise her to stay home until her fatigue and any other symptoms are gone and she's past the incubation stage from her train ride. While I want to encourage her to get back on her feet, our priority is to our customers."

Katharine had to agree. "Will you be able to open the store Monday?" This would be useful to know for Dr. Upton's patients.

"That's my intention," he said. "My downtown manager is reliable and can handle the store alone. I'll do my accounts in the office here while my wife deals with customers. She can call me out for complicated matters. She's not happy about working full time, but Marguerite might return by midweek, God willing."

Katharine circled back to the point of her visit. "Do you have any more questions for me?" Mr. Fielding seemed to be treating her mostly as a sounding board.

"I don't see I have a choice but to give this apartment idea a chance, mainly for Marguerite's sake. I'll lay out the ground rules to Miss DeLuca, and she'll have to follow them if she wants to stay. I suspect she likes the notion of independence. Women, today." He shook his head.

Katharine would've liked to stay and defend her sex, but she had to relieve John. She wished Mr. Fielding luck with his new tenant.

Down the street, the kickball game had expanded to include two more families of children. They formed a diamond pattern with a household group at each corner, two on the road and two on lawns.

Henry kicked the ball from their yard. John stood on the sidewalk in front of Irene's house next door, speaking with Gladys. Contrary to Mrs. Fielding's view, Irene and Gladys amicably shared a kitchen, by both women's accounts, although Katharine had heard no mention of Gladys' cooking. She earned a good income sawing wood at the Eau Claire & Bow River Lumber Company.

The afternoon was warm. Gladys draped her coat over one arm, no hat on her long frizzy hair. She was almost as tall as John, who wore his best suit. He turned as Katharine approached.

"You're home, and I take my leave." John bowed to Gladys. "I've enjoyed catching up."

"Me too," Gladys said. "When this is over, we'll invite you both to dinner. Your children can sleep with our bunch."

"Sounds like fun." John looked at Katharine. "I might ask Marguerite to dinner tonight to spare her from cooking."

"John, we have to avoid contact, especially right after her journey."

He scowled. "I'll be glad when this is over."

When this is over. Katharine would be glad when that phrase was history.

John dodged the ball on his way to Centre Street. The girl on the lawn across from Katharine's house kicked it to Irene and Gladys' group.

"I was sorry to hear about Vincent," Gladys said. "It must have been a shock. I didn't know him except to say hello. Too busy with work and our madhouse of children." Her face shadowed, a cloud passing overhead. "John also told me about his frightening experience. How lucky you were able to save him."

That was true.

"He sounded more upset about his club closing tonight," Gladys said.

"Is it?" He'd said at breakfast the owner might defy the health order.

"He got the call today."

"He'll miss playing with his band, but I'm glad the club is doing the right thing."

"I told him, if the weather stays fine, he should give us a concert out here on the street. We'll dance, kick up our heels— maintaining a proper distance, naturally."

Katharine looked up at Gladys' smiling face, which might be called handsome. Her long-sleeved blouse concealed the firm shoulders and arms that Katharine had noticed this summer when they worked in their backyard gardens. Gladys was close to Katharine's age, a good five years older than John, but a mature hand could steady him. The notion of John and Gladys as a couple was a definite improvement over John and

Marguerite. *When this was over*, Katharine might beat her next-door neighbours to a dinner invitation, though not only to play matchmaker. It was time to resume her friendship with Irene and make a new friend, Gladys.

One of the boys ran from the street to Gladys. "Can you play, Mama? We're losing."

"How can you lose when you're the biggest group?"

"John made a rule that it's us five against the other three groups."

"That isn't fair." Gladys looked down at her shirt waist and skirt that was divided to form loose trousers. "All right, after I change out of my work clothes." Her son raced back to his teammates. "Bloody hell," Gladys said. "These clothes need washing anyway." She strode to the porch, dropped her coat, and returned to the sidewalk. "Unlike poor Vincent, let's hope we all elude this nasty flu that's infiltrated our pleasant street."

"Yes." Katharine couldn't clear up that possible misconception until she heard from Detective Tanner. She wished the police worked as quickly as Hamish.

* * *

The chief poked his head in the doorway of Bertram's office. "Lab report's in." He plunked himself into the visitor's chair and slid a sheet of paper across the desk to Bertram. "They found nothing unusual. No unexpected ingredient in the whisky or on the bottle." He sniggered. "Women can get hysterical notions, especially at certain times of the month."

Bertram ignored his remark. "The hospital technician has been described as something of a genius. He might have caught a nuance in the data results that our technician missed."

"Our chap has the latest equipment."

"We don't know that it's better than the hospital's."

The chief cocked his head. "I appreciate this modern idea of listening to the public, but we still decide when to move forward or close a case."

Bertram pre-empted the chief's immediate closure by shifting gears. "I finally got through to the Ontario manufacturer. He denies violating any liquor laws."

"Naturally." The chief smirked.

"On the surface, it seems a legitimate operation. The Alberta government store clerk promises to send me their record of sales on Monday. They're busy with customers today."

"People need their drink for the weekend." The chief shuffled in his chair. "With your undercover work cancelled tonight, you might as well head home. We owe you the time off."

The club closure had left Bertram with empty hours to fill. After the chief left,

Bertram scanned the laboratory report, which stated that five samples had been taken from the bottle. Tests determined the liquid to be a blend of corn, rye, wheat, numerous spices, and other ingredients commonly found in Canadian whisky. No substances inconsistent with whisky production or inherently harmful to human life.

Bertram took out the case file and reviewed his notes on Mrs. Sterling's report. He still found her convincing and authentic. She'd mentioned in passing that her brother planned to meet the widow's train from Crowsnest Pass this afternoon. Bertram looked at his pocket watch: quarter past two. The train might not have arrived yet, the station was a ten-minute walk from police headquarters, and the chief had neglected to officially close the case. Why not detour there on his way home? An injured veteran in his mid-twenties might be easy to pick out in a crowd, although Mrs. Sterling hadn't indicated the nature of her brother's injuries.

Outside, Bertram headed west on Seventh Avenue in sunshine and unusual warmth for mid-October. He turned south on Macleod Trail and continued on Stephen Avenue. Normally, the bustle of pedestrians and vehicles on the city's main commercial street gave his spirits a boost. The flu had subdued the day's activity; the passing streetcar was half-full.

He arrived at the train station now dwarfed by the eight-story Palliser Hotel. Bertram thought of the grand railroad hotel, opened in June 1914, as Calgary's last blaze of glory before the Great War. In the station concourse, he wove by people to the arrivals board to check for the train from Crowsnest Pass. *Arriving 2:55 p.m. On time.* What luck.

The dozen or so people on Platform C appeared to be waiting for family and friends. Bertram's gaze landed on a man smoking a cigarette who leaned to one side. Was he easing the weight on an artificial limb? Smartly dressed in a suit, he looked the right age for John Wozniak, and his wavy hair was Mrs. Sterling's chestnut colour.

With a bellow of steam, the train hurtled into the station. The brakes screeched. The man dropped his cigarette and mashed the butt with his shoe. He scanned the train for passengers alighting and started forward toward a woman stepping down the train's stairs. She wore a black coat. A porter followed her to the platform and set a suitcase beside her. She handed the porter a coin as the man drew up to her. A large man ambled in front of Bertram and blocked his view of the pair's greeting. *Damn.*

They remained facing each other, the man's back to Bertram. A black veil covered the woman's face. The veil's movements suggested she was talking. Bertram was certain they were John and Marguerite.

John picked up the suitcase and passed behind Marguerite to walk beside the train. Bertram shuffled by them, as though he were seeking a passenger in the last carriage. Marguerite glanced his way, her expression hidden by the veil, and turned back to John. He didn't hold her arm.

Bertram reversed direction and followed them at a distance to the concourse. He lost them once in the throng but spotted them again. John's gait strongly indicated an artificial limb. Marguerite disappeared into the ladies' restroom. John stayed with her suitcase and took out another cigarette, which he smoked with short puffs. When she emerged, he butted it out. They continued toward the exit but then stopped at a café. She sat at a table while he went to the counter to place an order.

From his coat pocket, Bertram took out the pack of cigarettes he smoked on occasion for both pleasure and undercover work. Now, they proved useful for standing idly in the middle of a crowd heading for the station exit. Marguerite sat motionless and stared ahead beneath the veil, her body slim, her bearing regal.

John returned carrying a tray with two cups and a piece of cake. Marguerite raised her veil. Bertram couldn't make out her facial features from this distance. She looked at him again. His heart skipped. Did he imagine her questioning gaze? She turned back to John and picked up a cup.

Even if the pair went from here to the Palliser Hotel, this wouldn't be sufficient evidence to pursue the case. An illicit affair was a long way from murder.

Through the haze of his cigarette smoke, Bertram started toward the exit. When he was past the table, he halted to stamp out his cigarette and risked a final glance. Marguerite sipped from her cup, and John cut into the cake. A scar Bertram hadn't noticed before blemished John's left cheek. Did he have other, less visible, injuries from the war?

Back on Ninth Avenue, Bertram continued west to his home and remembered his promise to inform Katharine Sterling of the police lab expert's result. He dreaded hearing her disappointment that the police were close to abandoning the case. But he'd promised.

Chapter Eight

The telephone rang while Katharine was reading in the living room. She wondered if the caller was John. He was later getting home than she'd expected. Had Marguerite's train been delayed?

Detective Tanner introduced himself, referred to their meeting yesterday, and asked if she was doing well.

"Yes." His pause made her shoulders tense.

"We have the results of our laboratory analysis." He elaborated in a formal tone.

"The fact he didn't find something doesn't mean it wasn't there," she said when he was finished.

"Nevertheless, the police must rely on our own resources rather than those of outsiders."

"Why not, if the outsiders are better?" Perhaps Hamish could run the whisky through further tests. "Will you return the bottle to me?"

"Our standard practice is to keep evidence until a case is closed."

"So it's still open?"

"I'm waiting on other information and will let you know the outcome."

She hated his stiffness but softened her reply. "I'd appreciate that."

After they hung up, she paced the hall but came up with no arguments that might convince him to continue if his other information resulted in a dead end. She stomped out to the front porch and looked up and down the street—no sign of John and Marguerite. Had they gone to her house? If so, John deserved a reprimand for disregarding Katharine's request he minimize contact with their travelling neighbour.

She went to the kitchen and sliced turnips and potatoes for dinner with increasing force. No one listened to her: John, the police, even her children half of the time. If only Eddie were here to discipline them. She glanced out the back window to make sure Henry and Lillian were still playing safely in the yard. They squatted in the dead garden, ripped stalks off the vegetable plants, and dropped them in a pile, perhaps to jump into.

Katharine dumped the vegetables into pots of water and opened a can of mackerel. The front door clicked. *John.* She left the kitchen to meet him.

"Was the train late?" she asked.

"No. Marguerite needed to refresh herself afterward."

What did that mean? At least he'd come home without her.

"I need to get rid of this blasted leg." John brushed past Katharine.

She followed him into the living room. He sank to the armchair, rested his right leg on the coffee table, rolled up his pant leg, and yanked off the artificial limb.

"That's better." He sighed and massaged the stump.

She sat on the davenport across from him. "How was Marguerite's trip?"

John continued rubbing. "It went reasonably well. They buried Vincent to the cries and sobs of his mother and aunts. Marguerite said she spent her days murmuring assents to platitudes about Vincent. His mother kept insisting a mother's loss was greater than a wife's loss and yelled at Marguerite when she sympathized and agreed. Now she says she's fulfilled her obligation to Vincent's family and doesn't plan to see them again."

"Except when she visits his grave."

"Yes, well, she should be able to postpone that until spring, especially with the flu." John stopped massaging and rested his hand on his thigh. "I offered to take dinner to her and Clarence, but when we got to her house, he was making a mutton roast. Marguerite joked this was a miracle." He beamed. "Nice to see her smile again. They invited me to brave Clarence's cooking, but I couldn't stand this limb any longer."

Katharine viewed it as a positive that he wasn't comfortable enough with Marguerite to remove his leg at her house.

Footsteps pattered from the kitchen and down the hall. Henry and Lillian burst into the room. He ran to the toy box while Lillian leaped onto Katharine's lap.

"I'm hungry, Mama. Is dinner ready?"

Katharine glanced at the mantel clock. Quarter to five already. She slid her daughter to the floor. "The vegetables need time to boil."

"I spoiled my dinner with a piece of cake at the station," John said. "Lilly-pet, fetch me my sax so I don't need to stand up."

Katharine went to the kitchen, lit the gas burners for the potatoes and turnips, and got out the frying pan for the mackerel. Tonight, after the children were in bed, she'd try to draw more out of John about Marguerite's trip and his intentions for her—and hers for him. The doorbell rang.

A telegram about Eddie? Katharine tensed and lowered the heat on the burners.

"Mama!" Henry called down the hall. "The lady who taught us writing is here."

Marguerite? Katharine strode to the entrance and opened the door.

Marguerite stared at her. "Clarence told me a policeman came to the house last night. He said to ask you about it."

"Police!" Henry said.

Shuffling sounds from the living room suggested John was on his way.

Evidently Detective Tanner had followed up on Katharine's advice to interview Clarence. Now she wished she'd prepared a reply to his and Marguerite's inevitable questions.

Marguerite wore a black dress and no hat or gloves. Her hair was swept loosely off her face, her chin thrust forward in challenge.

"Marguerite." John drew up next to Katharine. "My sister did a damn foolish thing. She owes you an apology and explanation."

Katharine bristled, but the police might ultimately agree with John. She caught a whiff of vegetable aromas. "Marguerite, please wait in the living room while I settle the children for dinner."

"I want to hear about the policeman," Henry said.

"Me too," Lillian said.

"Later, after you eat."

"I don't want to eat." Henry pouted.

Katharine nudged both children toward the kitchen. "If you're good, you can have cookies for dessert."

"How many cookies?" Henry asked.

"Five cookies," Lillian said.

Bribery was a low form of parenting, but the children couldn't hear her explanation, whatever it might be. She'd give them a sanitized version after they were fed and plied with however many cookies it would take.

She coaxed them to set the table while she fried the mackerel and mashed the potatoes and turnips. Was there a way to describe her actions to Marguerite without implying that she suspected her of murder?

Once the children were seated and their plates filled, Katharine told them to stay in the kitchen until she came to get them.

"What if I need to go to the bathroom?" Lillian asked.

Why did they always have to push? "That's allowed," Katharine said. "You can also play in your bedroom but don't go past the telephone nook. I mean it."

They dug into their food, seemingly cowed by her firm tone, but that wouldn't last long. No time to waste time offering their visitor tea. She hurried down the hall to the living room and heard Marguerite's voice but couldn't make out her words.

Marguerite looked over from the davenport and stopped talking as Katharine entered. Since John sat on the armchair, Katharine took the rocker. The dying embers crackled in the fireplace.

Katharine stared over the coffee table and got straight to the point. "John had an episode Wednesday night. We thought it was the Spanish flu."

"Yes," Marguerite said. "He told me you saved him with the doctor's oxygen, instead of pounding his lungs to death."

Katharine let the insult go. "He started coughing after he drank from Vincent's bottle of whisky, which he brought from your house.”

Marguerite looked at John. “You took Vincent’s whisky?”

“You threw it in the garbage pail,” John said defensively. “I knew that when you felt better you wouldn’t want it wasted.”

“I thought it might be moonshine,” Katharine said.

Marguerite’s nose scrunched.

“Illegal liquor,” she explained.

“I know moonshine,” Marguerite snapped. “Vincent didn’t drink that.”

“Where did he buy his whisky?”

“Obviously from the government liquor vendor,” John said. “The only place in town to get it. They’ve got us in a noose.”

“*Non.*” Marguerite shook her head. “He buy it from our drug store with a doctor’s prescription. It’s legal.”

“That’s right,” John said. “The loophole in the oppressive liquor laws.”

Katharine ignored him and fixed her gaze on Marguerite. “I handle Dr. Upton’s patient files and don’t recall a whisky prescription for Vincent.”

“Dr. Upton treats his body, and another doctor treats his worries and trouble sleeping. Different doctors have different specialties.”

This was true and several Calgary doctors specialized in psychiatry. “Dr. Upton didn’t note a referral.”

"You have your nose in his files?" Marguerite said with a sniff.

"I type all his reports."

"Vincent can see any doctor he wants," John said. "He doesn't need Dr. Upton's permission."

Also true. "My point is," Katharine said, "when two people have identical reactions after drinking from the same bottle, there's reason to question the liquor's quality."

Marguerite folded her arms. "Our store operates legally and morally. You have no right to accuse us."

Katharine continued with her impromptu explanation. "I was concerned about others buying from the same batch, so I had Dr. Upton's colleague at the hospital analyze the bottle's contents. He found ..."

Marguerite leaned forward; her eyes narrowed. "What?"

"An ingredient in the whisky that was effectively poisonous. Since it might be moonshine gone bad, I brought the bottle to the police. They're rightly investigating to protect the public."

Marguerite balled her hands into fists. "So, they come to my house? They investigate my store?"

"I didn't know Vincent had bought it there."

"We do not sell moonshine." Marguerite rose and tottered. "This makes me dizzy." She sat again.

"Is it possible Vincent bought moonshine elsewhere?" John said. "He might have found it for a cheaper price than the store's."

"*Non*. We get an *employé* discount." Marguerite slowly stood. "I must go home."

"Sit a while longer if you're dizzy," Katharine said.

"Don't tell me to sit when you do such cruel things." Marguerite marched to the entrance.

John followed her. Katharine joined them on the porch.

"Thank you for telling me this." Marguerite's tone was now polite. "I must protect the store's reputation."

Bizarre. But this was better than being the object of Marguerite's wrath.

Marguerite barrelled down the stairs and across the street. Katharine and John watched to make sure she got inside without falling in her upset state.

"I didn't know she had such pride in the drug store," Katharine said.

"That's why she wants to manage it."

"I agree with Mr. Fielding about requiring professional qualifications. Fewer people will get sick or die due to wrongly prepared medicines."

"Marguerite's smart enough for the university program," he said. "But she told me school and she didn't get along. I don't think she graduated from high school or whatever it's called in France."

"I didn't know that."

He scoffed. "Now you do, and you can stop nagging her about higher education."

"I wasn't nagging ..." Yes, she had been.

Inside, Henry and Lillian waited in the hall.

"What about the policeman?" Henry asked.

Deception worked best when consistent. "He was investigating bad whisky that might have been mistakenly sold by Mrs. DeLuca's drug store."

"Moonshine," John added. "People make it in their backyards."

"Can we make some?" Lillian asked.

John grinned. "It will be our first class on Monday."

"No, it won't," Katharine said. "Now, let's go finish our dinner."

* * *

Bertram stalked down the hall from his living room into the study then through the kitchen and outside to his back porch. He blinked at the blinding sun in the southwest. *Why not, if the outsiders are better?* Mrs. Sterling's comment had stung, but she had a point and had implied her lab technician was brilliant.

A mad scientist? Bertram pictured Dr. Frankenstein in his lab. He shook the image from his head. Real life wasn't *Frankenstein* or Bertram's current reading, *The Strange Case of Dr. Jekyll and Mr. Hyde.*

He returned to the kitchen and paused at the telephone nook. The least he could do for his strange case was check out Katharine Sterling's "eccentric genius." He called the telephone operator and asked to be connected to the Calgary General Hospital.

The hospital receptionist answered and told Bertram that she hadn't seen Hamish McBride leave for the day. "I'll try the lab." She returned to the line a few minutes later. "No surprise he's still there. I'll put you through."

When Hamish came on the line, Bertram identified himself and the case. "I'd like to discuss your findings. When would be a convenient time for me to come to the hospital?"

"I have a few matters to finish before going home." The man spoke with a Scottish accent. "Could you be here in half an hour?"

"I could."

"Perfect."

The streetcar would get him there in time—unless there was a long wait. His bike would be more certain, and this could be the last warm day until spring.

Light traffic for a Saturday late afternoon made for an easy ride over the Centre Street Bridge to the north bank of the Bow River. Bertram turned east on Sunnyside Boulevard and pedalled to Bridgeland, where he'd helped contain a brawl early in the war. German immigrants tended to settle in Bridgeland. The majority lived quietly, but a few reacted to taunts about their loyalty to Canada and the British Empire. The pub owner had phoned headquarters about the altercation when Bertram was on call. He and his fellow officers arrived after the fighting stopped. One man had died after his attacker pulled a knife. They rushed a second man to hospital with massive head wounds. He recovered, but the doctors doubted he'd ever return to normal.

Bertram reached the Calgary General Hospital, a four-storey sandstone building. When it opened eight years ago, the newspaper said it was already too small for the city. The receptionist directed him to the basement laboratory.

Hamish McBride greeted him with a series of rolling *r*'s. "Pleasure to meet you Detective Bertram Tanner." Red hair, beard, bright blue eyes, McBride could be more Scottish only if he were playing the bagpipes and wearing a kilt rather than a lab coat.

"Call me Hamish," he said, as they entered the laboratory, which was about twice the size of the one at the police headquarters. Beakers, scales, and mortars and pestles littered the tables that lined the walls. A cleared table occupied the centre of the room. Bertram could imagine Dr. Frankenstein's monster lying on top, but they were the sole people in the room. He thanked Hamish for prolonging his workday in order to meet with him.

"My wife is used to it," Hamish said, and plucked sheets of paper from a side table.

"Would you mind if I take notes?" Bertram asked.

"Go ahead."

While Hamish read out his analysis of the contents of the whisky bottle, Bertram jotted technical words he didn't understand, asking for spellings as needed. The significant point was that Hamish had found a substance structurally similar to opium.

"Can I show your report to my technician for his comments?" Bertram asked.

Hamish clutched the paper to his chest. "It's my research."

"It would greatly assist our case."

"That isn't my concern."

If necessary, they could obtain a court order. "Please keep the report in a safe place for our future reference."

Hamish's hairy eyebrows rose. "Why in God's name would I dispose of it?"

Bertram had no doubt of the scientist's pride in and attention to his work, although self-confidence wasn't always justified. He scanned the laboratory room. "I expect the wartime economy prevents the government from providing you the most modern equipment."

"On the contrary," Hamish said. "They spare no expense for hospital research and

142

development of medicines. It's the one thing our government does right." He picked up a satchel from the table and slipped the papers inside. "I assume your next step will be to talk to George—Dr. Upton—the doctor who attended the death."

That would be a good plan. "Does Dr. Upton live north of the river?"

"Crescent Heights."

The suburb would be a short detour back to Bertram's home. "I could see him next if that wouldn't disturb his dinner."

"Don't worry about that," Hamish said. "He dines as needed."

Bertram assumed that meant no fixed schedule. Perhaps the doctor was unmarried. "Would you have his address?"

Hamish provided it from memory.

From the hospital, Bertram pedalled uphill to Crescent Heights, the ten minutes of strain and perspiration a reminder that he was no longer the young man who had joined the police force twenty years ago. He crossed Edmonton Trail to Dr. Upton's street, which was lined with bungalows that were larger than Mrs. Sterling's in Tuxedo Park. They were also more stylish, spaced farther apart, and had deeper front lawns with poplar trees. The breeze blew the yellow leaves to the ground. A man stood raking in front of a house with the doctor's address.

Bertram got off his bike. "Dr. Upton?"

"That's correct."

Bertram introduced himself and showed his badge. As he explained the reason for his visit, Dr. Upton's mouth kept opening wider. His grip loosened on the rake, which tilted sideways. A portly man with a handlebar moustache, the doctor wore a wool cap and knickerbocker pants for his leisure activity. Bertram estimated his age as mid-forties.

Dr. Upton motioned toward his house. "If you don't mind, I suggest we sit on the porch outside for mutual safety and to enjoy these last days of balmy weather."

Bertram walked his bike onto the property and leaned it against the porch railing. They went up six steps and sat on rocking chairs facing the street, where children played a game of hide-and-seek. A boy crouched behind a shrub in the neighbour's yard. Bertram took out his pen and notebook and asked permission to take notes.

Dr. Upton nodded. "I can't believe Mrs. Sterling went behind my back."

"I'm sure she didn't see it that way." Bertram would leave it to her to explain her reasons to her employer.

The doctor rocked back and forth. "When she telephoned me about Vincent DeLuca's breathing crisis, my first thought was Spanish influenza exacerbated by his pre-existing condition. In the war, he contracted tuberculosis, which permanently damaged his lungs."

"Mrs. Sterling told me this."

Dr. Upton continued rocking. "Perhaps my presumption led me down a path to misdiagnosis."

This had happened in Bertram's detective work, when the pieces of evidence pointed in a particular direction, and he didn't think to shift any pieces around.

"The sudden onset common to this strain of the flu makes it difficult to diagnose," Dr. Upton said. "Vincent had certain classic symptoms. Sniffles and a runny nose a few days before his acute episode of severe coughing. During our whist game Saturday evening, I recall him blowing his nose several times. This wasn't a feature of his medical condition."

Bertram jotted this down. The girl who was "it" in hide-and-seek spotted the boy behind the shrub. He raced across the street but couldn't beat the girl to the safe tree. Bertram supposed this children's game was better than most for avoiding influenza since the goal was to avoid physical contact.

"What were Vincent's other symptoms Tuesday night?" Bertram asked.

"Bloody nose," the doctor said. "Inability to breathe. Opiate overdose would cause the latter." He stopped rocking. "As tragic as it is to think of Vincent dying of influenza, the prospect of someone purposely poisoning his whisky is worse. Who would do that?" He looked at Bertram.

Bertram stared back. His job was to determine that answer.

"I see." Dr. Upton resumed rocking. "Normally I don't reveal patient information, but my patient is dead under apparently criminal circumstances. Although in my view, suicide is a moral matter between a man and his god and not a criminal one."

"What makes you think Vincent DeLuca might have taken his own life?"

Dr. Upton kept rocking. "If my friend Hamish is right and an opiate was added to the whisky, my guess would be it was laudanum. I wrote the initial prescription for Vincent's cough and, as a pharmacist, he continued dispensing it to himself."

"Is that normally done?"

"Yes, and acceptable ethically and medically. Vincent was aware of the dangers of combining laudanum and whisky. His medicinal dosage was small, and he assured me he limited himself to one drink a night, a reasonable risk we agreed. Odd that he'd pour laudanum into the bottle rather than into his glass, but troubled minds often don't consider those left behind or, in this case, the whisky left behind. Good Lord." His rocking stopped abruptly. "What if Marguerite had drunk it in her state of grief? She could be dead now." He shuddered. "That was selfish of Vincent. Abominable."

"Was he troubled?"

Dr. Upton took several breaths and calmed down. "Not that I knew, aside from a natural frustration with his chronic cough.

He took laudanum more sparingly than others would. A stoic, like many men who keep their problems to themselves. The young men fighting this Great War have endured and seen things you and I can't imagine. I was fortunate to be older when the war broke out."

Bertram had been thirty-four, on the older side to enlist. He was also fortunate that police work was essential for the home front, although many of his colleagues had answered the call to adventure. In addition, Nellie hadn't wanted him to go, and he'd had no desire to leave his life with her. So, he'd stayed home. Two years later, she became with child and died in childbirth. If he could go back, he'd enlist in a heartbeat, even if the war crushed him. Nellie would still be alive.

Dr. Upton rocked. "The more I think of it, the more I think it had to be suicide. Vincent lived a quiet life and had no enemies."

"From your observations, would you describe his marriage as happy?"

He glanced at Bertram; an eyebrow raised to his cap brim. "One never knows what goes on between a couple," Dr. Upton said. "Had he wanted to leave the marriage, there are less drastic options than suicide." The rocking halted. He stared at Bertram. "Are you suggesting Marguerite ...? She wouldn't. It's not in her nature."

In Bertram's cynical view, the gentlest person could kill given the right set of circumstances.

"Decency aside, she depended on Vincent's income," the doctor said. "Now, she's a woman alone in a country foreign to her. Why would she place herself in that situation?"

One answer might be a lover.

Dr. Upton's face flushed. "Marguerite a suspect? Impossible." He gripped the armrests of his rocking chair. "If you have no further questions, I must go in and prepare dinner."

Bertram closed his notebook. *Dr. Upton's flush. His defence of Marguerite. His horror at the prospect of her drinking the tainted whisky.* Was the doctor in love with Marguerite?

Throughout the conversation, Bertram had heard no sounds from inside the house. No woman had opened the door to find out what was keeping her husband so long. There appeared to be no Mrs. Upton, but Vincent's death had opened the door for one now.

Chapter Nine

After she kissed the children goodnight, Katharine joined John in the living room. Henry Burr warbled from the Victrola, "I'll Take You Home Again, Kathleen." John listened with his eyes closed. She set her mask-making materials on the coffee table and sat across from him on the davenport.

John opened his eyes. "Clever ploy with Marguerite, pretending your detective was investigating moonshine operations."

"A small falsehood to preserve neighbour relations," she said. "I'm glad the detective took me seriously enough to interview Clarence." She owed John the truth and told him about the police expert's conclusions. "If Detective Tanner's current actions fail, I suspect he'll close the case."

"The proper course," John said. "Marguerite isn't a killer."

He couldn't know that for sure. She hesitated but continued. "Another possibility is that Vincent took his own life. You knew him better than I. Do you think he was capable?"

"Anyone is, if they're cornered." John got up to turn over the record. He leaned against the sideboard. While he listened to "When the Corn is Waving, Annie Dear,"

Katharine looked at his scar and recalled her father's phone call about John's attempt to end his life.

"Your mother found him, his face covered in blood." Her father had slipped into Polish, which he did when upset. "She's devastated. Her baby."

John was their mother's favourite, her youngest child, the son who went to war against his immigrant parents' wishes. "Does it matter who rules Poland?" her father had ranted. "Germany, Austria, Russia? They're all the same."

Katharine's two older brothers agreed with him and remained safe on the farm.

Her father had ended the dreadful call with a promise to let her know if John's condition changed for the worse, despite the expense of telephone calls from Manitoba. It made her wish she'd stayed close to home to help her family when needed, but everyone said the new and growing city of Calgary was the place for opportunity. Eddie was drawn to that excitement, and she'd come to share his enthusiasm.

After the surgeons patched John up, he spent the winter at the farm. In the spring, Katharine proposed he come to Calgary for a fresh start.

"His companionship would benefit me too while Eddie's away," she'd added.

Her father had sniffed. "Don't expect John to be a help."

That prediction had turned out to be right, at least until this week. John's child-minding and cooking had been helpful.

John's fresh start had been up and down. Shortly after his arrival, Katharine had brought up his suicide attempt, finding their mutual silence on the subject a barrier between them. "Do you think you moved the rifle on purpose, changed your mind at the last minute?"

He'd thumped out of the room on one foot. She hadn't raised the issue again.

After Henry Burr warbled to a close, John put on a new record. "In memory of Vincent," he said.

"O Sole Mio" rang from the Victrola. The tenor, Enrico Caruso, shared Vincent's Italian heritage. John returned to his chair. Katharine rolled out the gauze and started cutting the material into mask-sized strips.

"Vincent had a dark side," John said. "He might be capable."

She looked up. "Dark in what way?"

"Marguerite alluded to it this afternoon when we stopped for coffee at the train station, and I could see what she meant." He stroked his moustache. "I liked Vincent at first—we had the war in common—but as I spent more time there, I started noticing him saying things to her that were thoughtless or cruel, indirectly."

"Such as ...?"

"Hard to come up with an example. It was subtle." He pinched the tip of his moustache. "For instance, one night she said she had to check their household accounts because she might have made a mistake in the calculations. Vincent said, 'Only might?' then laughed."

"Was he teasing?"

"On the surface it would seem," he said. "She's sensitive about her relative lack of schooling. Vincent knew that, and he was either thoughtless or purposely needling her sore spot."

"You tease me in similar ways."

"Yes, but when he said it, Marguerite's face blanched. I know she can overreact to any implied criticism."

"Such as my hint that her drug store deals in illegal liquor."

John smiled. "You'd react similarly if she accused Dr. Upton of treating his patients with the medical equivalent." He paused. "What if she said he'd injected someone with a quack medicine?"

"Any medicines he injects are proven." Although, she recalled one for a persistent respiratory infection that Dr. Upton had tried because Hamish called the medical establishment's dismissal of the drug shortsighted. The treatment hadn't worked, and Dr. Upton had resumed the patient's heroin injections. But they'd strayed from her original question. Was Vincent capable of suicide? "If Vincent chose to end his life with this drug, wouldn't he have put it in his glass of whisky? Why poison a bottle that someone might drink from later?"

John shrugged. "He probably didn't consider that, or care. People in that frame of mind don't think straight."

He would know.

"Plus," he continued, "Marguerite or Clarence or I were usually present when he poured his drink. If he'd dropped something in his glass, one of us might have seen it."

"Surely he could find a way to be alone in his own living room and doctor his glass of whisky."

"Interesting expression that, 'doctor.' But I guess he could have, if he'd wanted."

"You told me Marguerite drank whisky in the past," Katharine said. "Then Vincent couldn't be certain she wouldn't drink from that bottle after he was gone. Even in a distressed frame of mind, would a man leave behind a poisoned drink knowing there was a chance it would kill his wife?"

John rubbed the scarred side of his face. "You're saying, if Vincent chose to die, would he want to take Marguerite with him? Or not care if she lived or died after he was gone?" John's hand dropped to his lap. Enrico Caruso crooned to the end of the recording. The record made a wobbly, grinding noise in the Victrola. "Yes, I believe that's possible."

Katharine cringed at his matter-of-fact tone. "Murder is a large leap from cruel teasing."

"No larger than your leaps about Marguerite." He pushed himself to his foot. "Enough speaking ill of the dead. I'm going to bed early. It's been a sleepless week. Shall I put on another record on for you?"

"No." She needed silence to think.

* * *

Sunday morning was usually quiet at Union Cemetery with most people at church. Even now with the churches closed, Bertram was the only person in the graveyard. He gazed down at the double mounds of earth, one of them painfully small. Dry grass had sprouted during the summer and the mounds grew flatter each month. A year from now, evidence of Nellie's and their son's deaths would be gone, aside from the headstone with her name and the baby's name beneath hers.

Infant son Robert, Born—Died November 6, 1917

Bertram had named the child for his father, as he and Nellie had agreed, to continue the Tanner tradition of alternating names for each generation of firstborn sons. Now his father's male line would end with Bertram.

He read the inscription at the bottom of the stone, *Always loved. Never forgotten.* Nellie's mother had suggested those fitting phrases, but she had counselled against his leaving a space beside Nellie's name for his own.

"You're young enough to marry again," his mother-in-law had said. "She'd want you to move on without her."

Other relatives and friends had expressed or implied similar thoughts. Once, he'd had to walk away to avoid punching a cousin in the face.

Bertram was glad he'd left the space for himself on the stone. It was his promise to Nellie and Robert he'd be with them forever. The drive from Beiseker to Calgary was only double his walking time from his current home to the cemetery. He'd continue his Sunday visits, although switching to afternoons. Country neighbours noticed and cared if you skipped church.

The wind picked up and blew the yellow leaves from a poplar up the hill. Bertram spotted a new arrival at the far entrance on Spiller Road. Thankfully, the woman stopped at a grave out of earshot. He thrust his hands into his jacket pockets and told Nellie and Robert about his week. When he reached the part about Mrs. Sterling, his narration slowed, and he lingered on details.

"Strangely," he said aloud, "the case has come close to igniting my old flicker of interest." Sometimes his reports to Nellie and Robert showed him new ways of viewing problems, but today's account had revealed nothing that might convince the chief the case merited a full investigation.

While he spoke, a couple with a child crested the hill and walked toward him. Bertram ended his report with his ritual rereading of the epitaph. *"Always loved. Never forgotten."* He meant both with his heart.

To avoid talking with the couple, he took a side route down the hill to the path that continued to Twenty-Fifth Avenue. Under sunny skies, he crossed Macleod Trail and the Elbow River bridge to Mission then turned north on Fourth Street.

When he and Nellie had decided to buy a home, they'd looked at several in this neighbourhood. They cost less than comparable homes downtown, but he liked living a short distance from work and Nellie relished the city bustle. She'd looked forward to pushing a baby carriage along busy streets, where something of interest was always going on. They'd both assumed she'd soon be with child.

From Seventeenth Avenue, he veered onto the streets with Calgary's most prestigious homes. His secret wish for the previous night's planned raid of the club had been that it would unearth members of the city's elite. He'd love to catch one of them breaking a law they'd imposed on Calgary's lesser citizens. While Prohibition had diminished drunken brawls and their ensuing crimes, it had created an illegal alcohol trade that was arguably more damaging to society. Many homemade spirits on the underground market rotted people's guts. In addition, the law was impossible to enforce, especially since the government set liquor prices high to discourage people from drinking and also to rake in revenue. Word had quickly spread that liquor could be bought for less outside the government store. Citizens who were normally law abiding had no qualms about purchasing alcohol illegally from a colleague or acquaintance.

The large sandstone homes transitioned into middle-income residences on the fringe of downtown. Normally people would be spilling out of the churches at this time. Their closures had left the streets deserted, as though a plague had killed all human life. Bertram's most religious aunt believed Catholics had manufactured the Spanish flu to rid the world of Protestants and heathens. She dismissed his mother's arguments that Catholics were dying as frequently as the other groups and agreed with his father's jest that the heathens deserved the punishment.

"Your aunt hasn't left her house in a month," his father had said when Bertram telephoned yesterday. "She aims to be the last surviving Protestant in Beiseker."

His parents had been thrilled when he told them about his plan to move home when the war ended, and the troops returned with a soldier to replace him on the job.

He reached his Mewata neighbourhood, his body perspiring from the one-hour walk.

His sunny, sheltered backyard would be a pleasant spot for lunch. He stopped at the Jewish grocery store, which was open on Sundays. During this last year, he'd acquired a taste for the chicken soup that Mrs. Lieberman cooked in the back kitchen on Sundays and sold to her regular customers. In the store, she packed some in a container for him to take home.

From police work, Bertram had learned that Jews existed in Calgary. A number of them owned grocery stores, and robberies weren't uncommon. The Liebermans and two other Jewish families lived in Mewata.

Bertram and Nellie soon discovered their Jewish neighbours were largely the same as them aside from their observing the Sabbath on a different day, their food, the men's skullcaps, which they called yarmulkes—Bertram had asked about the spelling—their Yiddish language, and, now that he thought of it, a few other things. People were different, he had to admit, and yet the same beneath the surface trim. They ate, drank, loved, hated, feared, and killed on occasion. Lately, men had killed thousands of their fellow humans in the Great War. He might believe the influenza was God's curse for this if he believed God gave a spoonful of soup what mankind did. In Bertram's view, God had created man on a whim and left the creature to fend for himself.

Bertram entered his home, refreshed in the bathroom, got a spoon and a glass of water from the kitchen, and headed out to the back porch. He set his lunch on the table sheltered by Nellie's sewing room, which jutted from the second floor. He and Nellie had eaten outside at every opportunity. Calgary's summers were short.

He took his first bite—still warm. Mrs. Lieberman attributed the soup's particular taste to the kohlrabi bulbs she grew in her garden. Beiseker offered no such exotic treats, but his graveyard visits to Calgary could include a stop at the Jewish grocery store. The city's lighter traffic on Sundays would make driving through downtown easy. His plan was falling into place.

The soup finished, Bertram leaned back in his chair to enjoy the sunshine on his face. He and Nellie had been ready to make an offer on a home in East Calgary, on the opposite side of downtown, when their real estate agent suggested they look at a house in Mewata.

"*Mewata*," the agent had said. "A Cree word that means 'to be happy.'"

Nellie's eyes had brightened. "I like that."

They'd liked the house too, and Mewata was the same distance from Bertram's work as East Calgary. They'd changed their plan, put an offer on this house. They were happy in it for eleven years and joyous when they learned Nellie was with child. A miracle after the long wait.

A ringing startled him from his thoughts. He blinked in the sun. The telephone. He rushed into the house and answered.

"There's a woman here," Constable Jones said. "She asked to speak with you. Concerns a bottle of whisky."

Katharine Sterling? "What's her name?"

Rustling sounds suggested Jones was consulting his notes. "Mrs. Vincent DeLuca. Christian name Marguerite."

Bertram started. "What does she want?"

"She had an accent and rambled too much for me to follow. I told her to come back tomorrow, but she insisted I call you at home. She's persuasive."

"I'll be there in half an hour."

"I'll tell her to wait, then?"

"Yes. Don't let her leave."

Bertram ran outside, collected his dishes, and left them in the kitchen sink. Rather than walk to headquarters, he'd ride his bike through the sparse Sunday traffic and get there in half the time.

Chapter Ten

Katharine and the children finished lunch. They helped her clear the table and ran outside to the backyard.

While she was washing up, John shuffled into the kitchen. Around twelve-thirty was his usual time for getting up when he had no homeschooling duties. He wore his bathrobe, his hair dishevelled from sleep. She told him to help himself to soup. Outside, Henry and Lillian darted around the backyard, picking up fallen leaves and stalks from the garden plants.

John sat at the table. "What are your plans for today?"

"I don't know," she said. "I've already done the laundry." The war and her job had moved her laundry day from Monday to Sunday, the one day of the week she had time for the lengthy task. She longed to replace the tub and washboard with a washing machine but wouldn't have enough money until Eddie came back and found work. The church closure would enable her to spend the rest of the day on housework, but Sunday was supposed to be a day of rest, and the sunshine at the front of the house would make it warm enough to sit on the porch.

John glanced out the back window. "Why are they filling the wheelbarrow with leaves?"

"I expect it's a game they made up," she said. "Looks gentler than kickball."

When he finished his lunch, John joined them outside. Katharine washed his dishes and carried a kitchen chair to the front porch. Next door, Gladys sat on her porch with a book. Katharine asked what she was reading.

Gladys held up her book. "*The Shadow Riders*. It's by a writer who used to live in Calgary and set her story here. Who knew novels about Calgary existed?"

"Is it good?" Across the street, Clarence opened Marguerite's front gate.

"I find it ripping," Gladys said. "The female heroine is bold and spirited. The writer's a woman too. I'll loan it to you when I'm finished, if you like reading."

"I do, when I have the time."

Clarence crossed the street, ambled up Katharine's sidewalk, and held out a pot. "I believe this is yours," he said and thanked her for the dinner.

She told him to leave the pot on the porch for her to bring in later, wearing gloves. Experts believed flu germs could be contracted from sweat on surfaces.

"I hear you've taken up cooking lately," she said.

Clarence set the pot down. "If I have to keep making my own meals, I might as well take Mr. Fielding's apartment." He smiled. "But Pina, Vincent's cousin, got to it first."

"Is she moving in today?"

He nodded. "She and her friend with the car stopped by a half hour ago. She asked if she could have Marguerite's card table and a couple of chairs. Marguerite won't need them for whist as long as this flu hangs on, but I couldn't give them away without her consent." He looked toward Centre Street. "She should be home soon."

"Where did she go?"

"She didn't say." Clarence edged closer and kept his voice low, presumably so Gladys wouldn't overhear. "She's concerned about you sending the police to investigate the drug store."

"I didn't intend that." *Then why take the bottle to the police?* he might reasonably ask. She had no answer for her lie.

He glanced at Gladys, who looked absorbed in her book. "It's a touchy matter for Marguerite. This summer there was a furor about her preparing a customer's medicine. I gather she mixed wrong amounts of ingredients."

"That can be serious." Not something to lightly brush off.

"The man took violently ill but recovered," Clarence said. "They didn't tell me the details. It's what I interpreted from pieces of their discussion and arguments. In the end, it seemed Vincent agreed not to tell

Mr. Fielding. I consider that fair for a single mistake."

But pharmaceutical dispensing had no room for errors. "From my dealings with Marguerite, I find her generally competent and skilled at her work."

"That's my impression too," he said. "Sometimes she mixes up numbers and letters, a brain issue I've read about, unrelated to intelligence."

She nodded. "A patient of Dr. Upton told me her son has this problem with reading."

"Since you work in the medical field, I have a question for you." He paused. "Can dogs get the Spanish flu?"

She suppressed a scoff. Even doctors and scientists had little understanding of how this new influenza operated. "Not as far as anyone knows. Why?"

He shuffled from side to side. "Something Pina said Friday night, after the detective left. She was surprised that Vincent had a dog because he was severely allergic to them as a child. I told her people outgrew allergies, but now I'm wondering—if Vincent was prone to get the sniffles from dogs, might he be more susceptible than others to a dog's flu? It would explain why Marguerite and I didn't catch this Spanish dog influenza, so to speak." He smiled wanly and flushed. "An oddball theory."

"I've heard less plausible ones about this flu."

"The dog doesn't sniffle or sneeze, but flu symptoms might manifest differently in animals."

"This goes beyond my medical expertise," she said. "But could a dog allergy have caused the flu-like symptoms that preceded Vincent's breathing attack?"

Clarence rubbed his chin. "The creature was new to the house. Vincent would shoo it away, but perversely, it had a fondness for him. Looking back, his sniffling did begin around when Marguerite let the dog in. At the time, I didn't see the connection."

This allergy theory made sense.

"I suppose we're all looking for reasons," Clarence said. "Marguerite is convinced she passed her mild case of flu onto Vincent."

"She's had no symptoms other than fatigue?"

He shook his head. "And yet, despite that fatigue, she goes out all the time. Do you think it's her ruse to get me to cook?"

Katharine laughed. "That would be clever of her."

Vincent's allergy and Clarence's lack of symptoms were further evidence that the poisoned whisky had caused Vincent's death, but she doubted they would prompt Detective Tanner to step up his investigation.

* * *

Bertram ushered Marguerite DeLuca into his office. A black hat shaded her eyes. Her black dress, cinched at the waist with a flared skirt, looked more attractive than mournful. As he settled across the desk from her, she pulled out a thick folder from her handbag.

"These are the accounts and receipts for the last month from my drug store," she said. "You will see they are all correct. We purchase alcohol entirely from the government store and don't sell it without a prescription from a doctor whose name we recognize. Our sales are in line with other pharmacies our size. I know this from talking with the store managers." She slid the folder across the desk to him. "Please take care not to get the papers out of order."

He opened the folder. "Why are you bringing me these?"

"My boarder, Clarence Oxenham, and my neighbour Katharine Sterling told me you were investigating Fielding and Sons for the sale of homemade whisky. We would never sell this." Her nose wrinkled. Exposure to the flu hadn't inspired her to wear a mask.

Bertram pretended to peruse the papers to stall for time. Had Mrs. Sterling said this to avoid revealing she'd reported the incident to the police because she suspected murder? Surely Clarence had realized Bertram's questions concerned Vincent's death and not his business dealings.

Bertram skimmed the first pages. The figures looked orderly; the items were familiar alcohol brands. The list seemed comprehensive, but this didn't mean other bottles weren't traded under the table—illegally manufactured or nonprescription liquor or both.

Mrs. DeLuca watched him, beady eyed. He couldn't concentrate.

"May I keep this file to review later?"

"*Non*," she said. "I must return it to the store tonight."

Presumably, she had a key to the store and had borrowed the file while the store was closed. He reached for his pen in the holder to take notes.

"Don't write on them," she snapped. "They're our official records."

Bertram got a notepad from his desk drawer. "This will take me some time. You'll find it more comfortable to wait in the reception area. Constable Jones will make you a cup of tea. Better yet, it's a beautiful day for a walk. I suggest you return in an hour."

"*Non*. I'll wait here, *s'il vous plaît*."

She sat upright in the chair.

Her eagle eye on the file would make it hard for him to grasp these figures, but there might be an advantage to her staying here. "While I study these records, would you describe the events of Tuesday evening that led to your late husband's passing? This will help confirm the cause was indeed influenza."

She squinted at him. "You can read and listen at the same time?"

Probably not. "Yes, without difficulty," he said. "It's essential police training and experience." He couldn't recall any training for this but might have learned the skill on the job without knowing.

"I believe it began with me," she said. "Four days before, I served a customer who complained of headache, fever, and cough. His hand touched mine when I passed him the pill container. I should have washed my hands right away, but another customer came in, and I went to serve her." Her tone was wistful, filled with regret.

Bertram nodded in understanding. *Guilt.*

"By Saturday I feel tired," she said. "Vincent got a running nose. The night he died his cough was so loud I heard from the kitchen." She described her run to the living room and efforts to help him breathe. "I loosen his clothing, give him smelling salts. If I'd remembered more from working in the field hospital in my village in *France*, it might have saved him."

Bertram found her accented words added poignancy to her guilt and wondered if she tended to slip into French and awkward grammar when agitated.

While she spoke, he took notes, making it look as though he were copying words and figures from the drug store accounts. Apparently, he could do two tasks at the same time. Her report corresponded with those of Clarence and Mrs. Sterling. Thus far, there seemed to be no dispute about the facts. She reached the part where she flew into a rage and blamed Mrs. Sterling for killing Vincent.

"I went mad," she said. "Katharine pound his lungs too hard but not to kill, to try to save him. I blamed her instead of blaming me." She caught his gaze. "*Oui*, I blamed the whisky too, but not because I think it's moonshine. I don't know why I did that, but John had no right to steal from my garbage." She said that when Clarence later went to bed, John stayed to keep her company. He dozed in the living room. She spent the night restless, moving in and out of her bedroom.

She stared at Bertram, her eyes beneath the hat brim looking darker. "Until it happens, you don't know what it's like to lose a husband, even though ..."

What?

She shook her head, as though sweeping a thought from her mind. "Let us not talk of this. I came here for the future."

He hated to abandon his last silent question but decided to follow her thread. "Your future is the drug store?"

"I want to work there as long as I can," she said. "Vincent's family want me to live with them." Her nose wrinkled again. "My parents will want me to return to *France,* which is in ruins from the war. I don't believe my country will ever be the same again."

What would be?

"Vincent's doctor in *France* told us Calgary's dry air would be good for his lungs." She sneered. "What good did it do for him in the end? The dry air made his skin itch and nose bleed."

Bertram rubbed his dry hand. "Is your plan, then, to stay in Calgary?"

"If I am able," she said. "Mr. Fielding will dismiss me from my job if he thinks Vincent and I managed his store improperly." Her thin shoulders shook.

This was the crux, the purpose of her visit.

Desperation. Easy for Bertram to recognize after twenty years of police work. Most of the desperate souls he'd encountered had created their individual hells, but a few were innocent victims.

He closed the folder and slid it back to her. "I see nothing irregular in your accounts, but please keep them in case we request them later."

Her hands trembled on the folder. "Will you continue your questioning?"

Best to be truthful but leave her a little on edge. "We've almost completed this stage of our investigation, but new developments can arise."

She glowered at him and stuffed the folder into her handbag.

Katharine sat on her front porch, absorbed in sunshine and Jane Eyre's gloomy life. Next door, Gladys announced she had finished her Calgary novel and would pass it along to Katharine.

"Leave it on the porch next to the pot," Katharine said.

"Time to gather up my brood and take them to the park." Gladys went inside.

Katharine was happy to let her brood amuse themselves in the backyard. She returned to her book.

A motorcar approached from the direction of Centre Street. It drove past her, made a three-point turn, and stopped in front of Marguerite's house. A man got out and went up to the porch. Katharine recognized Mr. Fielding's brisk gait and recalled him saying he and his wife would visit Marguerite today to pay their respects and advise her to stay home from work until she was certain she wasn't contagious.

Mr. Fielding remained on the porch for a few minutes. Katharine glimpsed Clarence at the front door, probably telling him Marguerite was out. Mr. Fielding's trot back down the stairs was sprightly for a man in his fifties. During a drug store chat, Mrs. Fielding had mentioned that he skied regularly in Banff during the winter and competed in local races.

At his car, he waved at Katharine and strode diagonally across the street. "Beautiful day," he said. "Unfortunately, Chinook weather gives my wife migraine headaches, and she couldn't come with me to see Marguerite. Do you know where she went?"

"No idea."

"I'll try her again this evening."

He crossed back to his motorcar, drove east, and turned right on Centre Street, in the direction of his home in the Beltline.

John came around the side of the house. "I left the children to finish the moonshine."

"The what?"

He grinned. "They're pretending the dry leaves and stalks are fallen pieces of the moon. We collected them in the wheelbarrow to mix into a magic potion."

"That's sweet," she said and stifled a smile. "Or are we terribly wrong to let them play at making bootleg liquor?" In her periphery, she noticed a woman walking from Centre Street. "Is that Marguerite?"

John moved toward the sidewalk. Marguerite stopped in front of their house. She wore a coat and a velvet hat with a drooping brim.

"Lovely day for an outing," Katharine said.

"Yes," Marguerite said, with apparent disinterest in the weather. She carried a large handbag. "Yesterday you said you gave Vincent's whisky bottle to Dr. Upton's colleague at the hospital. The doctor is friends with Hamish McBride. Was it him?"

Katharine glanced sideways to check that Gladys and her brood weren't emerging from the house. No one else was on the street. Katharine left the porch to join John at the edge of the lawn.

"It was," she told Marguerite. "Do you know him?"

"Dr. Upton advised me last winter to have Hamish analyze one of my Chinese medicines. He is a smart chemist."

"What did he say about your Chinese medicine?"

"That it was benign, safe for customers. Vincent wouldn't let me sell powerful ones in the store."

Katharine stared at Marguerite, whose eyes were shaded by her hat brim. "Does this mean there are powerful ones?"

"I only give those to people when I can supervise the effects."

Who would fall under her supervision? "Vincent took them?"

"*Non.*" Marguerite sniffed. "He scorn Chinese medicine. If he'd tried it, the *fleur d'amour* might have helped his cough better than laudanum."

"*Fleur d'amour,*" John said. "I know that much French. Flower of love."

"Canadians call it crepe jasmine or pinwheel flower," Marguerite said. "My Chinese farmer grows the flower in his greenhouse. I buy the roots and leaves and grind them into powder but only for Clarence's tea. No one else."

"Why does Clarence take a powerful medicine?" Katharine asked.

Marguerite's lips pursed. "That's his private matter. You should know that from working for a doctor."

Marguerite was right. Clarence wasn't a patient of Dr. Upton's, and his health wasn't Katharine's business. She felt her face flush.

"Clarence seems healthy to me," John said.

"My medicine and cooking cure him." Marguerite's chin rose, perhaps with pride in her accomplishment. "His doctor used to prescribe morphine. Clarence switched to opium. He liked it better, but neither was as good as my treatment."

"Did he smoke it in an opium den?" John said. "I've heard there's a few in Chinatown."

Numerous immigrants had come from China to Calgary to work on the railroad and many had settled here. "Does your pinwheel flower medicine act similarly to laudanum?" Katharine asked Marguerite. "It must taste better since you serve it in tea."

Marguerite nodded. "It has a mild flavour and fragrance."

Could this be the drug with opiate properties that was added to Vincent's whisky? Marguerite probably stored the powder in her kitchen cupboard and prepared the tea every day. How easy for her or Vincent to sprinkle the powder into his bottle of whisky. Easy for Clarence too, if he had reason to do it.

"I'll be damned!" John said. "Is this the mystery ingredient Hamish thinks was in Vincent's whisky?"

Katharine nudged his elbow. *Be quiet.*

"What are you saying?" Marguerite turned from John to Katharine. "How would Clarence's medicine get into Vincent's whisky?"

Katharine looked away. John had already told Marguerite too much. Now she could go home to prepare an answer for the police that didn't incriminate her.

"I must go talk to Clarence," Marguerite said.

"I'll go with you," John said.

"*Non.* I do this alone." She stepped off the curb and beelined to her house.

"Laudanum or *fleur d'amour?*" John said. "Does it matter which it is?"

Was he truly unconcerned that one was a common medicine, the other particular to Marguerite?

John shrugged. "Since I'm not needed here, I'll go make moonshine." He limped over the lawn to the narrow passage beside the house.

Katharine went inside. Was this information worth bringing to Detective Tanner? It would help to have Hamish's opinion. He'd been known to work Sundays on his rheumatism tonic. She placed a telephone call to the hospital on the chance he was there.

"He's here. The man's obsessive," the receptionist said. "I'll put you through to him."

When Hamish came on the line, Katharine asked if he was familiar with the pinwheel flower Chinese medicine.

"No," he said. "I've been remiss in my study of Asian remedies, although I once analyzed one for your friend Marguerite DeLuca. Curiously, it derived from a type of daisy, her namesake."

"She said you told her the medicine was benign."

"That's right, and yet she claimed it was more effective than its Western counterpart. I suspect some Asian remedies are centuries ahead of our medicines. Why do you ask?"

She explained. "Since the pinwheel powder taste is mild, someone could have added an enormous amount to the whisky and the drinker wouldn't notice."

"That's it!" he said. "If the medicine acts similarly to opiates for treating pain, cough, and other ailments, I'd expect it to have a similar, but not identical, chemical structure—like the ingredient I identified. Katharine, I believe you've found the missing link."

She listened for noise from John or the children, not wanting them to overhear. "Would the police be interested?"

"That's your area, not mine."

After they hung up, she paced to the kitchen and decided Detective Tanner would want new information as soon as possible. Unlikely he'd be at headquarters on a Sunday, but the police protected the public around the clock. Someone should be on duty to take her call. She looked out the back window. John and the children still played "moonshine." Back in the hall, she telephoned police headquarters.

A man came on the line. "Calgary Police Services. Constable Jones speaking."

"May I speak with Detective Tanner?"

"He's not at the station now." The constable spoke with a lazy drawl. "What is the nature of your business?"

It was too much to explain. Katharine identified herself and added she'd seen the detective on Friday. "He'll remember me."

"I'll pass along your name."

"Can you do this immediately?"

"Yes, ma'am." He sounded condescending. "Thank you for calling."

"Detective Tanner would want—" The line clicked off.

She'd learn soon if the constable followed through, or if he didn't.

Chapter Eleven

Sunday dinner was leftovers in Bertram's kitchen. Four days a week, he paid his neighbour to prepare home-cooked dinners for him. She always made enough for two more meals, and he finished the remaining hodgepodge on Sundays. His challenge tonight was heating eleven different items on his five-burner range in the least number of pots to wash afterward. This week, his neighbour was on a mashed craze, so he combined the mashed potatoes, mashed turnips, and mashed parsnips into a yellow mush. He was taking out a second pot for the meat when his telephone rang.

His parents calling with news?

"It's your lucky day," Constable Jones said. "A second woman desires your company. This one doesn't sound French. Her name's ..." Shuffling noises signalled his search for a piece of paper. "Katharine Sterling."

Bertram's skin tingled. "What does she want?"

"Wouldn't say. She didn't come to the station. I spoke with her on the phone about an hour or two ago."

"Two hours?"

"I got sidetracked by a man who came in to complain about a bobcat in his yard," he said. "I expect this woman's matter can wait until tomorrow."

It could not. Immediately after Jones hung up, Bertram called Katharine Sterling. She answered quickly and thanked him for his response. In a soft voice, she explained what she'd learned from Mrs. DeLuca and Hamish McBride. Bertram's excitement rose with each word. Her quiet tones made him wonder if her brother was nearby.

"I'll speak with the chief tonight," he said.

A cheer erupted in the background.

"Meanwhile, please don't discuss this with anyone else."

"Including my brother?" she said.

Especially him. "Yes." Her brother was the one witness Bertram hadn't interviewed yet, and he wanted his testimony as untainted as possible.

"Then I'd best hang up before he and the children finish their crokinole game."

"I'll call you about any significant developments."

"If it's during my work hours tomorrow, could you phone me at my office? Dr. G. W. Upton Family Medicine."

Bertram agreed, signed off, and phoned the chief at his home, catching him in the midst of eating dinner. Bertram reiterated Mrs. Sterling's news.

"I'm afraid I don't see the urgency," the chief said. "Who cares about Chinese medicine?"

"Will you review the file in the morning?"

The chief sighed. "All right. Truth be told, I haven't read it yet."

It's time you did.

At headquarters the next morning, Bertram added Mrs. Sterling's information to the whisky case-file and brought the folder to the chief.

"Leave it on my desk," the chief said. "The mayor phoned and wants to see me later today. I'll look at your case as soon as I finish my preparation for the mayor's meeting."

Bertram returned to his office. With no other pressing work, he brooded on the case he was starting to dub *Tainted Whisky*. His thoughts turned to the suspect he'd interviewed first, Clarence Oxenham, who had means and opportunity.

Katharine Sterling and Clarence himself said he was a teetotaller, which gave him a perfect excuse not to join Vincent in a glass of whisky. Clarence was intelligent enough to be aware of his own medicine's side effects. He'd have had little opportunity to spike any glass Vincent poured for himself, but spiking the bottle would have been a simple matter of adding the power when his landlords were out. Clarence would have found it equally easy to dispose of the bottle had Mrs. DeLuca not beaten him to it.

Motive was the missing element.

Clarence clearly had some involvement with Pina DeLuca, Vincent's cousin. Bertram's understanding was Vincent was her sole relative in Calgary. Had the family assigned him to guard her welfare? Italian families were known to be tight-knit and protective of their women. What if Clarence and Pina were in love and Vincent had stood in their path?

Although, love hadn't factored into Bertram's impression of Pina and Clarence's relationship.

Then there were John Wozniak and Dr. George Upton, two men possibly in love with Vincent's wife. Was the love unrequited or returned?

The chief burst into his office. "I've completed my review and agree your case is worth a few more steps. First, check out the hospital's lab technician to ensure he isn't a quack."

Done that.

The chief set the folder on Bertram's desk. "If the man checks out, proceed with the remaining interviews, beginning with the doctor who attended at the scene."

Ditto for Dr. Upton's interview. Bertram was ahead of the game.

"I'll authorize a motorcar for you," the chief said.

Bertram reflected. "I find showing up in a motor vehicle intimidates people."

"That's the idea. Show power."

Or did one catch more flies with honey? "The people to interview today are easily accessible by streetcar."

"Suit yourself," the chief said.

Bertram checked his pocket watch. If he left now, the streetcar might get him to John Wozniak in Tuxedo Park by eleven o'clock.

* * *

On the streetcar, Bertram decided that after John he'd interview Mr. Fielding, the owner of the drug store that employed Vincent and Marguerite DeLuca. Fielding also saw the DeLucas socially at their whist games and might have comments about Vincent's mental state. Dr. Upton had implied the games were a regular occurrence.

Bertram and Nellie had played whist once a month with friends she'd met through work. They especially liked the newer form, bridge whist, which added the skills of bidding for trump and the successful bidder playing the dummy hand.

In the spring, these friends had coaxed him to resume the games. They'd also invited a fourth player, an attractive woman in her late twenties. Despite his annoyance at their attempt to set him up, Bertram had enjoyed the thrill of the game. He and the woman were paired for the last hand. She bid him up to four spades. When she set down her dummy hand, he didn't think they had enough point cards to make it. He sweated through every trick. It came down to the last one. His eight of hearts took their opponents' seven. Victory! His heart soared and then he remembered Nellie and their son. They lay underground while he frolicked above. He crashed down to below the earth.

The streetcar drove past unfamiliar buildings and an avenue number that was higher than Mrs. Sterling's. *Dammit.* He'd missed his stop. He got off at the stop right before the next hill, crossed to the west side of Centre Street, and walked south, the cool wind pounding his back. Dr. Upton's door sign said Open. Bertram longed to go in, but telling Mrs. Sterling he'd come to question her brother would needlessly disturb her workday.

He continued at a slow pace to view the window display for Fielding and Sons Drug Store. A Brownie camera and framed photographs of a man standing proudly in front of a motorcar, a woman perched on a mountain ledge, and people bathing in—he surmised—the lagoon in Bowness Park. All of them smiling, their happy moments recorded by the camera.

Medicine bottles were interspersed with the photos. A sign advertised Aspirin as a cure for Spanish influenza. Bertram had heard that some doctors prescribed large doses of the medicine to ward off the dreaded flu. Another sign flanked by bottles of Coca-Cola declared the soda The Temperance Tonic. In his youth, Bertram had guzzled Coke with friends for the buzz and floating sense of euphoria. These were gone since the company removed cocaine from the recipe.

Fielding and Sons was open now. Given Vincent's death, the store hours might be limited. If Mrs. DeLuca were working, this would be an opportunity to see her on the job. Bertram went inside.

Service counters fronted three walls of the spacious room. Immediately to his left, two customers waited their turns on chairs beside an icebox with sodas.

A woman—not Mrs. DeLuca—served a customer at the counter to the back of the store. Three closed doors were behind it. The glass case under her counter displayed cameras and bottles of various sizes. A man served a customer at the centre counter. Behind him, cabinets filled with medicines reached to the ceiling. The third counter, in front of the Centre Street display window, was topped with weigh scales and mortars and pestles that reminded Bertram of Hamish's hospital laboratory. A teenage boy stocked items in the counter's glass cabinet.

When the customer at the camera counter left, Bertram approached the female salesclerk. She wore a gauze mask, as did the two male staff. From the creases around her eyes, he guessed the woman was around fifty.

Bertram introduced himself and showed her his badge. "I'm investigating the death of your store manager, Vincent DeLuca."

The woman's eyes flickered. "Poor Vincent. Brought down in his prime, like too many of our young men. But why are the police investigating? Vincent died of the flu."

Bertram evaded her question. "Do you work full time in the store?"

"Half days before Vincent's death. Marguerite, his wife, assisted him in the mornings. My husband is the store owner." She motioned toward the man behind the centre counter.

"You are Mrs. Fielding?"

"Yes. Marguerite was in earlier today but was so tired I convinced her to go home. Poor girl, she could hardly stand. I urged her not to come in until she's completely better. If she has the flu, we must protect our customers."

Mr. Fielding ran up a sale at the cash register on his counter. A waiting customer edged forward to replace the first one. Bertram felt in his coat pocket for his mask and remembered he'd taken it out to clean without adding a replacement. Careless, when Marguerite might have passed on the flu to him yesterday.

"Was there something irregular about Vincent's death?" Mrs. Fielding asked.

"That's uncertain yet," Bertram said. "During the weeks leading up to his death, did you notice anything different about his mood or behaviour?"

Mrs. Fielding rubbed her mask, evidently forgetting that touching masks could spread germs to the face. "I can't say that I did," she said. "He was as charming as ever. Friendly and efficient with customers. They all liked and respected him. You couldn't ask for a better boss."

The dead were invariably perfect in people's minds. "What about Mrs. DeLuca?"

"Marguerite?" Her forehead wrinkled. "Nothing unusual about her either, although we'd merely cross paths as she left and I arrived at work. At most, she might update me on a customer's order."

Both turned toward a series of thumps on the floorboards.

The teenage boy loped behind the camera counter. "I've finished stocking the face creams and eau de toilettes, Mother. I'll see what else is in the storage room." He opened the middle door on the rear wall and disappeared inside.

"Selling those items for women was Marguerite's idea." Mrs. Fielding waved at the far counter, and her sweeping hand took in the length of her own counter. "As were developing amateur photographs—she's hired a local man to develop them in his basement—and selling cameras, Chinese herbs, sodas. I admit cold sodas were popular in the summer, but how are any of these items are related to what the store's name clearly states—drugs?"

No relation that Bertram could see, except that they might attract customers and increase the store's profit.

He glanced at the bottles below this counter and noticed labels with Chinese characters. "I've heard some Chinese herbs are as effective as Western medicines yet gentler on the body."

Mrs. Fielding sniffed beneath her mask. "Wouldn't their very gentleness be an indication of lesser effect?"

"Good point," Bertram said to be agreeable.

"Marguerite wants to turn the counter across the room into a soda fountain," she continued. "Mr. Fielding says other drug stores have done this and claimed success, but the renovation would be costly."

In his peripheral vision, Bertram saw Mr. Fielding's customer leave. "Since your husband is free, I'll talk to him now." He thanked Mrs. Fielding for her time, sidled toward Mr. Fielding, and repeated his introduction.

The drug store owner's eyes grew wide. "I was told Vincent died of natural causes, although this flu is far from normal."

"Is there a place we can talk privately?"

Mr. Fielding looked past his wife. "The office. I'll have Mrs. Fielding cover for me, although we might be interrupted if customers have questions that she can't answer."

"That's fine," Bertram said.

While Mr. Fielding spoke with his wife, Bertram strode between the icebox and camera counter to the back of the store. The boy emerged from the middle doorway carrying a box of soda bottles. He wove past Bertram to the icebox.

Mr. Fielding joined Bertram in front of the first door. "That's my youngest son, Thomas. It's good training for him to work in the store during the school closure."

The *Calgary Albertan* morning newspaper had announced this latest closure. Mr. Fielding opened the door and ushered Bertram into the office.

Dim light shone in from the window, which looked out to the back lane. A table with beakers, bowls, and mortars and pestles ran along the back wall. A safe occupied the space beside the door. Mr. Fielding slid a chair for Bertram toward the desk. Bertram sat and placed his hat and gloves on the mahogany surface. Mr. Fielding settled on the chair across the desk, a filing cabinet and shelves of pharmaceutical books behind him. A folder lay in front of him on the desk.

"Since you aren't wearing a mask," he said, "would you mind if I take mine off?"

Bertram nodded.

Mr. Fielding removed the gauze material and breathed a sigh. "That's better. I find them distancing from customers, but

Vincent's death has stunned us to the dangers of this vicious influenza." He set the mask beside the folder.

Bertram asked permission to record their meeting, took out his notebook and pen, and summarized the reason for his visit, implying the police expert found the opiate-like substance in the whisky and omitting the detail that a Chinese medicine prepared in this drug store was the likely contaminant.

"It's amazing what can be determined from chemical analysis today," Mr. Fielding said. "Can your expert tell if the whisky was legal or illegally made?"

"We are still waiting for further information," Bertram said.

Mr. Fielding shook his head. "I can't believe Vincent would buy whisky outside of legal channels, but, as you must know, some of our finest citizens flout the Prohibition laws. They scarcely view it as a concern unless they're caught."

"Your stores sell prescription whisky."

"Strictly for medicinal purposes." No defensiveness in his tone. "In some ways, spirits are less harmful than many of our everyday treatments, such as laudanum."

"Did Vincent have a whisky prescription?"

"If he did, I'd expect he'd have bought it from this store. Staff gets a ten-percent discount." Mr. Fielding scratched his whiskered jaw. "Under normal circumstances, I wouldn't reveal customer information, but a man, my trusted employee and friend, died." His voice broke on the last word. "Would you like to me to check the store sales accounts?"

"Please."

Mr. Fielding stood, turned around, and opened the top drawer of the filing cabinet. "We keep the accounts here for three months before transferring them to the main branch downtown. Let's start with the customer sales for October to date."

Back in his chair, he pushed the other folder aside and scanned the pages in the customer sales folder. "I see no record of Vincent purchasing whisky during these first weeks of October. How long does a bottle last a man? Let's have a look at September." He closed the folder. "For the sake of the store's reputation, I must admit I'll be relieved if he bought the whisky elsewhere by whatever means."

Someone rapped on the door and nudged it open. Mrs. Fielding apologized for disturbing them. "A customer needs to speak with you," she told her husband.

Mr. Fielding returned the October sales folder to the filing cabinet, excused himself, and departed, leaving the door ajar. Bertram turned the folder on the table around to read the label. *Utilities.* He opened it and skimmed the first page of figures. Electricity, heat, telephone. Unlikely relevance to the case. He closed the file before Mr. Fielding re-entered.

"Where were we?" Mr. Fielding said.

"September," Bertram prompted. He didn't know the size of Vincent's daily glass of whisky, but even "wee drams" from a bottle wouldn't last a month, especially since Vincent sometimes shared a drink with John Wozniak.

Mr. Fielding took the September customer sales folder from the cabinet. While he perused the contents, Bertram studied the laboratory equipment on the side table.

"Nothing for Vincent in September aside from his laudanum," Mr. Fielding said. "You're aware he took this?"

"I am. Do you prepare some medicines in this office?"

Mr. Fielding followed his gaze to the table. "The more potent ones containing heroin and morphine."

"I'm told morphine is ten times stronger than opium."

"True, but morphine can be more accurately measured and is therefore safer than opium if handled correctly."

"Did Vincent handle all the morphine preparation in this store?"

"Yes. My wife doesn't prepare medicines, and Marguerite is limited to mixtures no stronger than laudanum."

"Your wife told me Marguerite introduced Chinese medicines to the store."

He nodded. "She prepares them herself, but Vincent assured me none are dangerous."

Another knock on the door. This time Thomas peered in. "Father, you're needed out there."

Mr. Fielding excused himself again. Bertram asked if he could use the bathroom and was directed to the third door behind the camera counter.

The bathroom's small size suggested the storage room extended behind it. Bertram re-entered the main room as Mr. Fielding finished with his customer. He walked the man to the exit door, turned over the Open sign, and told his wife and son to break for lunch.

"It's not warm enough out to eat at the table behind the store," Mrs. Fielding said and suggested they bring their lunch bags to the waiting area chairs.

"I'll have my lunch in the office," Mr. Fielding told them.

Bertram took that as a cue to wrap up quickly. When they resettled at the desk, he asked Mr. Fielding how often he'd come to the Tuxedo Park store prior to Vincent's death.

"My office is in our downtown store," Mr. Fielding said. "I'd check on each branch about once a week. Fortunately, my downtown manager is completely capable. I've left the store in her hands and will bring my office work here until I find a replacement for Vincent. Qualified managers are scarce in wartime."

"It must help to have your wife and son here," Bertram said. "Mrs. Fielding mentioned that Mrs. DeLuca was in briefly this morning."

"She went home due to illness or distress, which is natural, under the circumstances." Mr. Fielding blinked several times, perhaps as he recalled those circumstances.

"She seems an employee with an innovative frame of mind."

Mr. Fielding smiled. "Marguerite and Vincent complemented each other well, in terms of the store's operation. He was skilled in the practical matters—his accounts are meticulous—while she has the vision."

"Your wife said she wants to put in a soda fountain."

His eyes crinkled. "It's not a bad idea. My extended time here has given me a better sense of the Tuxedo Park branch. This is the newest of my four drug stores and the largest one, in the youngest neighbourhood. The accounts show increased profits due to the addition of photo developing, ladies' products, and soft drinks. I have my doubts about Chinese medicine, but it might acquire a following."

Bertram segued to the personal. "I understand you saw the DeLucas socially."

Mr. Fielding nodded. "We met for whist most Saturday evenings. Mrs. Fielding used to play, but she was glad to concede her spot to Upton this summer. She doesn't enjoy cards and feels they lead to gambling, so we don't play for money. It also wouldn't be fair to Upton to take his coins every time." He chortled. "Vincent's and Marguerite's card playing reflected their business styles. He played shrewdly, while her bidding and play tended to be wild and unpredictable but sometimes successful, maddingly so when you're her opponent. Are you familiar with the new bridge whist, Detective?"

"I am," Bertram said. He might enjoy playing with Marguerite, as he was starting to think of her, probably because everyone he spoke with referred to her by her first name.

Mr. Fielding's hands left the table. He shifted in his chair. Time to call the interview to a halt.

Bertram rose and handed Mr. Fielding his card. "Please telephone me at police headquarters if you later think of anything that might assist us."

"I'll do what I can." Mr. Fielding's face darkened. "I've known Vincent since he was seventeen, fresh from Crowsnest Pass," he said as they left the office. "I hired him as an apprentice at my downtown store. He became fast friends with my second boy, who apprenticed at the same time. They went to college together, along with my eldest son." He stopped in the middle of the drug store. Mrs. Fielding and Thomas sat on the chairs by the exit, eating apples. "The three had barely graduated when war was declared. They all enlisted right away. Vincent was the first to return, albeit with a chronic illness that surely contributed to his death, however the means. The world is a heartless place."

Bertram couldn't disagree. He said goodbye to the Fieldings and went out into the cool air. Clouds loomed overhead, and the north wind had picked up. The sight of the apples had made him hungry, and he needed sustenance before his interview with John Wozniak. Restaurants were still permitted to remain open, but food from a grocery store would make a quicker meal. He spotted a grocery across Centre Street.

The store offered an appealing lunch plate: cold beef, cheese, bread, and pickles. He bought a Coke as well. No place to eat inside the store, but Mrs. Fielding had mentioned a table behind the drug store.

Bertram recrossed Centre Street, walked past the drug store, and ducked into the first lane. He guessed the blue Packard Touring motorcar parked behind the office window belonged to Mr. Fielding. The car sheltered a table and two chairs from the north wind rushing through the lane. Bertram sat on the less wobbly chair, devoured his picnic, and wondered where Katharine Sterling was now.

Did she eat at work? Go home for lunch? Would she answer her front door when he arrived? All of these questions warmed him.

Chapter Twelve

When the dishes had been cleared, Katharine told the children to take their arithmetic books and slates to the kitchen table. From their lunch conversation, it appeared school that morning had consisted of playing the piano, recess, and making soup, lightly salted this time. John was now delivering a pot to Marguerite. The children practiced their sums while Katharine washed the dishes.

She was placing the last bowl in the rack when the doorbell rang. A neighbour? A telegram? Her heart raced as she hurried down the hall.

Detective Tanner stood on the front porch. No telegram, but was his appearance good news or bad? His face was ruddy from the cold.

"I thought you'd be at work."

She folded her arms against the chill air. "I took my lunch hour later than usual."

"I'm here to interview your brother."

"He's stepped out for a few minutes. Please come in."

He entered, closed the door, and hung his fedora on a hall chair hook. She stole a glance in the mirror. A few hairs had escaped her bun. She tucked them behind her ears while he took off his gloves and draped them and his coat on the chair.

"Can I offer you a cup of tea?"

"Anything warm would be wonderful."

She waved him toward the living room. "Please make yourself comfortable while I put on the kettle."

On her walk to the kitchen, she realized the children shouldn't be in the house while a policeman interviewed John about their neighbour's death by suspicious cause.

"Who is there?" Henry asked.

She lit the stove for the kettle. "A visitor for Uncle John. We'll save sums for later. You two play in the backyard until he leaves." Fortunately, their outerwear was in the back porch and not the front closet.

"Is it a friend from his band?" Henry asked.

Katharine set the teapot, three cups, and three spoons on the serving tray. "They need to talk about a private matter, so you'll have to stay outside until Uncle John comes to fetch you." She took off her apron.

Lillian got up from her chair. "What if I get cold?"

"Your hat and mittens and boots will keep you warm." Katharine poured milk into the creamer jug and placed the sugar jar on the tray. "Henry, you help her dress."

"What if I fall and bang my knee and it's bleeding all over the grass?" Lillian said.

"Wipe it clean with a leaf."

"Is it Mrs. DeLuca?" Henry asked.

"No," Katharine said. "And don't disturb Uncle John. I mean it. If you do, I'll stay home from work tomorrow and we'll do sums all day. No recess or music or—"

They dashed to the back porch, playtime eclipsing Henry's curiosity and Lillian's worries.

Katharine poured steaming water into the teapot and carried the tray to the living room. Detective Tanner stood at the sideboard studying the portrait of Eddie.

"My husband," she said.

He whirled toward her. A flush rose up his neck, perhaps because she'd caught him peering into her personal life. She was curious about his too.

"Is he overseas?"

"In Flanders originally and France now. The letters censor his precise locations."

He nodded. "Has he been away these four years?

"Yes. I hope his portrait on the sideboard will make him less of a stranger to the children when he returns." And less of a stranger to her.

"How old are they?"

"Henry's eight, Lillian's six." Lillian's dolls were strewn on the floor. Blocks littered the coffee table. "I apologize for the mess. I've kept them home from school since last Wednesday."

"Where are they now?"

"Outside. John will be back shortly. He looks after them while I'm at work."

She set the tray on the sideboard, picked up the blocks from the coffee table, and dumped them in the toy box.

Detective Tanner collected dolls from the floor. "Do you play the piano?"

"Sometimes," she said. "Not well, and lately, it's rare that I have the time."

"Is that a saxophone case beside it?"

She nodded. "John plays at a club, which has closed for the flu."

"Sorry for all the questions." He chuckled. "A habit in my line of work."

"I don't mind. You can put the dolls in the toy box."

"This too?" Detective Tanner held up Lillian's sock. He passed it to her, his fingers grazing her hand.

She stuffed the sock in her pocket. "Normally, the house is neater than this."

"I find it comfortable," he said. "Are the needlepoints your work?"

She scanned her needlepoint pictures on the walls. All were country scenes except *The Blue Boy* and *Pinkie* needlepoint portraits that flanked the mirror above the fireplace. The hands of the mantel clock edged to one o'clock. She should leave in fifteen minutes.

"I made them before the war," she said. "It's hard to believe I had time for hobbies."

"They're lovely. They give the room your personal touch."

Katharine felt her face flush at his compliment. She placed the tray on the coffee table, bumping a remaining block to the floor. Since he sat on the davenport, she took the rocker. The fireplace embers could use a stoke. She let him pour his own tea and milk. He added a lump of sugar.

She stirred milk into her tea. "If John doesn't return in the next ten minutes, I'll fetch him from our neighbour's house."

"How long have you worked for Dr. Upton?"

"Four years," she said. "Shortly after my husband enlisted, I learned our doctor was looking for a receptionist. His former one had also signed up. I needed the money to be able to stay in our home. Otherwise, we'd have probably moved in with my parents in Manitoba."

He took a sip of tea. "Do you enjoy the work?"

"I do. There was much for me to learn at first, but I like meeting people, acquiring medical knowledge, and keeping Dr. Upton's office in order. He's been a good and fair boss."

"As he probably told you, I spoke with him on Saturday."

She started. "Dr. Upton didn't mention it, but we had a flood of patients this morning. That's why I came home late for lunch." Had the detective interviewed him without explaining her role in the matter as he'd done with Clarence? The front door clicked. "That's John now." She left her chair and met him at the entrance.

"Marguerite thanks us for the soup," John said. "But she's still angry with you for reporting her store to the police."

"John, Detective—"

"Did you know she went all the way downtown to show that detective the store accounts?"

"John—"

"Afterward, she looked more carefully at the accounts ..." He glanced beyond her to the living room; his eyebrows rose. "We have company?"

She followed his gaze to the detective moving toward them. "Detective Tanner stopped by to talk to you about the night of Vincent's death."

"Why?" John asked. "He's already got your version, Clarence's, Marguerite's. I can't add anything more." His eyes narrowed at the detective. "Have you questioned the doctor who made the faulty diagnosis?"

"I have," Detective Tanner said. "But we need statements from everyone who was there. People notice different details and were present at different times."

John had been alone with Marguerite for much of that night, after the doctor left and Clarence went to his room.

"Before I talk to anyone, I have to get rid of this blasted leg." John hobbled to the living room and bypassed the armchair for the farther-away rocker.

Detective Tanner returned to the davenport; Katharine sat on the armchair and moved the empty teacup toward John. She hadn't yet started to drink her tea. John yanked off the artificial limb and breathed a sigh. Usually, when company was here, he'd leave the leg on and grit his teeth through the discomfort. Either the pain was too much, or this was a ploy for pity from the police.

The detective took out a notebook and pen from his suit pocket. He looked at John, who was filling his cup with tea. "You said Mrs. DeLuca carefully reviewed the store accounts after she saw me?"

John dropped two sugar lumps into his tea. "To be clear, Marguerite didn't look at the store accounts before she took them to the police. Vincent handled them all. You can check the documents against his handwriting."

Katharine sipped her lukewarm tea. John's tone sounded challenging. Friendly and cooperative would be better.

John picked up his teacup. "Vincent told Marguerite he got his whisky by prescription from the drug store—she had no reason to disbelieve him—but there's no indication of this in the accounts. So he lied to her. Why? Because he pilfered it from his own store or got it on the underground market?"

"He might have bought from the government vendor." Katharine looked at Detective Tanner. "Have you checked into this?"

"We're waiting for their records."

Had he bought it by prescription from a different drug store to hide the shame of his mental or emotional problems? "Marguerite told us he was seeing another doctor," Katharine said. "Does she know his name?"

"No," John said. "She doesn't recall Vincent referring to him by name and saw no payments to another doctor in his household accounts."

"I would guess this doctor treats diseases of the mind," Katharine said. "There are several specialists in Calgary. I could get their names from Dr. Upton."

"That would be helpful." Detective Tanner wrote in his notebook. "I'll stop by Dr. Upton's office for the information after I leave here."

"I hope that's soon," John muttered.

Katharine stared at him. *Don't be hostile.*

John put down his teacup. He crossed his left leg over his thigh and bounced the leg up and down, seemingly blasé. "Marguerite and I agree it's one of two things. The first possibility is that Vincent bought moonshine that slowly deteriorated to poison. Maybe Clarence has a secret still somewhere and his Chinese medicine accidentally got in. Marguerite says he's frequently away during his nonwork hours."

Detective Tanner jotted another note. Did he really take that long-shot suggestion seriously?

John continued to rock his leg. "The other, more likely, possibility is that Vincent, in a burst of agony and despair, grabbed Clarence's medicinal powder from the kitchen cupboard and poured it into the whisky bottle while no one was looking and without thought for the consequences after he was gone. People don't think straight, in that frame of mind. I can attest to that." He looked at Katharine for her affirmation, and she couldn't deny this.

"Had Vincent experienced that frame of mind in the past?" Detective Tanner asked.

"Marguerite says he did a few times." John's leg stopped moving. "Once, he grabbed a knife, and it was all she could do to stop him from slicing his wrist. I wish she'd come to me then for help." He set his foot on the floor and picked up his teacup.

"This was recently?" Katharine said. "Since you moved here in April?"

John sipped, perhaps to avoid replying.

"Who else witnessed these incidents?" Detective Tanner asked.

Katharine realized she should stay quiet. This was the detective's interview.

"It happened when they were alone," John said. "Clarence was out, perhaps tending to his hideaway still."

Clarence's absence was convenient; John's comment, flippant.

Detective Tanner jotted a note. Katharine would give anything to steal a glance at his notebook.

John took another sip. "Suicide is a mortal sin according to Vincent's Roman Catholic family. Marguerite's family in France believe that too. She doesn't, but she wants to protect Vincent's relatives from this knowledge. What purpose would it serve to add to his mother's grief or prompt the Church to dig up his body and rebury it in unholy ground?"

"I see no reason at this stage to involve his relatives in the investigation." A shadow crossed the detective's face. A play of light in room?

A son's murder was arguably worse than his suicide even to devout Catholics, but Katharine could understand John's wish for the police to hide a verdict of suicide from grieving parents.

She finished her cool tea and checked the mantel clock. Time for her to leave. "I'm due at work but can stay if you need me. Dr. Upton will understand. I'll telephone him now."

"You've already helped enough," Detective Tanner said. "Please attend to your work."

She'd rather stay to hear John's responses and try to modify them. "Before I go, would you like more tea, Detective Tanner?"

"Thank you, Mrs. Sterling, but no." He placed his empty cup on the tray and rose with her.

"Why so formal?" John scowled. "I hadenough formal in the army." He stared up at the detective. "I'm plain John. What's your Christian name?"

Don't antagonize him, John. "It truly would be no problem for me to stay," Katharine said.

"It's best I talk to *John* alone," Detective Tanner said. "I can be Bertram to you both."

John crossed his arms, looking smug, while *Bertram* showed no air of defeat.

Katharine carried the tray to the kitchen. Outside, the children played in the yard, loading dead plant stalks and leaves into the wheelbarrow. She wondered which man in the living room had won the first round of their adult game.

* * *

Bertram would have liked to let Katharine Sterling stay, but he was here in his police role and detectives got better results when they interviewed witnesses and suspects alone. Between sips of tea, John Wozniak described the events of Tuesday night, his tone growing more agreeable as he went along. Bertram judged him an affable man. If this were a situation of death by influenza, he could accept that a grieving Marguerite had turned to John for comfort after he'd offered his companionship and assistance as a neighbour; a friend; and, since the recent health orders, a saxophone

206

player at loose ends with his club temporarily closed.

"Your sister mentioned you played at a club," Bertram asked, when John paused for a sip. "What's its name?"

"Charlie's Den," John said. "The owner is Charles Larriviere."

Bertram's hunch was right. This was the club in East Calgary that he was supposed to have raided Saturday evening. Had that operation gone through, this minute he might be talking to John in his jail cell.

John reached the point in his account where the morgue took Vincent's body away. So far, John's version of the events didn't deviate significantly from Katharine's, Clarence's, Marguerite's, or Dr. Upton's.

"Marguerite stoically bid him *au revoir*," John said. "The doctor's car followed the hearse, a mini procession down our suburban street. Then Clarence, Marguerite, and I went into the house, and her anger erupted. It was stressful but natural under the circumstances. She fired blasts at everyone and everything, including Katharine for her botched attempt at artificial resuscitation. In my sister's defence, Dr. Upton had told us she'd done as much as a person could, but Marguerite ..." He shrugged. "We all look for answers outside ourselves."

A profound remark from a man Bertram viewed as light. John took a drink of water.

Katharine had thoughtfully brought them both glasses before she left for work.

"Where are Henry and Lillian?" John had asked her.

"In the backyard making moonshine." She'd smiled at Bertram's puzzled expression.

"Good to put them to work," John had said with a chuckle.

Apparently, this was a children's game. Bertram had been tempted to ask about it, but this wasn't relevant to his investigation.

John confirmed Clarence's report that Marguerite had blamed her husband's last drink of whisky for his death. "She threw a glass that shattered against the wall."

"A single glass?"

"Or two or three. What's the difference? Clarence cleaned up the shards while I settled her down."

"That must have been difficult," Bertram said in an attempt to prompt details of John's calming process.

John shrugged again. "Not especially. She quickly blows hot and cold."

Bertram believed that from his short meeting with Marguerite. She was an attractive woman; her French accent added a seductive appeal, and volatility could be exciting. Probably many women would find John attractive were it not for his marred left cheek. His leg injury was more debilitating though. Bertram doubted John's job at the club contributed much to this household's income. Would the widow Marguerite be interested in a man who couldn't support her? Perhaps unfairly, Bertram judged her as inclined to be mercenary. Would she throw John over when she no longer needed comfort and help?

John said Clarence went to bed after they were assured Marguerite was settled. John stayed with her in the living room so she wouldn't be alone. They'd talked mainly of practical matters, such as what she'd say to Vincent's parents when she phoned them in the morning, a task she dreaded. They had disliked her from the start because she wasn't the nice, local Italian girl Vincent had left behind when he went to war.

"A common occurrence," John said. "A man meets someone overseas and abandons his sweetheart back home. Or he dies and leaves the woman alone."

Bertram glanced past John, at the portrait of Katharine's soldier husband on the sideboard. His image seemed to dominate the room in his absence. He was still alive, as far as Katharine knew, and he'd be a fool to throw her over. His departure had changed his wife from a woman with time for needlepoint to one who supported her family with her work in a doctor's office. In addition to *The Blue Boy* and *Pinkie* portraits, Bertram counted ten smaller needlepoint pictures on the living room walls. All of them featured people. Women working in gardens, men plowing a field, children frolicking in a meadow.

Music likely filled this room often. John would have leisure time for the saxophone, piano, and Victrola. The children evidently played in here. A sewing machine stood along the inner wall. Behind the davenport, bookcases faced each other. He'd like to see Katharine's reading tastes. John didn't strike him as a man who spent his time with books. This was a busy room, in the best sense, brimming with their activities.

John reached the end of his report on Vincent's death. "I didn't for one minute suspect anything irregular until my sister meddled. She meant well, but you'd be wise to leave things as they are and move on to your next case."

"Why is that?"

John finished his glass of water, perhaps to stall. "There's no earthly benefit to anyone. It won't bring Vincent back. Stirring things up will hurt people. What parents want to think their child was so despondent he ended his life, or worse, was murdered?" He caught Bertram's questioning stare. "Yes, I know you're looking for murder and you'll keep digging until you find it."

"Only if it's there."

"I'm not sure about that." John squinted at Bertram. "You could make a name for yourself, move up the ranks. I saw that happen in the army. A captain pinned a desertion rap on a corporal. The poor fellow was shot, and the captain moved up to major."

Bertram shuddered. That event seemed beyond the pale for this modern age, but he couldn't deny John's experience, and the police force wasn't immune to similar behaviour. He turned toward a knocking sound from the room behind him.

"Is that the children?" John hoisted himself from the chair.

Bertram returned both of their glasses to the tray, picked it up, and followed John to the kitchen on the pretext of helping; mostly he wanted a glimpse of Katharine's children. John opened the back door.

"I'm cold." A little girl hunched her shoulders and shivered.

"Faker." Her brother nudged her shoulder. John had referred to them as Lillian and Henry. "Is that your friend, Uncle John?"

"I hope so," John said. "Take off your overclothes, and let's make cocoa before piano lessons."

"Yay!" Lillian's smile was the image of Katharine's.

Bertram placed the empty glasses in the sink. He hoped he'd turn out to be John's friend, more for Katharine's sake than for John's. Bertram sensed she wasn't yet aware that he viewed her brother as a major suspect.

Chapter Thirteen

A lack of patients in the waiting room that Monday afternoon enabled Katharine to catch up on typing Dr. Upton's notes into files. If the bank were open, she'd scoot out to deposit the day's cash, but the manager had opted to close his branch today until further notice. She tucked the money from patients into her desk drawer, which had a lock. Smart thieves who noticed certain banks closing might deduce that nearby businesses would be forced to keep more cash than usual on-site.

Dr. Upton emerged from his examination room with a patient. Katharine took his notes and processed the payment.

After the woman left, Katharine seized the opportunity for a private talk. "Detective Tanner told me he spoke with you on Saturday."

"I was wondering when you'd bring that up. Rather a shock to have a police detective appear while I'm innocently raking my lawn." He pursed his lips. "An even greater surprise to learn you took the item to Hamish without consulting me."

"It wasn't an office matter."

"I attended to Vincent in my medical capacity—at your request, I might add."

She shifted the focus away from his blaming her. "You told the detective you weren't aware Vincent was seeing a specialist."

"Vincent is another one who went behind my back. I'd have referred him had he indicated he needed mental or emotional help."

She hadn't found Dr. Upton prickly before. Was he tired from a bad night's sleep? "Detective Tanner asked me for a list of Calgary doctors Vincent might have seen. Could you give this to me?"

"I believe I'm capable." The door rattled, and a patient walked in. "While you take her details, I'll look for their names."

He went into his office. Was he upset about his misdiagnosis of Vincent? Dr. Upton had a healthy dose of pride in his medical skills, but doctors dealt in too many unknowns to expect to completely avoid errors. He returned with a sheet of paper for her and led the patient to his examination room. Katharine scanned the list of three names. She'd learned to decipher his scribbles these past years of managing his medical practice. If she were a detective, she'd start with the doctor closest to Vincent's home and the drug store. She printed the names for Bertram.

More people arrived, bringing the lull to an end. As she processed a payment, she looked up at the sound of the door opening again. Detective Tanner entered. *Bertram to you both*, he'd said. He waited his turn behind a man at the reception desk. She quickly filled out the form with the man's symptoms and asked him to take a chair.

Bertram drew up to the desk. How would she get used to calling him by his first name when she could barely think of Dr. Upton as George after four years of working with him?

She handed *Bertram* the sheet of paper. "You're finished with John?"

"For now." A quiver to his lips made her conscious of the mask hiding half her face.

"I should wear a mask in a medical office," he said, as though reading her thoughts.

"Take one, if you wish." She nodded at the basket of them on the counter.

"I'll save those for your patients."

A woman and four children burst into the office, but Katharine wanted to learn more about the case and, more importantly, his interview with John. "What's your next step?"

"I'll review the entire file with the chief of police, and we'll take it from there."

That told her nothing.

The youngest child let go of his mother's hand, ran to an empty chair, and climbed on it. His siblings followed him and tried to push him off. The waiting room was headed for chaos. Bertram's lips puckered in apparent amusement.

"I'm afraid I have to serve my next patient," she said.

"I'll be in touch, as needed." Bertram left as the woman settled her children on the chairs, all of them coughing, sneezing, and wiping their noses.

Katharine bumped the family to the top of the next-to-be-seen list to get the rowdy and virus-carrying children out of the office as quickly as possible. She couldn't wait to get home to hear John's report of the interview.

Soon after the room grew quiet, Marguerite walked in, to Katharine's surprise. She scanned the patient list. Marguerite hadn't booked an appointment with Dr. Upton while Katharine was away at lunch.

"Can you fit me in today?" Marguerite's mask fluttered with her words.

There was still time before closing. "Certainly." Katharine found Marguerite's file in the top drawer of the cabinet and took out a fresh form. "What is the nature of your visit today?"

"I'll tell the doctor."

Katharine nodded. Some patients, usually men, refused to provide details and didn't consider that afterward she would type Dr. Upton's examination notes. She asked Marguerite to take a seat along the wall to her left if she was experiencing symptoms of influenza.

"I'm not sure if I am or not," Marguerite said. "Mr. Fielding told me I can't work at the store until Dr. Upton clears me of the flu, for the sake of our customers."

"Best to err on the side of caution." Katharine waved toward the chairs on Marguerite's left.

Marguerite sat on the one closest to the desk. "John says Detective Tanner came to see him today."

"You talked to John?"

"I stopped in on my way to talk to Mr. Fielding," Marguerite said. "John hopes the police will let sleeping ducks lie."

Did she mean sleeping dogs? The thought prompted Katharine to ask Marguerite how her dog was doing.

"I put him out to do his business yesterday, and he hasn't returned. Clarence jokes a cougar got him." Her lower face wrinkled the mask. "Vincent didn't like the dog. Pina, his cousin, says he was allergic to dog fur when he was a child."

"You've seen Pina today?"

"She came to ask for a cooking pot. Her bank has closed for this horrible flu. I hate it." Her eyes flashed. The mask highlighted their almond shape. "Maybe it's right the dog should pass to the next world after Vincent."

"It's sad when anything dies in a brutal way."

Marguerite shrugged. "That's nature."

Dr. Upton emerged with his patient and called the next one in. As he turned around, he stepped back at the sight of Marguerite but continued to his examination room. Katharine put the Closed sign on the door so no more patients would arrive.

During Marguerite's fifteen minutes with Dr. Upton, Katharine finished typing the other patients' files.

Marguerite re-entered the waiting room with the doctor. "No flu," she said in a buoyant tone. "I'll tell Mr. Fielding I can work tomorrow." She thanked Dr. Upton and glided out of the office.

Dr. Upton handed Katharine his notes. *Fatigue and stomach upset. Mild hysteria due to stress following the death of her husband.* He advised rest, no prescription.

"Her temperature is normal," he said. "I believe her symptoms are a natural bodily response to the personal tragedy."

Katharine silently agreed this was a reasonable diagnosis.

* * *

When Bertram arrived at headquarters, he asked Julia to telephone the three medical specialists.

"Will do," she said. "The government store finally supplied their records for import from the Ontario distillery and subsequent sales in Alberta. The document arrived by post this afternoon." She handed him an envelope.

He thanked her. "Is the chief free?"

"He's still out with the mayor."

"Let me know when he returns."

Bertram went into his office to study the sheets of paper that listed the past year's activity for Vincent's brand of whisky. The government store had imported an average of eighteen bottles of Godfrey's Finest Blended Whisky per month and sold them all to drug stores. No private sales. Roughly one third went to Fielding and Sons, and half of these to the Tuxedo Park branch. From Bertram's knowledge of liquor prescriptions, Tuxedo Park's sales of about three bottles per month of a particular whisky wasn't excessive. He would request Fieldings' records to make sure the figures balanced. His telephone rang.

Julia came on the line and connected him to one of the specialists. The doctor said he worked from a home office but had cancelled this week's appointments due to the flu. Bertram explained the situation.

"I hesitate to reveal a patient's name," the doctor said.

"The man is dead. Your information is essential to our investigation."

The doctor paused. "Vincent DeLuca? I don't recall him, but I might forget someone I saw on a single occasion, especially if this were months or years ago."

Bertram doubted this was the case since Vincent would need at least a monthly prescription for whisky. "Could you check your appointment calendar for the past year?"

"It's upstairs in my office. I can get back to you within the hour."

After the call, Bertram opened his notebook, titled the next page *Tainted Whisky Case*, and wrote *Action one: obtain Fieldings' record of Godfrey's whisky purchase and sales.* If the store's stock showed a discrepancy between the two amounts, it would suggest Vincent was stealing supply. A bottle every month or so might easily go unnoticed.

John's comment about Clarence's secret moonshine production seemed at best wishful thinking, and at worst a deliberate attempt to mislead the police, but Clarence's activities away from his home and work were worth investigating to unearth a motive. Bertram noted this second action.

Did Marguerite or Clarence prepare his herbal tea? Since Vincent scorned Chinese medicine, Bertram doubted he would mix the drink. If Vincent's fingerprints were on the jar, this would point to suicide. Action three would be to request the jar of Clarence's medicine powder for fingerprinting.

The whisky bottle had probably been handled too frequently for meaningful fingerprint analysis, but the police lab had no use for it anymore. Bertram's fourth action would be to order the return of the bottle to check for prints.

Julia appeared in his office doorway. "I've tried the other two doctors several times but got no answers."

"They've probably cancelled their appointments as well and closed their offices. Could you try them at their homes?"

"I'll do my best."

When she left, his thoughts shifted from medicines to Dr. Upton, a pudgy man in his mid-forties. Would Marguerite, an elegant woman twenty years younger than him, find Dr. George Upton attractive? Crescent Heights, where he lived, was a tonier neighbourhood than Tuxedo Park. He probably owned his house, rather than rented like Vincent and Marguerite. From Marguerite's perspective, Dr. Upton had money. If he adored her or treated her better than Vincent had, this would be icing on her cake. Bertram's fifth action would be to confirm Dr. Upton's single status and get a greater sense of his feelings toward Marguerite and the nature of their relationship. Had he recently joined their regular whist night as an excuse to spend time with her?

Action six involved similar questions about John Wozniak. His feelings for Marguerite, their prior relationship, plus the frequency of their past meetings.

Bertram tried to think of a seventh action. *Lucky seven.*

His telephone rang. "I have a second doctor on the line," Julia said.

This doctor also told him he'd cancelled appointments and was reluctant to confirm names of patients. His office was in the Calgary General Hospital. In the end, he admitted he didn't recall treating Vincent DeLuca, but he agreed to check his appointment schedule the next day and phone Bertram with the result.

After he hung up, his phone rang again. "The chief's back," Julia said.

Bertram found the chief in his office, grimacing at a stack of papers on his desk. "I go out for a few hours, and the work piles up. What can I do for you now?"

Not the best time to burden the chief. Bertram sat across the desk from him and briefly summarized the government store's report as well as his interviews with Clarence, Hamish, Dr. Upton, Marguerite, Mr. Fielding, and John.

"You've been busy," the chief said.

"Thanks to my head start on Friday and the weekend."

The chief squinted at him. "Very well. I'll give the case a thorough look tonight and decide if there's sufficient evidence to continue with it or not."

"I'll have Julia type my interview notes and give you the file before she leaves."

"She might as well bring it home with her. Save me the trouble." He frowned at the pile on his desk.

With luck, the comforts of home would improve the chief's mood this evening.

Bertram's sole action for tonight would be to review his notebook for anything he'd missed.

* * *

Katharine arrived home from work while John and the children were playing on the living room floor. They'd stacked blocks in front of Lillian's dollhouse to defend the miniature dolls from attack by Henry's toy soldiers. John told Katharine that Marguerite had given them a chicken that needed to be used. He and the children had chopped chicken and vegetables during afternoon cooking class. The chicken stew was simmering for dinner.

She went to the kitchen and tasted the stew gravy. Not bad, nor too salty. She had to thank Marguerite for this meal with meat. Cooking class was a practical addition to the children's schooling, and not just because it relieved Katharine of the task. One day Lillian would probably run a household, and Henry might remain a single man. Thanks to cooking class, his meals might be more interesting than Dr. Upton's.

After she changed into her warm underwear and housedress, Katharine set the table, sliced bread, and stirred the pot occasionally. When the stew was ready, she called everyone to dinner. The children bounded into the room.

She stopped John in the hall. "How was your talk with Detective Tanner?"

"Bertram," he said. "Before long we'll be calling him Bertie."

That was a stretch. "What did he ask you?"

"We're not supposed to discuss it." He ran his finger across his lips to indicate silence.

"Even after we've told him what we know?"

"Ask Bertram. I'm not familiar with police rules." He hopped to the kitchen.

She longed to press him on the subject but not with the children present. During dinner, John mentioned their other afternoon class—piano lessons—and suggested they have a concert before bed. The children left the table before she and John were finished their meals and ran to the living room to continue the dollhouse siege.

Katharine resumed the hall conversation. "My impression, John, is the police want to get each person's version before they've had a chance to influence each other. Criminals, in particular, might cook up a story."

"A little chicken here, potato there ..."

His levity irritated her, but the analogy applied. "Together, their story blends. Apart, one of them mentions an ingredient that doesn't fit in the stew or raises questions."

"Is this a metaphor?" he asked. "The children and I haven't got to studying them yet."

"But once the police have our individual pieces, we can discuss among ourselves."

"If we want to," he said. "I don't. I got my fill of these damn suspicions with Bertram today." He scraped up his last bits of food.

She let the matter go but would try once more to get him to talk after the children were in bed. "While I wash up, you organize the troops to clean up the damage." The thought reminded her of Eddie. Still no letter in today's post.

By the time she entered the living room, no evidence remained of the dollhouse war. John's disciplining skills were improving, and the concert was impressive. Lillian played a simple one-hand tune. Henry played Mozart's Minuet in F Major, K2 with both hands, few errors, and a touch of flourish. Perhaps he'd become a musician like his Uncle John, rather than a bricklayer or soldier like Eddie. In terms of both safety and remuneration, bricklayer was easily the best of those three careers, but she'd choose musician over soldier for her precious son.

The three urged Katharine to wrap up the concert with a piano piece. She declined in favour of John.

"I don't have the sheet music for it," he said, "but I've been learning this new song by ear."

They all sang along to "Hail! Hail! The Gang's All Here." She wouldn't view her problems as lightly as the song suggested until Eddie left his soldier gang and returned to their family in this room.

John shifted to another song while Katharine coaxed the children through their bedtime routine, negotiating them down to two stories. Weary from the effort, she returned to the living room. Bach music flowed from the Victrola. John sat on the rocker beside the crackling fireplace, his eyes closed, listening.

She got her mask-making basket from the sideboard. The masks would be better and more quickly made on the sewing machine, but she'd rather relax on the davenport and sew them by hand. Before the war, in the evenings, she'd sit here and read, do needlepoint, or darn socks while Eddie built items for their home, including several in this room—the bookshelves, lamps, toy box, and coffee table.

When John opened his eyes, she broached the subject of the police investigation. "After talking to you, Detective Tanner—Bertram—came to the office for the names of specialist doctors that Vincent might have seen. It's odd that Vincent wouldn't ask Dr. Upton for a referral, but perhaps he trusted Dr. Upton with his body and not his mind."

"The mind is a tricky business," John said.

"I'm starting to wonder if Dr. Upton is good for routine illnesses but not necessarily complex ones. Vincent might have brought up a difficult problem and found Dr. Upton didn't understand."

"Sadly, we'll never know," John said, as the doorbell rang. "Who's that? Marguerite?"

A telegram? Katharine set her mask-making materials on the coffee table.

John left the rocker and held on to furniture and walls on his way to the entrance. "It's you," Katharine heard him say in a tone of surprise. "Come in out of the cold."

Katharine went to hall. Pina DeLuca entered.

"Could I use your sewing machine tomorrow?" Pina asked. "Marguerite suggested it. She doesn't have one."

"What are you making?" Katharine asked.

"Cushions for my apartment. I bought fabric and stuffing at the dry goods store."

"Normally I wouldn't mind at all," Katharine said, "but with the flu numbers rising, the city advisory is to keep to our separate homes."

"Let's discuss this in comfort." John headed back to the rocker.

Pina took the armchair. Katharine sat on the davenport and supposed they were reasonably separated. She asked Pina about her move.

"We spent all day yesterday driving items from my boarding house to the apartment," Pina said. "The place comes with a stove and fridge and two beds. We moved one to the living room to use as a sofa. The cushions will be a backrest. Marguerite loaned me her card table and two chairs and Vincent's dresser, which we cleaned out. Today, I shopped for cushion materials and food and dishes and other things. It's a lot of work and money to live on my own. I didn't think of that before moving in." She paused to take a breath. "And now, I'm out of work until this flu is over. I'll still get a partial salary. Clarence says the bank should pay my whole salary since they're still holding onto people's money and no one can take it out. But here, I'm stuck in the suburbs with nothing to do. I didn't especially like my landlady and boarding-house roommates, but they were people to talk with." Pina paused again.

Katharine could appreciate that talking was an important need for Pina. "At least you're close to Marguerite and Clarence for visits," she said, to lift Pina's spirits.

"That was the point for my mother," Pina said. "She pushed me into the move."

Katharine hadn't expected that. "My mother would have discouraged me from living alone."

"She knew the sin you'd have gotten into," John quipped.

Pina raked her fingers through her cropped hair. "Sin is a top concern for my mother too, but it's a distant second to looking after family.

"You mean Marguerite?" John asked.

Pina nodded. "I phoned Mama yesterday to tell her about the move. The apartment has no phone, of course. Another inconvenience. I used my friend's phone at his house."

"You can use ours from now on," John said.

This was becoming friendlier with Pina than Katharine liked with a flu raging through the city.

"Mama thinks it will help Marguerite to have a relative nearby, especially if she's right about her condition."

Katharine glanced at John, who looked as startled as she was by the implication.

Pina's arched eyebrows rose. "Mama claims she can tell that a woman is with child before the woman suspects herself."

John's jaw dropped.

"Something about a softness in her face," Pina said. "Yesterday on the phone, she told me that after I left the Pass, she cornered Marguerite and asked about her condition."

John cleared his throat. "Marguerite is ...?"

"Marguerite denied she's in the family way," Pina said.

"She saw Dr. Upton this afternoon," Katharine said. "He told me—and I typed his examination report—that he'd diagnosed her with—" To say more would be a breach of confidentiality.

"Let me guess." Pina sniffed. "Hysteria, the catch-all for every woman's ailment. Mama would insist her diagnosis is better than any doctor's."

"Marguerite hasn't told me about this." John shook his head. "I don't believe she's carrying a child."

But her fatigue and stomach upset were common early signs of pregnancy. Dr. Upton knew to look for this in all his younger female patients. He shouldn't have missed it.

Chapter Fourteen

Tuesday morning, Bertram strode into headquarters and stopped at the reception desk to talk with Julia, who wore a mask.

"Chief's orders." She explained that the previous evening, her younger son had developed a high fever and complained of a sore throat, headaches, and body aches. Terrified he'd contracted the flu, she called the doctor, who rushed to the house. The boy's symptoms were subsiding by the time the doctor arrived. He thought they indicated a normal grippe. No one else in the family showed signs of Spanish influenza. The chief decided it would be fine for them both to come into work today. Shaken into awareness of the flu danger, he'd ordered all staff to wear masks while inside, until further notice.

"A proper safety measure," Bertram said. He'd been negligent in this matter, partly due to his indifference to his own well-being.

Julia nodded at a tray of masks on her desk. "My mother scrounged these from her ladies' hospital volunteer supply. I've set them out for visitors."

Bertram plucked one from the tray. "Is the chief free for me to speak with him?"

"Be prepared for a grumpy mood." Julia grinned. "No one at our house got much sleep last night."

Bertram remembered the whisky bottle and asked Julia to have the lab send it back for fingerprint analysis.

She nodded. "I'll also try your third doctor at his home again as well as his office. He might have gone in to do paperwork."

"Thanks. Any stabbings or other altercations from last night for me to deal with?"

"Quiet as the proverbial mouse."

Monday nights had typically been slow even before Prohibition and the flu closures.

Bertram continued to the chief's office. The chief noticed him through the glass and picked up the mask on his desk. Bertram tied on his own mask as well and took the seat across the desk.

"Julia told me about your grandson," Bertram said. "I trust he's better this morning."

"Hopping around like nothing happened. Caused us all a major scare."

"I can imagine. Did you have a chance to review the Tainted Whisky file?"

"Last night? With my family in crisis?" The chief glanced at the folders on his desk. The pile didn't appear to have shrunk since yesterday. "I'll get to it after these priority matters. And why do you young officers insist on giving police files pretty names?

Have you been reading too much Sherlock Holmes?"

Bertram did read Holmes, and thirty-eight wasn't young. "It helps us keep track of the cases."

"If you can't keep track in your head, you aren't qualified for police investigation."

Bertram brushed off the chief's orneriness. "It would greatly help the investigation if you could find the time for the file this morning."

"Hrmph. Damn masks." The chief pulled on the gauze. "They get caught in my beard."

Bertram slipped out of the room. At the reception desk, Julia told him the Sunalta robbery trial was postponed because the defendant claimed flu symptoms. Her eyes crinkled at the convenient excuse.

Bertram had no new cases that needed attending, and the plan for his undercover work at Charlie's Den was fully in place for whenever the club reopened. He could read his notes on the Tainted Whisky case again, but last night's review had brought no new insights, and another pass through was unlikely to do more. Since it was doubtful the chief would read the file in the next couple of hours, Bertram had time to check out something nearby.

What about action one—Fieldings' store records for Godfrey's whisky? The Fielding and Sons downtown branch was a five-minute walk from headquarters. Bertram recalled passing the store whenever he'd detoured to Stephen Avenue to shop on his way home. Mr. Fielding would be in Tuxedo Park, but Bertram could talk to his capable store manager. At worst, it would be no greater waste of time than sitting here doing nothing productive.

He told Julia he'd be back in less than an hour and stepped out to lightly falling snow. Newcomers to Calgary often were stunned and appalled when winter arrived before the end of October. Bertram tried to assure them the cold would be gone with the next Chinook wind. He enjoyed southern Alberta's varied and unpredictable weather.

Stephen Avenue bustled less than usual for a weekday morning. Fewer shoppers and people on their way to work. A tumbleweed rolled down the street, reminding him the untamed countryside wasn't far from this frontier city. He arrived at the sandstone building that housed Fielding and Sons.

A woman stood behind the counter, occupied with a customer. While waiting his turn, Bertram studied the tall cabinets crammed with medicine bottles and the counters cluttered with mortars and pestles and other drug store paraphernalia. The brighter lighting and spacious open area of the larger Tuxedo Park branch gave it a modern flair. This downtown store had an icebox with sodas but sold no photographic equipment, face creams, or perfumes. Chinese medicine would be far from anyone's mind in here.

Behind the counter, a framed certificate hung on the wall. The University of Alberta Faculty of Medicine declared Ethel Gibbons qualified to practice pharmaceuticals. It would take skill to understand the properties of every medicine and mix the appropriate amounts for treatment, while being cognizant of potential side effects that ranged from irritating to potentially fatal. No wonder pharmacists had college degrees.

When the customer left, Bertram introduced himself to the woman, whose nametag read *Miss Ethel Gibbons*. "I spoke with Mr. Fielding at your Tuxedo Park branch yesterday and want to follow up with some questions."

"Mr. Fielding is in his office now if you'd like to speak with him."

"His office here?"

"Yes."

A bonus.

She led him to a room at the back of the store.

Mr. Fielding looked up as they entered. "Detective Tanner?"

Miss Gibbons left them alone.

"I'd thought you were working in your Tuxedo Park branch," Bertram said.

"I am. Have a seat." Mr. Fielding pulled up a chair to the desk.

Bertram sat across from him facing three portraits displayed on the wall. He guessed the soldiers in dress cap were Mr. Fielding's sons: three young, handsome, confident-looking boys unaware of the slaughter ahead. They reminded Bertram of the portrait of Katharine's husband on her sideboard. Below the first two portraits were certificates from the Ontario College of Pharmacy, issued to James Fielding and Arthur Fielding in 1914. Arthur, Mr. Fielding's second son, had been Vincent DeLuca's close friend.

"Marguerite saw Upton for a checkup," Mr. Fielding said. "She told me he cleared her of the flu and recommended work and routine as the best medicine. She returned to the store today. I'm taking the opportunity to spend a few hours here catching up on paperwork."

Dim light shone from a window that looked out to a lane. This office was similar to the one in Tuxedo Park, with shelves of ledgers and pharmaceutical books, a safe, a filing cabinet, and a table with medicine-preparation equipment.

"Marguerite can't compound strong prescriptions without me present," Mr. Fielding continued. "But she can prepare simple ones, take new orders, distribute medicines I prepared yesterday, and sell patent and over-the-counter medications and our other drug store add-ons." He paused. "What can I do for you this morning?"

"Could you supply a written account of your company's purchase and sales of

Godfrey's whisky, the brand Vincent DeLuca drank?"

"We don't tabulate brands separately, but I'll have my secretary do this for Godfrey's distillery. We purchase two brands from them. One called Godfrey's Pure Medicinal reassures customers they are buying medicine, while Godfrey's Finest appeals for opposite reasons. I suspect the labels are the sole difference between the two." He smiled. "My secretary could get you the information tomorrow morning. Would that be soon enough?"

"Perfect," Bertram said. "Would it have been possible for Vincent DeLuca to help himself to bottles of whisky without entering them into your Tuxedo Park store's sales accounts?"

Mr. Fielding's jaw tightened. "This crossed my mind after our talk yesterday, but I hate to think it of a trusted manager and a friend who is gone from us."

"If he'd wanted a free bottle every month or so, how would he accomplish this?"

"As a store manager with sole responsibility for incoming and outgoing items?" Mr. Fielding scratched his chin, apparently reflecting. "He'd need to alter a figure at some point in the chain. Supply in, supply out, or surplus supply at the month's end. Meticulous as we are, I suppose a small amount could go unnoticed. We rely on trust to a large extent, rather than excessive checks and balances. Perhaps that is an old way of doing business."

"Could you find the irregularities through a careful examination of your books?"

Mr. Fielding glanced at a bookshelf holding some ledgers. "I could but have no desire to tarnish Vincent's memory or press charges for a minor theft."

The police couldn't charge a dead man in any event. "We might request your books."

"Then I would comply."

Bertram recalled another action item. "Like all of us, I'm sure you're looking forward to a return to happier moments, such as your weekly whist games. Will you be looking for a single man like Dr. Upton for your missing fourth?"

"Not necessarily." Mr. Fielding's face relaxed as the conversation shifted to card games. "A woman to balance our foursome might be the ticket, especially one attractive to Upton. The old bachelor is becoming fussy and set in his ways." He chuckled.

With the doctor's single status confirmed, Bertram segued to an unrelated question to bring the interview to a close. "Are those your three older sons on the wall?"

Mr. Fielding twisted around. "One in the trenches, one the cavalry, and Arthur, the RFC pilot. He's been reported missing."

"I'm sorry."

"My wife and I hope to welcome all three of them home this winter or spring. You met our fourth son, Thomas, at the Tuxedo Park branch. My dream is for each son to eventually manage one of my four stores. I've planned the Tuxedo branch for Arthur, the cleverest of my boys. It's a wicked war that would take the best and brightest."

War does that.

Mr. Fielding's face grew red. "This damn flu follows a similar path of killing the young and strong and sparing those of us past our primes. What reason is there in that?"

The world wasn't reasonable.

"Pardon my rant." Mr. Fielding's shoulders shook with his effort to compose himself. His tone softened. "I support the war but get angry at its threats to my family and dreams. When it's over, I look forward to putting my plans in place, God willing."

God often has other plans.

Bertram returned to headquarters, the snow falling heavier and blowing now. Inside, Julia told him the chief wanted to see him. Bertram found the chief's glass door ajar, a sign he wasn't concentrating on work.

When Bertram sat down, the chief slid the Tainted Whisky folder from the edge of his desk to a spot in front of himself. Since the chief's mask lay on his desk, Bertram didn't put his on.

The chief set his palms on the folder. "I've finally had a chance to review this case and see no purpose in your further investigation."

"I've outlined a number of actions and—"

"All the solid evidence points to your wounded veteran succumbing to the Spanish flu," the chief said. "Or if the hospital technician is to be believed, using a readily available drug to end his life. A sad tale that happens too frequently. It will get worse when our boys come home and struggle to adapt to the lives they left behind." He tapped the folder. "This man is a canary in our new world's coal mine, foreshadowing what's to come."

"That's nonsense." Bertram realized his arms were crossed. He left them in place. The chief's prediction about the returning soldiers might be right, but this didn't mean it applied in Vincent's case. "Let me at least conclude my actions. They'll give us a better picture of the true situation."

The chief leaned his chair back. "I spent yesterday going over the police budget with the mayor. We can't waste our resources on frivolous investigations."

"A suspicious death isn't frivolous."

"Suicide is serious, but it's between a man and his god, not a matter to prosecute."

"I know that." Bertram unfolded his arms to look less petulant.

The chief leaned forward. "I appreciate your enthusiasm for the case. It's good to see your old zest for police work back, but I can't keep the case open for that reason."

"Of course not." Worse than the chief closing the case would be him letting Bertram continue out of pity for his sad plight. Perhaps this was simply the chief's bad day following an alarming night. Bertram scrambled for a last plea and forced himself to calm down. "Will you sleep on this and reserve your decision until tomorrow?"

The chief's hands returned the folder; his forehead lines rippled. "Bertram, you've served the force admirably for twenty years. For that, I'll give it another night, but no more."

* * *

While processing patients and typing forms, Katharine spent her morning wondering how to confront Dr. Upton about Marguerite's condition without implying the medical diagnosis of a miner's wife in Crowsnest Pass might be more accurate than his.

Toward noon, a regular patient mentioned she'd stopped by the drug store on her way to her medical appointment to pick up her photographs and was shocked to learn of Vincent's death. "Marguerite looks to be holding up well."

"Is she at work?" Katharine asked.

"Busy as ever. I enjoy dealing with her and hope she'll stay on the job, but since she

240

was only there to assist her husband, I assume she'll move on to something congenial to a widow."

What could be more congenial to a woman alone than work? Since Katharine couldn't think of a way to approach Dr. Upton without causing offence, she decided to stop by the drug store on her way home for lunch in an effort to find out the truth from Marguerite. If she snapped at Katharine, that would be nothing new.

Outside, the north wind whipped snow down the street. Katharine was relieved to duck into the relative warmth of Fielding and Sons. Mrs. Fielding and Marguerite were both masked and served customers at the main counter. Katharine was glad when Marguerite's customer left first since she didn't have time to chat with Mrs. Fielding.

Katharine began by mentioning Pina DeLuca's visit the previous night and her request to use her sewing machine. No need to add that she'd agreed to let Pina come to her house on condition she mask and avoid interactions with the children and John.

She focused on Marguerite's eyes, a variety of brown shades. "Pina also told me about her mother's talk with you in Crowsnest Pass."

"Psshh. That's not your concern, and her mother is a gossip. I knew she'd tell Pina that foolishness." Marguerite glanced at Mrs. Fielding and sidled away from her.

Katharine followed on her side of the counter. Both stopped at the far end.

"We have old women like her in our village in *France*," Marguerite said. "They make guesses that are true half the time because women there are always *enceinte*, and it's the same with Italian wives in Crowsnest Pass. It's different for us in the city."

Marguerite had a point.

"But after she told me this," Marguerite said, "I went to Dr. Upton to be sure. Talk to him if you want."

Katharine pretended to believe her. "You must be relieved not to be with child. Raising one without a husband is hard. I've learned that too well these past four years."

"*Oui*." Marguerite's eyes flickered, slightly but enough to satisfy Katharine that Pina's mother had guessed right. "Are you here to buy something?"

"Not now."

Marguerite looked past Katharine. "If you're finished, I have a real customer waiting."

Katharine left the store and fought snow on her walk home. How could Dr. Upton have been wrong about this? Marguerite had gone to him with a suspicion she was with child. She'd had a husband, was of child-bearing age, and had symptoms—fatigue, upset stomach, and possibly others she'd only told him. Upon physical examination, her condition should have been obvious to

Dr. Upton. Diagnosing the obvious was his forte.

Assuming Marguerite was with child, was it possible she'd convinced Dr. Upton to cover up her condition? He had the highest medical ethics, but Marguerite was skilled at persuading men who were smitten with her. Had he lied to Katharine and falsified his report in Marguerite's medical file? Moreover, was her condition of interest to the police?

Bertram might want to know about this. If nothing else, a telephone call to him would provide a pretext to learn where the case was headed.

Chapter Fifteen

Bertram sat at his office desk eating his lunch when Katharine phoned with her suspicions about Marguerite and Dr. Upton. "There's no proof I'm right about either one," she said, "or that it affects your case in any way."

"Can you think why they would want to conceal her condition?"

"She seems determined to work. If Mr. Fielding knew, he might insist she stay home and rest. Most employers would."

Nellie had worked during the early months she was with child. Later, Bertram had wondered if this had contributed to the disastrous ending, but he couldn't see the connection. People longed to attribute reasons to random events.

"I'm surprised Dr. Upton would go along," Katharine said. "He's always been proper about medical ethics." She paused. "I have thought he might be sweet on her, as the phrase goes, which would incline him to want to please her."

Bertram mentally added a check beside action five on his list—confirm Dr. Upton's feelings for Marguerite. Was Katharine calling from home during her lunch hour? It made sense she wouldn't want the doctor or his patients to overhear. Bertram heard no noise from her family in the background.

"Incidentally," she said. "John noticed Clarence outside smoking this morning and went over to ask why he wasn't at work. He said his intestinal problems were acting up and he couldn't stomach a streetcar ride. Those problems might be why he takes the Chinese medicine."

"That could be helpful to know," Bertram said, although this wouldn't convince the chief not to close the case. He'd postpone telling her that development in hopes the chief's good night's sleep reversed that decision. "Thank you for calling. I'll phone with any news from our end."

After he hung up, he finished his sandwich and cookie. His leap ahead of the game had worked earlier in the case and might again. Since he had no other work that required attention until the sales records from Fieldings' drug store arrived tomorrow, Bertram decided to pursue his Tainted Whisky case threads.

He told Julia he was leaving to check on some matters related to the Sunalta robbery. "Might as well prepare in case the culprit's alleged flu symptoms resolve."

She nodded. "That makes sense."

How easy it was to lie with barely a twinge of guilt.

The streetcar to Tuxedo Park was more crowded than he'd expected for a midafternoon Tuesday when half of the city's businesses and institutions were closed. He overheard a passenger telling another he'd left work early before the storm worsened. Bertram was headed in the opposite direction—away from his home.

He got off at the stop across from the medical office and drug store. Should he question Dr. Upton or Marguerite about her condition? At this point, it was a personal matter that had no bearing on the case unless Marguerite had known or suspected she was with child when Vincent died. Would a dependant woman in that condition kill her husband? Possibly, if a lover had fathered the child.

Since Clarence was home alone and actions two and three related to him, these threads would be better ones to tackle now.

Bertram walked down Marguerite's side of the street and glanced at Katharine's house. No activity outside or face in the windows. He rang Marguerite's doorbell, his shoulders hunched against the cold wind, and was about to ring again when Clarence opened the door.

"Detective   ...?"   Clarence   said. "Marguerite is at work."

"I have a few questions for you."

"Come in. It's freezing out."

Inside, Bertram placed his coat, hat, and gloves on the hall chair and removed his boots. "I heard you were home from work today."

Clarence gritted his teeth. "Seems my gastrointestinal tract misses Marguerite's cooking. Katharine Sterling's soup can't compare with French vichyssoise."

Bertram bristled on Katharine's behalf. He followed Clarence into the living room, which looked even starker than before. The card table that had stood under the front window was gone, along with a couple of chairs. Clarence sank to the closest armchair. He looked pale.

Rather than sit beside Clarence in the other armchair, Bertram carried a wooden chair from the side wall to the space in front of the cabinet and front window. This way he could face Clarence and keep his distance. Gastro problems could be flu symptoms rather than Clarence's chronic condition, and they weren't wearing masks. Bertram had left his in his coat pocket. The last time he was here, Clarence had moved Vincent's word-cross puzzle papers from the card table to the cabinet behind Bertram to make space for the tea service tray. Bertram wouldn't have minded a warm tea now.

Clarence rubbed his abdomen. "Since my tea might have been the murder weapon, does this make me a suspect?"

"Do you think this was murder?"

He shrugged. "Or suicide, the murder of oneself. From your perspective, I had means and opportunity."

Would a guilty man point this out? A smart man like Clarence might do it to appear innocent. "What about motive?" Bertram asked.

"You tell me how I benefit from this." Clarence looked around the room. "I had a comfortable home with Vincent and Marguerite. She still wants me to stay here, but is that realistic when ... Oh hell. How long does she think she can she keep her secret?"

Bertram took out his notebook and pen.

"Marguerite is with child," Clarence said. "She cajoled Dr. Upton into keeping this to himself so she can work as long as she's able. Why are men like me with twisted bowels permitted to do physical labour while women with babies inside them are treated like delicate flowers?"

Bertram shook his head to indicate he agreed this was inconsistent.

"Vincent's family wants her to live with them in Crowsnest Pass so they can raise their grandchild," Clarence said. "That's the plot, Pina says. Now she understands why her mother was eager for her to move to Tuxedo Park, to help the family manipulate Marguerite. Pina says she's not cooperating and wants Marguerite to choose her own path."

"Have you talked to Pina recently?"

"Yesterday and less than an hour ago. She's bored to tears here in the suburbs, especially with her bank closed. Pina told me that her mother 'sensed' Marguerite's pregnancy at Vincent's funeral. Marguerite first insisted it was *impossible* but later admitted the truth to me. Those old wives can be sharper than old doctors."

Bertram finished his notes, couldn't think of more questions about Marguerite, and moved on to action two: learning about Clarence's unknown activities to unearth a motive for him to kill the hand that had fed his gastrointestinal tract. "Do you enjoy suburban life? How do you keep yourself occupied when you aren't working at the Ogden Shops?"

Clarence cocked his head. "Political and union meetings. Occasional bars with friends. I won't say I patron the odd brothel since they're illegal. The Socialist Party's not illegal—yet." His smile seemed challenging.

"You've told me you don't drink."

He patted his stomach. "Marguerite insisted I stay off booze while taking her Chinese medicine. It reacts badly with liquor, as Vincent discovered. I drink soda when I'm out at bars. Detective, you're fishing in the wrong pond. I'm not the person you want to hook."

"Who is?"

Clarence winced and clutched his abdomen. "Blast this Fabry Disease. It's been stable for months, and now it flares." The agony on his face looked genuine, although the pain was also convenient for evading an answer.

"Fabry Disease?" Bertram asked.

"A rare inherited condition I've had since childhood. Doctors don't know how to treat it except with morphine that left me craving the drug all the time. Detective, I'm afraid I need to use the toilet. Do you have more questions?"

"Whom would you suggest I try to hook?"

"Anyone but me." Clarence hoisted himself from the chair.

Bertram rose and noticed piles of paper littering the sideboard at the back of the room. "Are those Vincent's word-cross puzzles?"

Clarence followed his gaze. "His accounts. Vincent recorded all the household expenses. I'm helping Marguerite go through them. She reads English but tends to mix up numbers and letters." He clutched his abdomen again. "Excuse me, I need the toilet before my bowels explode all over this room." He darted into the hallway.

Bertram listened to his footsteps recede down the hall and went to look at the papers on the sideboard. The top sheet listed monthly expenses for rent, electricity, and coal. On the next page, the same neat, masculine-looking handwriting itemized food by the week. Bertram noted cabbage, bok choy, carrots, potatoes, and tomatoes purchased from Mr. Wong. No mention of Chinese medicine, which might be outside the realm of household supply. Bertram saw no reason to request these accounts for his investigation.

He heard footsteps and turned as Clarence re-entered the room and stopped between the armchair and wall, presumably having made it to the toilet in time.

"One final thing," Bertram said. "I require your jar of Chinese medicine for fingerprinting. This is a new police procedure—"

"I've read about it," Clarence said. "The jar's in the kitchen. Marguerite's prints and mine will be on it. I don't recall seeing Vincent touch the jar, but how would you identify his fingerprints since I assume you don't have them on record?"

"Process of elimination."

"Of course." Clearly, he understood the general procedure—fingerprint every suspect.

In the hall, Bertram got his gloves from his coat pocket and put them on while walking to the kitchen. Clarence opened a cupboard above the sink.

"Let me handle it," Bertram said. "If you have a spare jar, I'll pour the powder into it to leave with you."

"The tea isn't helping me these days, but she keeps empty jars on the top shelf."

Bertram took out both jars, one with a label in Chinese characters. He poured the brown powder into the empty jar, leaving some behind for analysis in the police lab, and tucked the labelled jar into his pocket.

They returned to the front entrance, where Bertram put on his hat, overcoat and shoes.

"With luck," Clarence said, "you'll deduce Vincent's fingerprints on the jar, which would strongly suggest suicide. Failing that, I can't say I hope you catch your killer. I oppose capital punishment and find it ironic that so many believers in God don't reserve life-and-death judgments for him."

"Is that why you won't point your finger at the killer?"

Clarence grimaced and grabbed his stomach. "Bloody hell. I need the bathroom again. Please let yourself out."

Convenient.

* * *

Katharine and Dr. Upton stepped outside to blowing snow. She locked the office door behind them. The wind whisked them around the corner. Fielding and Sons was still open. Dr. Upton had suggested they close the medical office early so he could drive home before the streets got icy. She left him at the lane and trod carefully over the slippery sidewalk to her home.

Piano music flowed from the living room. The music stopped as she took off her boots and hung up her coat and hat.

John hopped toward her. "Good news. I think." He waved at the telephone nook. A few envelopes sat on the table.

"A letter from Eddie?"

He nodded.

"At last."

Her heart pounding, she seized the envelope addressed in Eddie's bold script. He was alive! She peered at the cancelled French stamp depicting a Red Cross ship and nurse but couldn't make out the postmark date.

"I knew Eddie's luck would hold after he survived Passchendaele."

"Where are the children?"

"Out back playing in the snow."

"I should read it before I tell them, in case there's something ..." A letter written by Eddie himself wouldn't be all bad, but a serious injury would account for a delayed message.

"I'll leave you alone," John said.

In the past, she'd read Eddie's letters privately the first times, wanting to savour his words for herself and hide her initial responses and tears. But these past six months, she and John had become partners in this great misery.

"Let's both go to the living room." She got the letter opener from the table drawer.

"Rip it open."

"I don't want a piece of this shredded." She slit the envelope seam.

They sat in the living room, John on the armchair, Katharine on the davenport, where she could see Eddie's portrait on the sideboard. She studied the envelope's address. *Mrs. Edward Sterling.* The capitals large and reaching high, the letters sloped to the right, the *g* finished with a flourished tail. She could look at this for hours, and there was so much more inside.

John remained uncharacteristically quiet and didn't urge her on. He and Eddie had got along instantly from the day Katharine and Eddie had started seeing each other. John looked up to Eddie as a big brother. Glad to have John with her now, she lifted the single sheet of paper from the envelope. *September 15* was written at the top. Over a month ago.

The paper shook as she read aloud. *"Dearest Katharine, Henry, & Lillian, Wonderful that you and John are enjoying fine summer weather. Your description and pictures of the picnic and swimming in Bowness Park made me long to be with you all."* She glanced up. "He's replying to a letter I sent and pictures the children drew for him in July. I wrote others in August that wouldn't have reached him by mid-September."

"Personal mail is lower priority for the army than fighting the Huns," John said.

"Rightly so, hard as that is for us at home." She returned to the letter. "He continues with comments on other things I mentioned. The garden, my work, your saxophone playing. He says it's good you've found something that interests you."

"Rather than mope around the house and get in your way."

She hadn't been that candid about John in her letters, but Eddie had correctly interpreted. "Then he gets to his news," she said as she flipped over the page. "*Life in the trenches remains the same, except for a growing buzz that the kaiser is on the verge of surrender.* The next sentence is blacked out."

"Bloody censors."

"*War isn't what I'd thought it would be,*" she read. "*The prospect of home and the future sustains me. You'll be glad to no longer have to go out to work or repair leaky faucets or cranky stoves or other matters I'll be there to take care of.*" She stopped reading. "Have I complained about doing these things in my letters?"

"Probably."

"What if I want to keep working for Dr. Upton after Eddie gets home?"

"Eddie won't allow it."

She squinted at him. "How do you know?"

"The old Eddie wouldn't have," John said. "I can't speak for the new one, whomever he might be."

The new Eddie would be a partial stranger to her, and a complete one to Henry and Lillian. Katharine sniffed aromas from the kitchen. Would the new Eddie do women's household tasks, like John? She continued reading. "*Remember our plan to raise the roof to build bedrooms for the children? The minute I'm settled, John and I will start work on that. We'll need the extra space."*

"He needn't worry I'll live with you forever," John said.

"He didn't mean that." Or had he? Did Eddie think they'd need the extra space for John, or for more children? She was thirty, young enough to have several more. Did she want another child? She couldn't work for Dr. Upton while caring for a baby. As for John, she'd grown used to him being here and didn't want him to leave. Would Eddie find her brother's presence an intrusion?

"Is something wrong?" John broke through her thoughts.

"I don't think Eddie's return was real for me until now." Her eyes blurred as she read the final paragraph. "*These have been the worst four years of my life and in some ways the best. Every man in the trench is my brother, bound together for the same cause. I'll miss the intensity, the passion, but I look forward to ordinary days surrounded by you and our children. I hope my ramblings make sense. I've run out of space. Love, Eddie.*" He'd crammed in the last sentences at the end of the page in tiny letters.

"That's philosophical for Eddie," John said.

It was, including parts he'd left unsaid. *War isn't what I'd thought it would be.* Would Eddie be like John and gloss over the horrors he'd seen? She reread the last paragraph and shivered. In effect, he'd said his time with her could never match the passion, camaraderie, and sense of purpose he'd experienced in the war. She and their children were the dull and ordinary.

Voices sounded from the kitchen—the children. Katharine had wanted this letter so much; now, she found it unsettling. "We'll read it to them after dinner." She slipped the letter back into the envelope, which she placed on the sideboard next to Eddie's portrait, and went to help the children get out of their overclothes. John followed.

"We pretended the snow was falling pieces of moonshine," Lillian said.

So innocent. Katharine wiped her damp eyes.

John stuck a fork in the boiling potatoes. "They seem done." He mashed them while Katharine scooped pigs' feet and broth into serving bowls.

She found pigs' feet tolerable but hoped they'd be gone from this kitchen after the war. When they gathered around the table, she offered to say grace. "God bless this meal and Eddie—our husband, father, and brother—who is alive and well in France."

During dinner she told the children about their father's letter. "He can't wait to come home and be with us all."

"You'll find him stricter than me," John said.

"Who isn't?" Katharine shot him a glare. They had to build an image of Eddie for the children that wouldn't create fears about the upcoming change in their lives. She shifted to current matters. "Did Pina come by to use the sewing machine?"

"She did," John said. "We kept our distance from her by doing sums in the kitchen."

"Then she taught us a dance," Lillian said.

Katharine swallowed some potato. "That doesn't sound like distance."

"A modern dance where people don't touch," John said. "She dances better than she sews, judging by the cushions she took home."

"Will she need to make more?"

"She says two are enough for now." John helped himself to more pigs' feet. "This is tasty. Good work, Henry and Lilly-pet. I'll take a pot of leftovers to Marguerite. She'll be tired after her full day of work. She didn't put in those hours even before ..."

Vincent's death. And her pregnancy.

After John left for Marguerite's house, Katharine snuggled with the children on the davenport and read them their father's letter, leaving out his unsettling reflections on the war. Both were pleased that he liked their drawings and loved the idea of having their own bedrooms.

John returned as she was hustling the children into their bedtime ritual. "Marguerite thanks us for the food. She has no appetite but set a plate out for Clarence."

"Is he feeling better?"

"He ate some and went to his room to rest," John said.

Katharine shooed the children to the bedroom and bathroom. "Do you think his illness is the real reason Clarence didn't enlist? If he told people this, instead of citing his anti-war principle, they'd sympathize instead of giving him white feathers for cowardice."

"Maybe he didn't want sympathy for being sick," John said. "Or he wanted to take a stand against a war he disbelieves in. I'd call that admirable—and smart. Most of us had to live with rats in the trenches and watch our mates get blown to pieces before the truth sunk into our heads."

That might have been the most John had ever told her about the horrors. Would she get more out of Eddie so he wouldn't bear them alone and she would understand his experience?

She left to read the children their stories and hear their prayers. After she tucked them in, she followed the piano music to the living room. John stopped playing.

"Keep going," she said. "That's a lovely, sad tune. Who's the composer?"

"Me." He pressed a few discordant keys. "It's garbage. I can't find the melody for this section."

"Keep working on it."

He stumbled through the next notes, but the song had promise. She got her mask-making kit from the sideboard and paused at Eddie's portrait.

The doorbell rang. *A telegram? Please not so soon after encouraging news.* She went to the front entrance and opened the door.

Marguerite stood on the porch. "It's Clarence. He's dead."

Katharine's voice caught. "Are you sure?"

"Please call the doctor or morgue." Her tone remained flat.

Katharine stepped back from the freezing air. A week ago, to the day, Clarence had appeared on her doorstep with a similar request.

John thumped from the living room. "What is it?"

Marguerite glanced toward her house. "I must go to him."

"I'll go with you." Katharine grabbed her coat from the closet. "John, it's Clarence. He's seriously ill. Phone Dr. Upton. Tell him to come immediately but drive safely on these icy roads."

"There's no hurry," Marguerite said. "It's too late for him."

Katharine threw on her coat and caught up with Marguerite as she stepped onto the street. Marguerite skidded but regained her balance.

"I'll take your arm." Katharine slipped her hand under Marguerite's elbow. No resistance. "What happened?"

"After he finish dinner, Clarence went to his room for two hours. I worry and open his door to check. His chest looked moving, but I go closer ..."

They passed through Marguerite's open gate to her porch. It was possible she was wrong, and Clarence still had a spark of life.

"Which is his bedroom?" Katharine asked.

"The back one."

Inside, Katharine ran down the hall and turned on the bedroom light. Clarence lay supine on the bed, his body still. She steeled herself, approached him, and pressed her ear to his chest. No sound. She took her mask from her pocket and placed it under his nose. No fluttering. No pulse in his wrist or neck. His skin was cool. *Too cool.*

She rolled him onto his stomach and positioned herself on the single bed as best she could to administer artificial respiration. *Hands in a butterfly position.* She pressed her palms to his middle back. One, two, three. Pause. Again. No response. Again. Nothing. Again. She was too late but had to try.

Her arms ached with the effort. *Too late.* Minutes that seemed hours passed.

The doorbell rang. One, two, three. Pause. Voices, noise in the hall.

"Where is he?" Dr. Upton burst into the bedroom.

Relieved, Katharine retreated from the bed. The doctor bent over Clarence. She slunk out of the room, down the hall to the living room.

Marguerite sat on the armchair by the fireplace. Katharine dropped to the adjacent chair.

"He's dead," Marguerite said.

"I think so." Katharine raked her loose hairs back, but they kept falling on her cheek. "Were his symptoms the usual ones he had with his disease?"

"Yes, before my cooking and tea cured him. Your meals made him sick again."

Katharine bristled at Marguerite blaming her unfairly a second time. And it had been mostly John's and the children's cooking.

Clarence's symptoms could indicate Spanish flu. He hadn't breathed on the mask or on her, but no one knew exactly how this flu spread. In this instance, it was safer to leave her mask off.

"What will I do now?" Marguerite scanned the room. "I can't afford this rent without Clarence's payment."

Selfish of Marguerite to think of herself, but understandable. "You could take in another boarder," Katharine said. "What about Pina?"

"*Non.* She's a spy from Vincent's family." Marguerite stared out the front window. "I might marry John."

Katharine started, but evidently John and Marguerite had a mutual attraction. "Has he asked you?"

"Not yet. Dr. Upton has more money." Her nose pointed upward, her jaw firm.

"Do you love either of them?"

"Love and marriage aren't the same."

Dr. Upton appeared in the living room archway. "He's gone."

"*Mon Dieu.*" Marguerite moaned.

Dr. Upton brushed past Katharine to Marguerite. "How tragic for this to happen to you a second time."

"Clarence is the one who died," Katharine snapped.

"Yes. Quite." Dr. Upton sidled toward the window and faced them both. "It appears his heart failed. This man wasn't my patient, but, Marguerite, you once alluded to him having a pre-existing condition."

"Fabry Disease," she said.

"What's that?" Katharine asked.

"Good Lord," Dr. Upton said. "I've heard of it but haven't encountered a single case in my many years of practice. I'll have to consult his doctor to determine cause of death." He looked at Katharine. "Mrs. Sterling, could you please phone the morgue?"

She nodded and rose from the chair. Dr. Upton took her place. Marguerite ignored his presence and continued to gaze out the front window.

"Please accept my condolences," he said and leaned toward Marguerite. "If there's anything I can do ..."

Katharine left them alone and went out into the night and falling snow. If she had to sacrifice a man to Marguerite, she'd choose Dr. Upton over John.

Across the street, John stood on the porch wearing his overcoat. "Dead?" he asked.

"Yes. I'll call the morgue."

"I'll go check on Marguerite."

"Dr. Upton is with her."

"He'll leave with the body and hearse."

Don't count on it this time.

John beelined to Marguerite's house. Katharine hoped Marguerite would choose money over John's less tangible qualities.

Inside, Katharine stamped snow off her boots and phoned the morgue. Did Clarence have family to contact? She'd forgotten to ask in the midst of everyone's greater concern for Marguerite.

Still dressed in her coat and boots, Katharine checked on the children. Both slept peacefully, bundled under their covers. She left them, went out the back door, and traipsed through inches of snow to the shed to get the shovel for clearing the sidewalks before she left for work tomorrow. *Two deaths a week apart.* Would the police want to know? Bertram might be another person to call tomorrow.

She carried the shovel to the front porch and waited for the hearse to arrive. Within twenty minutes, it rumbled past her house, made a U-turn, and parked in front of Dr.

Upton's Ford Model T. The hearse driver got out. Two silhouetted figures emerged from Marguerite's front door, one man tall and slim, the other stout. They helped the driver take a stretcher from the vehicle. John and Dr. Upton each held a handle at the rear of the stretcher; the driver held both handles at the front. They all disappeared into the house, and ten minutes later they carried out the stretcher with a bulky shape on top.

After Clarence's body had been loaded into the vehicle, the hearse drove toward Centre Street. Dr. Upton and John remained on the sidewalk, talking. Then Dr. Upton got into his car and John returned to Marguerite's house. The Model T Roadster drove off. Katharine retreated to the warmth of her home and her children, asleep and ignorant of adult stupidity.

Chapter Sixteen

After breakfast, Katharine sent the children to the living room to play while she went out to shovel snow.

"Can we help?" Lillian asked. She still wore her nightgown.

Getting the two of them dressed and retrieving their shovels from the shed would double the time needed for the task. "You can help Uncle John later today."

Apparently satisfied, Lillian settled on the living room floor and cut out paper dolls from last season's Eaton's catalogue. Henry vroomed a toy car around the coffee table. Katharine put on her coat, boots, and gloves and went out to the front porch.

Gladys hoisted snow from the city sidewalk in front of the house next door. Had she and Irene noticed the vehicles on the street last night? They'd want to know that their neighbour had passed away. Gladys waved hello.

Katharine carried the shovel to the sidewalk, the hem of her coat trailing through the half-foot drifts. Snow fell lightly but persistently from the sky that was heavy with cloud. She stopped a half-dozen feet from Gladys and told her about Clarence.

"Dear God," Gladys said. "I had no clue he was sick." She shook her head, her frizzy hair dotted with snow. "I can't believe we missed all the commotion again."

"Irene must be a sound sleeper." Irene and her three children slept in the front bedroom, Gladys and her two boys in the back one.

"I used to meet Clarence now and then on the streetcar or walking to and from our homes," Gladys said. "We shared a lot of common views. Namely that unions will get us workers decent wages and benefits and our politicians are idiots. At least the US had the sense to stay out of the war for almost three years."

"They don't have our loyalty to King and Empire."

Gladys sniffed. "Look where that landed our naïve boys."

War widows, like Gladys and Irene, had reason to be bitter about the war. If it took Eddie, God forbid, Katharine might despise the cause as much as they and Clarence did.

"Since I've started on the sidewalk," Gladys said, "I'll clear the section in front of your house."

"Thanks, but I might as well stay busy. I can't leave for work until John comes back from Marguerite's." Gladys was bound to find out John had spent the night there, especially if he crossed the street during the next five minutes. "We didn't feel right leaving her alone after a second death."

"Irene lost her two children in the same space of time," Gladys said, in a distant tone.

Five years ago, both children had died from scarlet fever, while Vincent and Clarence had died from unrelated causes—unless Marguerite had sprinkled a lethal dose of the Chinese medicine into Clarence's food. But why would she?

"Will Marguerite look for a new boarder?" Gladys said. "A widow with children would liven up her home. Our five keep us hopping."

Gladys would also learn before long that Marguerite was with child, but it wasn't Katharine's place to reveal that secret.

Katharine scooped snow off the city sidewalk. When Eddie returned, he'd handle most of the shovelling, as he'd done before the war. The damp snow was heavy today, but she liked the excuse to get some exercise in the fresh air and chat with a neighbour. Gladys waved goodbye and went into the house.

Of course, when winter set in, Katharine would shovel and walk to work in darkness, sometimes in temperatures as low as forty degrees below zero. On those mornings, she'd prefer staying warm inside while Eddie shovelled.

The twenty-five feet in front of her house cleared, she started on the sidewalk to her door. Marriage had to be about more than avoiding tasks like shovelling in winter, checking the roof and drain spouts in spring, mowing the lawn and tending the garden in summer, and raking the leaves in fall. Actually, she enjoyed these tasks, and her marriage with Eddie had been about much more, including their nights in bed. After four years apart, would that joy still be there when he returned?

"Good to see you being useful." John's voice made her turn around.

"How did you get here so fast?"

"I skipped lightly across the street." His face looked merry for a night of consolation.

"How is Marguerite?"

"Fine, under the circumstances," he said. "She viewed Clarence as a friend, but that's not the same as losing a husband."

"Is she going to work today?"

"Yes, but an hour later than usual. She asked me to phone Mr. Fielding to let him know, and phone Clarence's workplace, his father in Montreal, a few friends from his union and political groups. I have the list here." He patted his coat pocket. "Fortunately, Henry and Lillian are used to amusing themselves under my tutelage. Our first lesson today will be to shovel Marguerite's sidewalk so she won't have to trudge through snow to work."

Heaven forbid she get the hem of her stylish coat damp. "You'll have a busy day. I could stay home from work if you need help."

"I'm sprightly thanks to a few solid hours of sleep last night."

In Marguerite's bed? Surely not when Clarence, her friend, was barely cold.

John went into the house, almost bounding up the stairs. Katharine resumed shovelling, with more force than before. Most poisons and toxic doses of medicines attacked the gastrointestinal tract, which seemed to be Clarence's body's weakness. Marguerite would know the properties of every drug in her store. Had she taken one home and doused their breakfast and dinner food, which she was too nauseous to eat?

Katharine finished clearing the porch and rested the shovel against the wall. Inside, the children sat on the entrance floor, yanking on their boots. While Henry put on his overclothes, she bundled Lillian into her jacket, pulled her wool cap down over her ears, and wrapped a scarf around her neck.

John appeared in the hall with the small shovels he'd got from the shed. Katharine took off her boots to not dirty the hall floor and waited until the front door closed behind them all before calling police headquarters.

A woman answered. "Detective Tanner should be here in fifteen minutes. Can I pass along your message?"

Katharine would be on her way to work then and might miss his call. It'd be better to phone him from the office. "I'll try again later."

Her boots back on, Katharine set off for work. Across the street, John shovelled Marguerite's driveway while the children threw snowballs at each other. She would admire his responsibility to their neighbour if she thought Marguerite genuinely cared for John and hadn't murdered one or two other men.

Katharine arrived at the office. The building windows were dark. Dr. Upton was later than usual, perhaps due to the road conditions. She entered, flipped the door sign to Open, but left the lights off to survey the room in shadows. To her right, the chairs in the main waiting area formed an L shape; the widely spaced chairs on her left were for patients with flu symptoms. After the pandemic passed, she'd leave those chairs there for all patients with potentially contagious illnesses and require them to wear masks. Such small innovations added up.

When she'd started working here, the filing system and records were a mess. Dr. Upton's former receptionist, his nephew, shared his uncle's disregard for organization. She'd found patients' folders alphabetically misfiled and *Mac* and *Mc* surnames spelled indiscriminately; reports within folders only loosely followed chronological order. More serious was the absence of a process for patient follow-ups and referrals. In lulls during her first months of work, she'd reviewed every patient file and discovered sixteen omissions. Most weren't critical, but her review got one patient to a specialist in time for her ovarian cancer to be treated; now, the woman would be alive to raise her four children.

Katharine would miss so many aspects of this job, but her post-war work of looking after a household and bringing up the next generation was also important.

She turned toward the click of the door. Dr. Upton burst in and switched on the light. He started. "I didn't see you here. Why in blazes are you standing in the dark?"

She deflected his question. "How was the driving?"

"Miserable." He brushed snow from his overcoat. "I passed two accidents, skidded several times, and almost hit a lamppost. We Calgarians can't handle the season's first snowstorm. The streets will be gruesome when everyone has a motorcar."

It would be years before she and Eddie could afford one. The streetcar and her feet were all she needed, although leisurely family drives to Banff and the foothills countryside would be lovely.

Dr. Upton scanned the room. "No patients yet?"

"I expect a slow day due to the storm," she said. "Thank you for attending so quickly last night."

"It's my job." He looked down at the floor and then at her. "How is Marguerite this morning?"

"Well enough to go into work."

His jaw tightened. "I admire her persistence but hope she doesn't push herself too hard."

In her condition, Katharine mentally finished his sentence. No point in pressing him about his false medical report. Clearly, he'd conceded to Marguerite's request simply because she'd asked him to. Undoubtedly, John would have done the same in his place. "What is Fabry Disease?"

"I looked it up in my medical text at home," he said. "It's an incurable condition that can affect numerous parts of the body—kidneys, brain, heart, and more. Gastrointestinal pain was Clarence's primary symptom, according to Marguerite. She provided his doctor's name. I'll phone him this morning."

"I hope you'll order an autopsy."

"Why?" His eyebrow raised to his fur hat. "When cause of death is due to a chronic condition, there's no need."

A man walked in, and Dr. Upton strode to his office. Katharine took the new patient's medical details and opened a file for him. He said a friend had recommended Dr. Upton but didn't know if he had space for more patients.

"We'll squeeze you in," she said. Since she'd started work, their patient list had steadily increased despite the many men in the neighbourhood away at the war. The practice hadn't simply become more efficient—numerous patients had said they preferred her friendliness to the previous receptionist's curt manner. And more than a few appreciated her advice on medical treatments. But she was raised to believe her life's work should be about sacrifice and not vanity.

More patients trickled in. Time to stop musing about herself and attend to her duties. At the first opportunity, she'd phone Bertram to tell him about Clarence's death and relay her new suspicions, which would probably prove unfounded.

* * *

Bertram sat across the desk from the chief and braced himself for the verdict.

The chief set his hands on the case file. "I slept on it, as promised. In fact, I reviewed the entire case a second time and saw nothing to change my mind."

Case closed. Despite his preparation, Bertram felt his heart sink. "There's obviously a chance this was murder."

"We can't waste our resources on long-shot speculations."

"This shot is far from long," Bertram said. "I'm not talking about expensive procedures."

"You recommended fingerprinting."

"We can hold onto the bottle and jar while we gather more evidence from interviews and not run the prints through the lab right away. I'm the only resource you'll waste, and I have nothing else to do while the city is half-closed. Throw me at this long-shot case. If something sticks, the mayor will pin a medal on you."

Bertram leaned back in his chair, trying to look relaxed. It was true that his alternate plan for today was paperwork that Julia would file in the basement storage room never to be seen again. He hoped the chief's ambition would trump his stubbornness or blindness. Or laziness. Had the chief really reread the file?

The chief linked his fingers and twiddled them as though he were giving the matter thought. Bertram held his breath.

The twiddling stopped. "Bertram, I realize you've had a hard year, but now that your spark is back, it will propel you forward. The next good case that comes along will have a greater probability of success and give you the recognition you deserve."

Don't stroke my pride after I did that to manipulate you and failed.

The chief leaned forward. His eyes brimmed with sympathy and commiseration, like a father speaking to a child whose pet rabbit had died. "Since you have no critical work, I suggest you take the rest of the day off. When was the last time you had a holiday?"

His holiday last year was spent grieving and taking care of the myriad matters that followed his loved ones' deaths. This year's time away from work had been weekends in

Beiseker, where everyone he met asked how he was doing in tones as pitying as the chief's were now. The worst were those who spoke of his future as though he'd left the grief behind.

"Go!" The chief waved him off. "Have fun, play in the snow. I order it."

Bertram stormed out of the office. Julia sat typing at her desk. There was nobody else nearby. He stopped to tell her the chief's decision on the file, found himself venting, and squeezed his hand, pressing his nails to his palm to make himself stop.

"I'm sorry," he said, and felt his face grow hot. "I forget he's your father."

Above her mask, her eyes crinkled. "Dad's mind is like a brick once it's made up."

"Perhaps he's right, that I grew too close to the case."

"For what it's worth, I think it has merit."

"You've read the file?"

"I typed it."

His heart lifted at her encouragement, but it didn't change the fact that the chief had the final word. "I suppose I can force myself to dive into tedious paperwork."

"Or take the day off on the chief's orders."

"I'm too old to make angels in the snow." Something occurred to him. He could visit other "angels." He wanted, needed, to speak to them. "On second thought, I believe I will skip out for the rest of the day. Mark it as vacation time and hold my messages until tomorrow."

"Shall I phone you at home if it's top priority?"

"I can't imagine anything crucial coming in, but yes. I'm not completely AWOL."

"Have fun." She waved him off in a movement similar to the chief's. Fun was far from Bertram's mind.

He left headquarters and took the quickest route from downtown to the cemetery, down Macleod Trail, his coat collar raised against the falling snow. The storm clogged incoming traffic. Motorcars were stuck in drifts. A milk-wagon horse reared in frustration.

The wind hurled snow at Bertram and battered the Tainted Whisky case into perspective. One man had died, possibly by murder. This morning's newspaper estimated the Great War had killed close to fifteen million soldiers and civilians, directly and indirectly, and wounded over twenty million military personnel. Experts predicted another fifteen million people might die of the Spanish flu. Bertram could hardly grasp these numbers. In the midst of this worldwide slaughter, one murder was like a single snowflake. He might capture a killer or confirm Vincent DeLuca had killed himself, but the killing would never end. Cholera and typhoid epidemics ravaged cities and towns. Countless diseases took down their victims. Motorcar accidents killed drivers and pedestrians. People died on their jobs or from causes beyond anyone's control, like Nellie and Robert. All tragic.

The chief was right. Why avenge a single death? A death that was less gruesome than that of a man blown to pieces on a battlefield. Bertram's decision to leave the police force was equally right. His work was pointless. He'd been foolish to think pursuing the Tainted Whisky case made a whit of difference to the world. Had he sought redemption through this work because he couldn't pummel his wife's and son's killers to death? That bordered on delusional.

He arrived at Union Cemetery. Snow covered the field of graves; no footprints marred the blanket of pure white on the path up the hill. He was the first person here today and the only one present. That rarely happened on his Sunday visits.

The headstones draped in snow looked like ghosts. Dampness seeped through his boots as he tramped to their graves. With luck he'd catch a chill and die. He'd join them beneath the snow and earth.

Engulfed in blowing white flakes, he reached their stone and wiped off the snow with his glove. A strange name stared at him, the letters blurred. Not Nellie and Robert. Where were they?

He gripped the stone beside it, brushed off snow. *Tanner,* Nellie's name and dates, the space for Bertram, and underneath

Infant son Robert, Born—Died November 6, 1917.

They lay here, forever, but Bertram had forgotten the way to them.

That was his crime. He'd forsaken them in his passion for the case and, he had to admit, in his attraction to Katharine.

The living buried the dead and moved on. His choice in this merciless world—join one side or the other.

* * *

When she finally got a break from patients, Katharine phoned police headquarters and asked to speak with Detective Tanner.

"He's off today," the receptionist said. "I'll have him contact you tomorrow or put you through to another officer."

Katharine recognized the woman's voice. "You told me earlier he was due to come in today."

"Who is calling, please?"

"Katharine Sterling, regarding a case he's handling."

The receptionist paused. "Do you have a message for him?"

"I'd rather speak to him directly."

"One minute. Here he is walking in now." The receptionist sounded surprised. "I'll hand you over to him."

Katharine listened to muffled voices until Bertram came on the line.

"Good to hear from you," he said.

She warmed at his welcoming tone. Why was he at work on his day off? She told him about Clarence. "An autopsy would be valuable. Can the police request one if the doctors don't?"

"We can with sufficient suspicion," he said. "This is worth looking into. Thank you for calling."

"I didn't know you were off work."

"Seems I'm on it," he said with a laugh. "I'll be in touch once I know the next steps."

She looked forward to that contact more than she ought to have, given it would result from Clarence's misfortune.

For the rest of the morning, Katharine pondered her motives for pushing Bertram to investigate the two deaths. She assured herself her main one was to be at peace with John's involvement with Marguerite. During their months of living together, she and her little brother had developed a closeness, which would be ripped apart if her suspicions about Marguerite remained. A second motive was to see justice served. Vincent and Clarence had died before their times. If murderers ran free, human life had no value.

But beneath those two prime motives, darker desires lurked. The thrill of a murder case and her attraction to Bertram. This would be Katharine's last chance for excitement before Eddie returned to pick up the life they'd had before the war. She had to find out if that life was the one she still wanted.

Chapter Seventeen

"That reminds me," Julia said when Bertram hung up the phone, "the third doctor on your list called. Since I thought you were off today, I took the liberty of asking if he'd treated Vincent DeLuca. After some hesitation and a search of his records, he told me hadn't."

"I'm not surprised," Bertram said. "If Vincent had a doctor's prescription, he'd most likely buy whisky through his store with his ten-percent discount."

"Perhaps he didn't want his colleagues to know he suffered from a mental disorder? Many people feel ashamed about this."

That was possible. "Vincent's staff consisted of his wife and Mrs. Fielding, the wife of the store owner. She might tell her husband about her manager's condition."

"Especially if she thought it impacted his work. A boss would want to know this."

"Speaking of bosses," Bertram said. "I'll go talk to the chief."

"Good luck." Julia's eyes crinkled above her mask. "Despite his hard head, he generally sees reason where it exists."

That had been true in the past. Bertram loped to the chief's office and rapped the closed door.

The chief started at the sight of him. "Didn't I send you home?"

"There's a new development." Bertram sat on the visitor chair. Since the chief didn't put on a mask, Bertram removed his and placed it on the desk. From his glimpses of fellow officers and clerical staff, it seemed everyone at headquarters complied with the chief's mask order except the chief. Bertram told him about Clarence.

When Bertram finished, the chief leaned back in his chair. "Let me get this straight. A man with a chronic disease dies of complications from that disease, or the flu, or a combination of both. What's suspicious about that?"

"It's the second death in that household in a week."

"Sadly, the Spanish flu will make this a frequent occurrence."

"The first man didn't die of the flu."

"Not according to our lab report."

"It's wrong."

The chief glowered.

Bertram took a deep breath. It never helped to antagonize the chief. "Let's at least request an autopsy on Clarence Oxenham if the doctors don't."

"If medical experts don't think it's required, why should we?"

"We're experts in a different area—suspicious deaths."

"Doctors also look at irregularities, but let me know if they request one."

A partial score for Bertram. "When I spoke with Clarence yesterday, he hinted that he suspected someone of killing Vincent."

The chief's chair clunked forward. "Why would you talk to him about a case we'd closed?"

"You were going to reconsider," Bertram said. "I viewed the case in limbo."

"Hrmph."

"When I arrived, Clarence had been looking through Vincent's household accounts. Nothing of interest there, but what if Clarence discovered something questionable in Vincent's other records and confronted a person involved?"

"Did Vincent keep other records?"

"He was an orderly man," Bertram said. "Clarence made a point of mentioning that he didn't believe in capital punishment. This might suggest he suspected the individual of a capital crime. Telling me could send someone to their death. Perhaps Clarence dealt with the matter in another way."

"Such as ..."

"One that led to his own death."

The chief shook his head. "Speculations."

"You've trusted my hunches before."

"We both know you haven't been yourself this past year." The chief's gaze darted sideways, perhaps embarrassed by his understandable pity and distrust.

Bertram straightened. "I'm myself now."

"Your hour away from work was hardly a holiday," the chief said. "Take a week off. Spend time with your family in Beiseker. The countryside will be soothing."

Bertram had recently thought similarly while he plotted his departure from a life spent chasing criminals to one of a country grocer. But was soothing the life he wanted?

"In short," Bertram said, "no further action."

The chief pursed his lips. "If the doctors order an autopsy, we'll review it, of course."

Wait and see. Don't take initiative. Such dedication to pursuing crime. Bertram mentally spewed sarcastic thoughts all the way to Julia's desk but put a lid on his anger at her father. "No further action," he said. He remembered something. "Earlier, the chief cited budget restraints. Has the mayor put pressure on him to reduce police spending?"

"No more than usual that I'm aware." Her brow knit. "It's not like the chief to nip a case in the bud, although he has a tendency to skim through details and miss the trees for the forest." She laughed. "But that's supposed to be good, isn't it?"

"Who knows?" Bertram's fuming mind was too muddled to grasp metaphors. With the Tainted Whisky case closed, there remained one legitimate action on his list. "When I'm in my office, put me through to the police lab."

A youthful voice answered his call.

"Please release the whisky bottle I sent for analysis directly to me," Bertram said. He had no clue what he'd do with the bottle, but evidence for closed cases had been known to disappear. Hell, that had happened with active cases too.

"I threw it out."

"You did what? Why?"

"You can talk to my uncle."

Bertram listened to muffled voices and fumed again.

The lab technician came on the line. "My nephew passed along your request. The chief advised us yesterday to dispose of the bottle."

So, the chief had no intention of sleeping on his decision. "Could you retrieve it?"

"Sorry. It's on its way to the landfill. My nephew said he heard the bottle break when he threw it in the dumpster."

Bertram slammed the phone earpiece into its holder. The chief had been humouring him. Or worse, he'd lied. But why? Was he covering up the case? If so, was it the whisky aspect? Illegal liquor sales? During the first year of Prohibition, a few police officers had received kickbacks to close their eyes to people and establishments violating the laws.

But the chief had cleaned this up. He was cracking down on illegal liquor and had offered Bertram's services for the provincial unit's raid on the club.

Had he selected Bertram less for his experience than the fact he was off his game and might botch the job? The raid had been set to go ahead when the club followed the municipal order to close due to the flu, an unexpected compliance. Was the club owner tipped off? By the chief?

Bertram had worked with the chief for twenty years. His daughter, Julia, was impeccable. His wife was a prohibitionist. At her urging, the chief had voted for Prohibition. But who benefited the most from Prohibition? Moonshine producers, people who sold illegal liquor, and those who received kickbacks for permitting their activities.

The chief had told Bertram to take a week off. *Blast that*. He'd spend the rest of the day clearing up the paperwork he'd let slide and then snoop around the East Calgary club where John Wozniak played the saxophone.

* * *

"We might as well close early," Dr. Upton said.

Katharine agreed. She couldn't remember the last time the waiting area had been empty at 4:00 p.m. "Everyone must be at home, hiding from the storm."

"Clarence Oxenham's doctor finally returned my call." Dr. Upton said. "We

287

consulted and agree he died a natural death from a serious medical condition."

"An autopsy—"

"—would be a needless affront to the body, may he rest in peace."

How could she argue with two doctors?

Dr. Upton went into his office to pack up for the day. Katharine finished typing the examination report for Mrs. Jones, the day's last patient, placed her payment in the desk drawer with a lock, and turned the door sign to Closed. Katharine and Dr. Upton left the office together. Snow still fell steadily, but the wind had let up since her walk back after lunch. The window sign on Fielding and Sons was turned to Open.

"I wonder how Marguerite is managing today," Dr. Upton said.

Katharine glanced at his profile but couldn't read his expression beneath his muskrat hat. "You could go in and ask her."

"I wouldn't want to intrude."

Did John and Marguerite's involvement make him feel shut out? Katharine could try to learn Marguerite's view of the issue. "Since I have extra time, I'll stop in to say hello."

"If you wish."

She suspected his indifference was feigned and he'd welcome her account of the visit tomorrow.

The store was almost as empty as the medical office. At the camera counter, Marguerite chatted with Mrs. Jones, perhaps filling time while waiting for Mr. Fielding to prepare her prescription. Mrs. Fielding sat with her son behind the main counter. She left him to ask Katharine if she could be of assistance.

"I'm here to talk to Marguerite," Katharine said.

"Poor woman, to go through that experience again."

"Poor Clarence," Katharine said with force.

"I didn't know him well," Mrs. Fielding said. "Those rare times he came into the store, he'd talk with Vincent, but once—I don't like to speak ill of the dead—he made a sardonic comment to me about the war. Marguerite tells me now that he had a grave medical condition that disqualified him from military service, but that's no excuse to disrespect our brave boys overseas."

Katharine had to respect this viewpoint of a woman with three sons fighting in the war. "Any news about your son?"

Mrs. Fielding's eyelashes twitched. "Still missing. If you don't need me, I'll get back to Thomas' schooling."

Marguerite took out an item from under the counter to show Mrs. Jones. Mr. Fielding emerged from a back room, handed a bag to Mrs. Jones, and came over to Katharine at the main counter.

"Terrible business about Marguerite's boarder," he said. "He'd usually greet Upton and me briefly on whist nights then retreat to his room to read. That room is available now, sadly, for Vincent's cousin. If she wants to move in, I'll waive her apartment rent for the time she's been there."

"That's generous."

"It's only a few days' rent," he said, but looked pleased by his own kindness.

"Mrs. Sterling," Mrs. Jones said from Marguerite's counter. "I didn't notice you come in."

Katharine joined her and Marguerite.

"These remedies Marguerite gets from the Chinese farmer are fascinating," Mrs. Jones said. "I've bought one for my rheumatism."

"Make sure you tell Dr. Upton what you're using," Katharine advised her. "Even mild herbal remedies might interact with your prescribed drug."

"I've told her this already," Marguerite snapped. "And I've told you, I don't sell medicines to customers that aren't safe for them to take."

"Marguerite's farmer also sells fresh vegetables, fruits, and eggs," Mrs. Jones said. "She gave me his name and location less than an hour's walk from here."

"He gives his hens better food and uses superior manure," Marguerite added.

Katharine had to agree this might improve his produce. As Mrs. Jones left, Katharine recalled that when Clarence died, she'd been too annoyed with Marguerite's selfishness to express her sorrow for his passing. Katharine offered her sympathies now.

"He called my cooking a miracle for his stomach." Marguerite touched her slim waist. "But the smell of food made me sick. He'd be alive if I'd kept cooking."

"You don't know that." Especially if she was adding a toxic ingredient to his food. A nasty thought when Marguerite's regret seemed genuine.

"I'm starting to cook again. Too late for him."

Katharine dared a pointed question. "Are you close to three months along?"

Marguerite's eyes flashed above her mask. Would she continue her denial? "I think so," she said. "I hate this child."

Katharine stifled her surprise and judgment. From her experience with Dr. Upton's patients, she'd learned women didn't always respond to prospective motherhood with instant joy. "I realize the baby adds to your difficulties."

"I don't know how much longer this baby will let me work, although Mr. Fielding says I can hide my stomach behind the counter and stay until I give birth on the pharmacy floor."

Katharine doubted Mr. Fielding had phrased it that way, but it was good of him not to insist Marguerite stop working when her condition showed. Evidently, her situation was no longer a secret.

"The baby is fussy," Marguerite said. "It makes me tired, won't let me eat or cook or drink wine. What if it confines me to bed when I get heavy? The Spanish flu is worst for women who are *enceinte*."

Her worries were valid. Growing evidence suggested pregnant women suffered from this influenza more than any other population group in terms of death rates and severity of symptoms. A large percentage lost their babies. The flu aside, pregnant women often required bedrest for their baby's or their own survival. Katharine could tell Marguerite that she'd love her child the instant it was born, but that wasn't always true and might not be helpful now. "Maybe your baby got its fussiness over with during your first trimester and will let you sail to the end. That was the case for me with my daughter." Katharine hadn't quite sailed with unborn Lillian, but she'd found her last six months easier than the nausea of the first three.

Marguerite looked skeptical and wisely so.

Why did women do it? Katharine mused on her way home, although she wouldn't give up Henry and Lillian for the world. They were outside in the front yard playing in the snow fort they'd built. Both hurled snowballs at their five neighbours in their fort next door. Irene's eldest threw a snowball at Lillian. She recoiled into Katharine, who wrapped her arms around her daughter.

"Mrs. Murphy says we all have to stay in our yards," Lillian said. "But it's not fair, five against two."

"Life isn't fair," Katharine said with sympathy. "Why isn't Uncle John out here helping you?"

Lillian glanced at the front door. "He's talking to the lady."

"What lady?"

"The one who sews cushions."

Pina?

Inside, Pina and John were seated in the living room. Both turned toward Katharine when she entered.

"We were talking about Clarence." Pina's voice filled with sadness. "Who or what else matters today? I've been distraught since John came over and told me this morning."

Katharine sat across from them on the davenport.

"I didn't leave the children alone," John answered her silent question. "They came with me and played on the high school yard while I went in to see Pina."

Katharine had often taken the children to the school playground across the street from the library and the Methodist Sunday school in Pina's building.

"I knew his damn Fabry symptoms had returned," Pina said. "But he seemed in good spirits when I stopped by yesterday. He morbidly joked that John must have doused the meals he'd brought over with a poison that caused stomach upset."

John snickered. "Fortunately, I don't take stomach drugs or Katharine would have her Scottish scientist test them."

This wasn't funny, especially since she'd notified Bertram about Clarence's death and suggested it was suspicious. "Did you call the people on Marguerite's list?" she asked John.

"I've talked to Clarence's father in Montreal twice," he said. "His mother died of the same disease."

"That's why Clarence didn't want children," Pina said softly. "He wanted the sickness to end with him."

"His father decided to have him buried in Calgary," John continued. "The place of his future, rather than his past. He said Clarence would want that. Pina's offered to make the arrangements."

"Gives me something to do," Pina said.

"His boss and buddies were shocked," John said. "He'd told no one he had a debilitating illness."

"He hated pity," Pina said. "I think that's partly why he emphasized his moral opposition to the war as his reason for not enlisting. He could have used his disease to avoid people calling him a coward."

"No one's handed me a white feather." John touched his right thigh. "In some ways, it's easier to have a sickness or injury you can't hide." He glanced at the mantel clock. "You're home early, Kath."

"Slow afternoon at work despite the storm easing up." She sniffed savoury aromas wafting from the kitchen. This coming home from work to prepared dinners was a treat. She'd encourage John to continue cooking class when Marguerite was back at her stove. Since Pina showed no signs of leaving, Katharine offered to make tea.

"The ladies' drink," Pina scoffed. "Do you have something stronger?"

The only liquor in the house was the half-bottle of sherry in the kitchen cupboard. "It's early, not quite five o'clock."

"Close enough."

"All we have is wine."

"Perfect."

John rose. "While you ladies enjoy your drink, I'll go see if Marguerite is home and wants me to bring her another poisoned dinner."

In the kitchen, Katharine got the sherry bottle from the top cupboard. A bottle of red wine stood behind it, along with a bottle of whisky. Neither had been there last week when she and John toasted Vincent's memory. John's only opportunity to buy them legally from the government vendor would have been on Saturday afternoon when he met Marguerite's train downtown. But most stores closed Saturday midday.

Katharine set the sherry bottle on the serving tray with two glasses and a bowl of almonds to eat so the alcohol wouldn't make her lightheaded.

* * *

Snow covered the lawn of the two-storey house in East Calgary owned by Charles Larriviere. No sign announced the place as Charlie's Den. Bertram guessed someone had shovelled the sidewalks about an hour ago, judging from the quarter inch of snow that had accumulated since then. A missed opportunity to talk with that person.

Sunset darkened the sky, but no lights shone from the house windows. Bertram pressed the doorbell. When no one answered, he turned the doorknob. Locked, as he'd expected. Lights streamed from the neighbouring homes. He went to the one next door. An elderly gentleman answered. Bertram took out his badge and identified himself.

"You cops finally shut down the operation," the man said. "It was about time."

If the chief had tipped off the club owner, Bertram supposed the police still deserved credit for closing the place. "I see someone shovels their sidewalks."

"The neighbour on their opposite side," the man said. "I told her that makes her complicit in their crimes, but she needs the money. Has the operation closed for good?"

296

"We're working on it. Aside from shovelling, have you noticed any activity at the house this past week?"

"A truck pulled up one afternoon," the man said. "Two men carried boxes out of the house. From the weight of them, I suspect they contained liquor. They loaded the boxes into the truck and drove off." He scratched his chin. "That's all I can think of. Otherwise, the place has been dead quiet."

Bertram thanked him and walked to the shoveller's house. A woman answered his doorbell ring. Children's voices sounded from a room behind her. She confirmed her neighbour paid her a flat rate to maintain the front of the property.

"It keeps the house looking good," she said. "Not an eyesore on the street. You wouldn't know anything fishy was going on, except for Saturday evenings. Then there's cars parked out front, taxicabs pulling up, men staggering out, sometimes yelling and singing in the middle of the night, music blaring out the windows. I didn't complain because it earned me a few extra coins. I suppose he'll sell now if you've closed it."

"When was the last time you saw the owner, Charles Larriviere?"

"Charles Smith, his name is."

An alias.

"The first of the month, when he paid me," the woman said. "We don't talk about his business. He doesn't seem to live in the house otherwise. A waste of a good home."

Bertram wrapped up the interview and crossed the street to the house directly opposite the club. Three children were building a snowman in the front yard. A fourth ran out of the house carrying a bowler hat for the snowman's head. The others added stones for its eyes and twigs for its nose and mouth.

A woman came to the door. She looked to be about thirty, like her neighbour across the street as well as Katharine Sterling. A generation of women minding the home front while their husbands fought and died overseas.

"I reported the house to my alderman last week," the woman said. "He told me he advised the mayor, and the house has been silent since then. It's good to see our city council and the police doing their jobs."

"Has there been activity of any nature at the house since the closure?"

"Not that I've seen in the evenings or on the weekend. I work weekdays."

A child brushed past Bertram and into the house, which was filled with cooking aromas. If this woman could work, raise children, and cook, he should be able to manage a few meals a week. He'd start by buying groceries this weekend and prepare his own Saturday and Sunday dinners.

Bertram thanked her for taking the initiative to contact her alderman.

"I should have done it sooner," she said. "The Saturday evening parties started about five months ago. I delayed reporting it until fall because, well, I liked listening to the music through the open windows. Free entertainment on a Saturday night." She smiled.

John's music. Bertram would like to hear him play, and he didn't begrudge this hard-working woman her small enjoyment. He left her house and continued to the one next door. Something he hadn't yet done with the Tainted Whisky case was canvass Marguerite's neighbours to see if any had witnessed a person entering her house in order to tamper with the whisky. An oversight on his part probably because he'd focused on a perpetrator who lived in the home—Marguerite, Clarence, or the victim himself—rather than on a non-resident, like Dr. Upton and John Wozniak. Both men had an interest in Marguerite. One of them might be her lover who'd acted on his own without involving her in the dirty deed. John could have had an opportunity to tamper with the whisky before he left Monday night. Either man might have entered the house later that evening or Tuesday while Vincent, Marguerite, and Clarence were at work.

Monday night would be risky. Footsteps could disturb the three residents sleeping in their beds. Had Dr. Upton left the medical office for any reason on Tuesday morning? Bertram would ask Katharine about this the next time they met.

He recalled her saying she'd started keeping the children home from school on Wednesday, the day after Vincent's death. John could easily have slipped into Marguerite's house by the back lane on Tuesday while the children and Katharine were away. Bertram had noticed a trend toward downtown residents locking their doors, but people in the suburbs generally felt as safe as those in small towns. He hated to think Katharine's brother was a killer, but his job was to explore that possibility.

Chapter Eighteen

Katharine carried the tray into the living room and set it on the coffee table.

Pina stood beside the piano studying the bookshelves. "Clarence loved reading," she said in a wistful tone. "He acquired the habit when he was bedridden as a child."

They returned to their seats: Katharine on the davenport, Pina on the rocker by the fireplace. Katharine poured them each a glass of sherry, leaving some in the bottle in case Pina wanted seconds.

Since Pina seemed a forthright person and she'd mentioned Clarence, Katharine took the opportunity to satisfy her curiosity about their night together. "If it's not too personal, were you and Clarence friends, or more than that?"

"Friends and occasionally more when the mood suited us."

Katharine sipped her wine, trying not to appear startled. "I can't imagine that kind of friendship. How do you manage emotional entanglements?"

"We simply didn't get tangled." Pina paused. No flushed face or other indication she was embarrassed by the questions. "I admit there were moments during or after 'the act,' when I'd feel a kind of love for him.

He and I talked about this, actually. He called it a trick of the body to lure us into raising the next generation."

Katharine hoped she wasn't flushing. "You don't want that? Children, I mean?"

Pina's nose wrinkled. "I enjoy my nephews and nieces for a few hours at a time, but all day and night for the rest of my life? My mother doesn't understand. She thinks there's something wrong with me."

"I wouldn't say that." Katharine recalled a young woman who came to the medical office. After Dr. Upton examined her, she made it clear to Katharine she intended to terminate her condition. Katharine wrestled with her conscience and, in the end, decided the moral and practical choice would be to help the woman go through the procedure safely. Katharine convinced Dr. Upton to locate a qualified doctor, called the woman to give her his details, and never saw her again. She prayed the woman suffered no ill effects. "Do you worry you might find yourself with child?"

Pina frowned, her first sign of distress about the topic. "I insist the men wear French letters or pull out before they spill their seed."

Katharine gulped the last of her wine. She'd known Pina less than a week and she hadn't discussed this much with anyone else, including Eddie. Pina finished her drink, and Katharine emptied the bottle into Pina's glass.

"Do you have more?" Pina asked.

"A bottle of red wine in the kitchen."

"I'll help you start it."

One glass of wine was enough for Katharine, but she fetched the new bottle. Back in the living room, she paused to look out the front window. John and the children stood in the fort, pitching snowballs at their neighbours. Evidently, Marguerite was still at the drug store, or she'd sent John home after he delivered the food. Katharine wondered if he'd spend the night with Marguerite again. Probably John, himself, didn't know yet.

She returned to the davenport and decided to treat herself to a second glass of wine. Perhaps, they'd discussed Pina's love life enough. "I think it's especially good for Marguerite to have you living nearby now that Clarence is gone as well."

"He might be a greater loss for her than Vincent."

"Why do you say that?"

Pina swirled her glass, creating wavelets in the wine. "Vincent was my younger cousin—nine years is a big gap when you're children. He was a pest, like most little boys, but when he came back from the war to Calgary, I made friends with him and Marguerite. As adults, the gap narrowed." She paused for a drink of wine.

Katharine took a sip, waiting for Pina to get to her point.

"The three of us had fun at first," Pina said. "We went out to clubs, dance halls, restaurants. One night, I drank too much and confided I'd had an abortion."

Katharine forced her face into a neutral expression by reminding herself of her pragmatic approach to Dr. Upton's young female patient. Work in a medical office had made her less shocked and critical of people's actions than she'd been in the past.

"Both told me it wasn't important," Pina said. "It didn't change their view of me, they insisted, but a few weeks later, when Vincent and I argued about something, he joked he'd 'tell on me' to my mother. At least, I thought it was a joke, but he joked about it again later, a touch sharper. After the next 'joke,' he asked me for a loan, which I gave him. When I later mentioned repayment, he implied that if I pressed him, he'd spill the beans to Mama. It was subtle. Marguerite was there for every conversation but seemed unaware he was doing anything. Sometimes, I wonder if I imagined it."

"You didn't." Katharine remembered another one of Dr. Upton's patients. He'd referred the woman to a doctor who specialized in emotional problems, and she'd ultimately left her husband who'd treated her in similar belittling ways that were almost undetectable.

"It would break my mother's heart to learn this," Pina said. "She'd view it as murdering an unborn child and an affront to family and God, in that order. Vincent never did give me my money back," she said with a scoff. "And it was a reasonable sum."

"Marguerite might honour his debt."

"She has enough troubles without that." Pina jerked upright. "I suppose this gives me motive to kill Vincent. I confess, I imagined whacking him once or twice. That's why I avoided spending time with them this past year. What I'm trying to say is, Vincent wasn't a nice person. Clarence, for all his faults, was a decent human being, and his rent money is a monetary loss for Marguerite."

If Vincent was murdered, had his character led to his end? Katharine drank more wine. "Mr. Fielding told me he'd waive your rent if you want to move in with Marguerite."

"No." Pina shook her head. "I like her in small doses, but her endless cooking and cleaning and drama would send me climbing up walls. Maybe she reminds me too much of Mama." She smiled wanly. "Also, I don't think she's as hard up for money as she lets on. She and Vincent lived frugally. I think he squeezed me for a loan more from meanness than need. On the train to the Pass, Marguerite told me she had almost enough savings to buy a small house. With her shrewdness, she'll live in comfort."

"Provided her condition doesn't force her to leave work or cause her serious medical problems."

"God must be a man to inflict that 'condition' on the female sex."

They giggled.

Rustlings at the front entrance suggested John or the children had come inside. Katharine glimpsed them all through the archway. Henry and Lillian threw off their overclothes and raced to the back of the house.

"I promised them cookies and cocoa." John stepped into the living room. "I could use some myself after that snowball fight. We were winning until Gladys came home from work and joined the other team. Her snowball landed hard on the side of my head." He rubbed his right cheek. "Now, I have matching wounds."

From this distance, his face looked unscarred and glowed rosy from vigorous exercise outside in the cold.

"Is Gladys the lesbian?" Pina asked.

Katharine started. She'd learned the term from a novel. Eddie had been intrigued when she read him the paragraph in the book. But Gladys ...?

"That's right," John said. "She works in a lumber yard."

"Many women do men's work these days," Katharine said. "That doesn't make them lesbians."

John's eyebrows raised. "You know what that is?"

"I'm not so innocent." She looked at Pina. "Have you met Gladys?"

"Clarence told me about them," Pina said. "I forget her friend's name."

"Irene," John said. "Both used to be married to men but found their true callings during the war."

Irene too? "Before the war, Eddie and I had dinner with Irene and her husband dozens of times," Katharine said. "They seemed a normal couple."

"What's normal?" Pina sniffed.

Gladys and Irene both had children. Each woman slept with her own children in separate bedrooms. Or had Katharine assumed this? Did the women share one bedroom and their five children the other one?

"Often women don't realize their preference until they find themselves dissatisfied with marriage," Pina said with an air of expertise. "Or they marry in hopes it will change their natural inclination."

"Happens to men, too, I hear." John smirked.

Katharine finished her wine, annoyed at their smugness about her unworldly life. *Gladys and Irene.* If they were a couple, how hard it must be for Irene, a deeply religious Roman Catholic. The Pope declared her nature a sin.

"I'm off for my cocoa and cookie," John said. "I'd invite you two along, but you look happy with your wine."

"That reminds me," Katharine said. "When did you buy the whisky and new bottle of wine?"

"A week or two ago, I guess."

She squinted at him. "They weren't there Wednesday night."

"He bought them from me," Pina said.

John's gaze shot to her. "Don't tell her more. She's friendly with a cop."

"I'm not friends with Bertram," Katharine said.

"See?" John said. "They're on a first-name basis. Anyway, I've got to grab my treat before I head over to Marguerite's. She stopped by on her way home and said to bring dinner at six." He left the room with a spring in his step.

Katharine poured herself more wine. What was she doing? She'd never drank three glasses at one time, but it tasted good, and she relished the respite from worries and responsibilities. "Why would you sell John liquor?" she asked Pina.

"I don't make any profit," Pina said, with no defensiveness.

"Is it moonshine?"

"No." She cocked her head. "If I tell you, will you promise not to tell your cop friend?"

Katharine's head felt light. "I can't promise before I know what you'll say."

"Bertram." Pina set down her empty glass and crossed her arms. "Is he the detective who talked to Clarence and me?"

"Probably." Katharine wanted to know what Pina would say and doubted her actions were seriously criminal. "All right, I won't tell Bertram." This wouldn't stop her from contacting another officer, if necessary.

Pina unfolded her arms. "My friend, who helped me move, buys liquor from legitimate producers. He marks up the price—not as much as the government store—and sells it on the side. It helps pay for his car. As thanks for moving all my stuff, I took some of his bottles to sell to friends but don't take any money for myself."

"And you happened to mention this to John when he went to your place with my children?"

"They were playing outside across the street."

Right. Katharine had forgotten. She rubbed her fuzzy head. Footsteps in the hall foreshadowed John's return from the kitchen.

He held a pot in his hand. "I'm off to Marguerite's. With luck, you won't see me until the morning. I'll be back in time for you to leave for work."

If Katharine's brain were clear, she'd worry about John and Marguerite and about Pina selling liquor illegally to John. Those worries would have to wait until she was sober.

* * *

Between the storm and the influenza restrictions, Bertram figured that everyone in Tuxedo Park was home tonight. So far, his canvass of the houses that lined the lane behind Marguerite's house had yielded a one-hundred-percent response to his doorbell rings, aside from a home with a quarantine sign on the fence, an ominous reminder of the sickness infiltrating the city. But no one had seen a person in the lane during the hours a killer might have entered her backyard and gone into the house.

"That was over a week ago," an older man said. "I hardly remember what happened yesterday."

The police had missed the critical few days after a suspicious event to collect witnesses' information. Bertram's contrary side was glad they'd bungled the case. Clarence had got him thinking about the death penalty. Bertram believed it worked as a deterrent and an "eye for an eye" was fair, but few killers were so evil they deserved to hang. John Wozniak, for instance, a man damaged by the war, might have let passion carry him into a dark tunnel. Each neighbour who saw nothing unusual in the lane added to Bertram's relief.

He approached the corner of Centre Street. The last home to canvass was a two-storey farmhouse-style building that must have predated the suburban development. If the residents responded with a negative, it wouldn't prove John or Dr. Upton hadn't been there, but Bertram had promised to update Katharine on the case, and this reassurance might help counteract the chief's stance that her concerns weren't worthy of police time. A dog barked as he rang the bell. The woman who answered looked to be in her sixties.

Bertram identified himself and held out his badge. "I'm investigating an incident in your neighbourhood." He raised his voice to drown out the dog's barks. "Did you notice someone in your back lane between the hours of 8:00 p.m. Monday, October 14, and 2:00 p.m. Tuesday, October 15?"

"Last week? I don't get out much lately." Her brow knit in thought. "I expect I was home all that time except possibly for a short trip to a store. My back lane? We've got a high fence and the most I see of anyone is the top of a tall man's hat, but I don't recall noticing that lately. Would you like to ask my husband?"

"Please."

"I also don't remember our dog barking for no apparent reason, but I can't say he didn't bark." She turned and shouted for her husband.

Their high fence would less likely conceal John than a shorter man like Dr. Upton.

The husband appeared and confirmed he was home during the hours in question. "I'd have gone out to the back porch for a smoke a few times."

"More than a few." His wife snorted.

"The dog always comes out with me for a run around," he continued. "Don't remember him barking at anything."

Bertram held his breath. "Was anyone else in the house during those hours, who might have seen someone?"

"Only us," the woman said.

He exhaled, thanked the couple for their time, and jaywalked across the street to Katharine's house. Large snowflakes fell lightly; the temperature had warmed during his hour and a half in Tuxedo Park. On Katharine's porch, he checked his pocket watch—almost eight-thirty—and rang her doorbell.

The door opened. Pina DeLuca stood in the entranceway.

"I ... Is Katharine home?" he asked.

"You're the detective," she said. "Bertram. I was at Marguerite's on Friday when you talked to Clarence."

"I remember."

"Katharine's putting the children to bed, if you don't mind waiting." She stepped back to let him enter.

Inside, he took off his hat, brushed the snow from it, and set it with his coat and gloves on the hall chair. He removed his boots. "Is John home?"

"He's at Marguerite's." She led him into the living room. "Katharine should be finished soon. How long can it take to read children stories and tuck the monsters in?"

Bertram had no idea—his spirits sank at the reason—and perhaps eight-thirty wasn't late for children's bedtime when schools were closed. Pina sat on the upholstered rocker near the fireplace. He took the davenport across from her, which gave him a view of the archway to the hall, and offered his condolences about Clarence.

"It's still a shock." Pina's face darkened. "I knew his sickness was ultimately fatal but assumed he'd always be here."

Bertram understood. Humans irrationally lived as though death weren't inevitable. "When was the last time you saw him?"

"Yesterday afternoon," She glanced at the sewing machine that stood against the inner wall. "When I came here to make cushions, John said Clarence was home sick from work. On my way back home, I stopped in to see how he was doing."

"Did he say anything that struck you as interesting or unusual?"

Her eyes narrowed. "Is that a police question?"

"Unofficially." But he was mentally taking notes.

"I can't think of anything, aside from his joke about John poisoning the meals he brought over to the house."

"John was taking him food?"

"To save Marguerite having to cook for him while she was grieving and too nauseous to eat. Do you know about her condition?"

"I was told." So, John had opportunity to poison the food with a medicine that in large doses would destroy a fragile gastrointestinal system. Had Clarence's comment been more than a joke? "I visited Clarence not long after you that day."

Pina's arched eyebrows rose. "Why?"

Footsteps in the hall rescued him from a reply. He rose to greet Katharine, who halted under the archway.

Pina stood. "He's here to probe us with questions. Since he's finished with me, I'll leave you two to talk alone."

As the women walked to the front entrance, Bertram stepped between the sewing machine and armchair to eavesdrop.

"Thanks for the wine, conversation, dinner, and musical evening with your children," Pina told Katharine. "It took my mind off Clarence."

"Thank you for washing the pots and pans 'drums,'" Katharine said.

"I finished your second bottle of wine in the process."

Both giggled, and Pina departed.

Two bottles? Bertram wondered if they'd been friends before the two deaths or if the tragedies had brought them together.

Katharine returned to the living room and sat on the armchair. She didn't look flushed or intoxicated from drinking. Perhaps she'd consumed her last drink well before the children's entertainment.

Across from her on the davenport, Bertram got the bad news over with. "Clarence's death didn't alter the chief's decision not to investigate." He couldn't implicate his boss by adding his suspicions about the chief's kickbacks. Looking back, he thought the only thing that had prevented the chief from slamming the Tainted Whisky case shut from the start was the fact he hadn't read the file until yesterday.

"I had hoped to learn the truth before John ..."

Became more involved with Marguerite. Bertram silently finished her sentence. It would be relevant for him to ask if she thought her brother and Marguerite were intimate now and before Vincent died. But the question might antagonize her, and Bertram wanted her to feel he was on her side, which he was in truth.

He realized that telling her that no neighbours had seen her brother lurking in the back lane would reveal that he viewed him as a suspect. "I've done some additional investigating on my own but have come up with nothing that adds a great deal. Do you recall if Dr. Upton left your medical office for any reason the Tuesday that Vincent died?"

Her mouth quivered.

"This is unofficial. You're not obliged to reply."

"No," she said. "No, I want you to investigate every angle but hadn't suspected Dr. Upton. I'm sure he dreams of winning

Marguerite, but I don't believe he'd go that far." She rubbed her jaw. "Tuesday? Over a week ago? It's hard to recall."

He waited, relieved that he hadn't given offence. Despite her intelligence, Katharine seemed unaware that a deep exploration by the police might point to John as the killer. Bertram admired her trust in her brother.

"Dr. Upton rarely leaves the office between his morning arrival and his departure at the end of the day," she said. "I don't recall last Tuesday being different from normal."

"Does he start work before or after Vincent and Marguerite did?"

"Before," she said. "The drug store opens a half hour later than us and closes an hour or so later, but Marguerite only worked part-time. She'd be home in the afternoon."

Evidently Katharine understood he was looking for a time of day when Dr. Upton could have stolen into their home. "You told me you and the doctor stagger your lunch hours."

"I take mine a half hour earlier and always come home," she said. "In theory, he might have left the office during that time frame, but most days I leave him with a patient."

"I agree it's a slim window." In contrast, John Wozniak's window was wide open.

Katharine ran her fingers through her hair, loosening the braid that flowed down her back. "Had Dr. Upton gone to their home for a nefarious reason, he'd have been wise to exit the back door of the medical office, follow the lane behind my house to First Street, and circle back to Vincent's rear door, rather than enter their lane from Centre Street, where he'd be more noticed."

"Good point," Bertram said.

She looked at him sideways. "Do detectives suspect everyone connected with a case, regardless of their character?"

"People aren't always what they seem."

"Including me, I suppose."

"Not you." *Yes you, but in the best possible ways.* Her comments were leading toward dangerous ground, where he might shift from indirectly accusing her employer to her brother. "I've detained you long enough."

Both rose and walked to the hall.

"Do you have to get home to a wife and family?" Katharine asked.

He missed a step, startled by her interest. "Sadly, no." At the front entrance, he had an urge to tell her everything. About Nellie, their son, this wretched past year. He stifled the desire. "I'll advise you of any developments."

"I hope they'll involve more than pursuing Dr. Upton," she said. "His faults stop short of killing a man."

Two men if Clarence was murdered as well.

Bertram left her home and shuffled toward the streetcar. Katharine's description of the doctor sneaking through the back lanes had given him the idea to follow that route into Marguerite's house to search for papers related to Vincent's business dealings. If those papers existed, they might contain clues about the two deaths. Overnight, Bertram would consider the practicalities of doing this. And the ethics.

Chapter Nineteen

Katharine, Henry, and Lillian grabbed their shovels from the front porch to clear the half inch of snow that had accumulated overnight. The snow had stopped falling, but clouds hovered. Katharine was dressed for work in hopes John would come home as promised, which he'd done the last two times he'd spent the night with Marguerite. He'd shown he could keep his word, *but everyone's a suspect*, Bertram had all but said. This might include her, despite his polite denial, and it would certainly include John.

She scraped the shovel over the pavement, hurled snow onto her whitened lawn, and cursed Bertram for planting a seed of doubt about her brother. Rather than encourage her to urge Bertram to halt his investigation to keep John from the gallows, she wanted the police to pursue the case to its end to exonerate John in her mind. Ninety-eight percent faith in her brother wasn't enough.

Gladys emerged from Irene's house next door, waved at Katharine, and began shovelling their front porch. Katharine wouldn't be able to talk to either woman now without thinking of their union. But was it more unholy than some marriages Katharine had observed? Dr. Upton had treated several women who came in with bruises he suspected were caused by drunken, angry, cruel husbands. Marguerite's marriage to Vincent had seemed far from ideal and had potentially given her a motive to kill him.

Henry dropped his shovel, formed a snowball, and threw it at Lillian. She shrieked and tossed a snowball back at him. Across the street, John came out of Marguerite's front door. His spirited walk across the street suggested all was well with Marguerite from his perspective. Katharine had to leave for work and would get the details from him later.

She held out the shovel to John. "I'll be back for lunch at the usual time."

"Cooking class today will be chicken soup," he said. "Marguerite thinks she might manage a bowl of broth."

"Is she going to work today?"

He nodded. "I left her preparing her *toilette*."

Gladys pushed her shovel toward them. Katharine left them to talk, got her handbag from inside the house, and disrupted the snowball fight to kiss the children goodbye. Aside from a numbness in her head, she felt no effects from drinking the previous day. She walked up the street, thinking that the disappointing aspect about Gladys' preference for women was that she couldn't replace Marguerite in John's heart. Another hope squashed by real life.

Katharine rounded the corner and opened the door to the medical office. It would be easy for hooligans to break a window, pick this flimsy lock, and search all her desk drawers. They could get the money from the locked drawer by banging it with a crowbar. Dr. Upton's private office had no lock at all. Thieves might have no interest in his stethoscope or sphygmomanometer, but he kept a small supply of medicines to give to patients of meagre means. John had mentioned that some people at his club used heroin and cocaine for recreation. Several patients had asked Dr. Upton for prescriptions of high doses of Aspirin to ward off the Spanish flu. Dr. Upton refused their requests. A myth, he said, but people were desperate for a cure; that drug would have value on the street market as well.

She put her handbag in the bottom drawer of her desk and checked the money drawer, although she'd checked it twice before leaving yesterday, and there were no signs of a break-in. Still locked. The Fieldings had a safe in their office and a modern pin tumbler lock for their outer doors. When she'd suggested they upgrade the medical office security, Dr. Upton hadn't seen the need. They made less money than the drug store, and Katharine made daily trips to the bank when it was open. Normally, less than two dollars remained on-site at the end of the day, but who knew how long the flu would shut the bank down? She'd taken her daily salary home, but Dr. Upton insisted on leaving the rest of the gross take in the office for calculation at the end of the week.

Dr. Upton breezed in and paused at her desk. "Roads are better today. Prepare for a flood of patients."

"I was thinking," she said. "Would Fieldings' keep our patients' payments in their safe? Our money could be tucked in a corner."

"No harm in asking."

"I'll go over during a lull here after they open."

A woman with a crying baby entered. The next hour saw a stream of patients but not the predicted flood. Midmorning, Katharine left two regular patients alone in the waiting room while Dr. Upton attended to a family of six. She told the ones waiting she'd be back before he finished the family's lengthy appointment.

Next door, Marguerite stood behind the main counter serving a customer. No Fieldings in sight. The glass cupboards were packed with bottles of medicines that would be worth a lot on the street. The cabinet below Marguerite featured a large display of Abbey's Effervescent Salt, touting the mild laxative's benefit of combatting the Spanish influenza germ. Abbey's too had appeal to thieves, as would cameras and other nonpharmaceutical items.

When the customer left, Katharine went up to the counter and wasted little time with greetings. "With the bank closure—"

"Mr. Fielding called after I arrived at work," Marguerite said. "His son died in *France*."

Katharine inhaled. "Their missing son?"

"That was a lie. He was never missing." Marguerite's tone was harsh. "He died of pneumonia."

"I'm so sorry for them." A thought rushed into Katharine's shocked mind. "Did it develop from the flu?"

"Mr. Fielding guessed that too." Marguerite said. "He thinks the army lied so the Germans intercepting letters wouldn't know our soldiers are weakened by Spanish flu."

Many espoused this hush-up theory, and it made sense.

"Now they tell the truth because they know we've won the war. Mr. Fielding told me to keep the store open or not, whatever I want. I can serve customers but not dispense medicine." Her eyes glowered above her mask.

Katharine sympathized but still believed there was a need for qualifications. "You could go to college and get your pharmacy degree after your baby is born if you found someone to look after the child."

John. He didn't have a day job. John could move with Marguerite to Edmonton or Toronto and had experience minding his nephew and niece. Much as Katharine hated the thought of him with Marguerite and would miss him if he moved away, if they were gone, she'd worry less about one or both being a killer. They could murder each other for all she cared. *Not true.* She loved John, whatever he'd done.

But this was wrong to think of herself when the Fieldings' loss was worse. She remembered the purpose of her visit. "I came to ask if you'd have room in your safe for the money we receive from patients during the bank closure?"

Marguerite's brow furrowed. "We might, but I would need Mr. Fielding's permission."

"Don't disturb him about this until he's ready to think of work," Katharine said. "Please give him and his family my condolences if you speak to him. Dr. Upton's as well. Mr. Fielding can't have called him about his son yet or Dr. Upton would have told me."

"Men keep their pain inside," Marguerite said. "John is different that way."

"He isn't with me."

Marguerite sniggered. Evidently, she'd drawn out John better than his sister had. "John says you think I murder Vincent and convinced the detective to think the same."

Katharine tried to keep her expression neutral. Damn John for revealing this to Marguerite.

"Are you and Detective Tanner lovers?"

Katharine stepped back. At the rear counter, a customer studied the cameras. No other people had entered the store.

"Of course not," Katharine said. "Why would you suggest that?"

Marguerite's enigmatic gaze made Katharine bristle. Scratch the idea of John running off with Marguerite and helping her through college. Katharine loathed that prospect, and she'd do her best to prevent the woman from manipulating him into it.

* * *

Ethics be damned. Bertram rapped his office desk. He'd spent last night and this morning debating the pros and cons of breaking into Marguerite's house to search for evidence of illicit liquor purchase and sales. Bertram still hadn't decided.

This would be an illegal search, but obtaining a warrant for a case that officially didn't exist would be impossible. Any evidence he acquired would be inadmissible at trial. But there would be no trial unless he acquired evidence to push open the case.

Would he want to push if any discoveries he made pointed to murder committed by Katharine's brother? Not necessarily. He'd consider burying evidence against John as well as Dr. Upton, Marguerite, and anyone else for good reason.

Did that make him a terrible cop? Probably, and further support for his decision to quit the police force in the spring.

Burying evidence. In the past, Bertram had despised cops who did this. Now he saw there might be good reasons for it. But the chief's reason was wrong if he was receiving kickbacks to shut police eyes to illegal liquor activities and had buried a suspicious-death case related to the illegal trade. Vincent's papers might bring some of this to light.

The cost to Bertram of getting caught on an illegal search would be firing or suspension without pay. He dreaded the dishonour in the eyes of his colleagues, family, and friends.

But could he let a killer go free, one who had killed twice and might kill again? That wrong overshadowed the personal cost of an illegal search. If John turned out to be the killer, Bertram would have to weigh the wrong of burying the case.

Why put himself through this mess? He had the chief's blessing to let the case go.

Curiosity, Bertram supposed. A need to see something through. A desire to help Katharine learn the truth about her brother and the woman John loved, for want of a better word.

Love. Bertram had known Katharine a short while. He wasn't in love with her, but his feelings for her taught him he could love again if he wanted. For that, he owed her this much. Ethics be damned.

He checked his pocket watch. Marguerite would be at work. Since she might go home for lunch or leave work early this afternoon, there was a small window between two and three o'clock.

* * *

Bertram got off the streetcar at the stop before Marguerite's street and followed the back lanes to her house. The windows were dark. He turned the knob of the back door. It opened, proof that an outsider, like Dr. Upton or John, could have entered and tampered with Vincent's whisky and Clarence's medicine.

No sounds from inside.

A creature slithered past him and into the house. The dog scurried down the hall. Bertram followed its route to the living room. The mongrel gazed up at him and barked. Presumably it lived here. Bertram patted its shaggy head. Thankfully, the mutt calmed and settled on the floor.

The sideboard was clear of papers. Bertram checked the drawers. No papers, but he found a pile in the adjacent secretary desk. Word-cross puzzles. Squares, words, and letters crossed out. Vincent's draft creations. Another desk drawer held the lists of housekeeping accounts that Bertram had previously checked.

He crossed the hall to the bedroom that had to belong to Marguerite, judging by the hairbrushes, jewellery, and cosmetics on the vanity. The dog trotted in, leaped up to the bed, and curled into a ball. Bertram rifled through drawers with women's underthings and overthings and lifted the mattress to look beneath, prompting the dog to jump to the floor and bark. *Damn it.* The mutt was loud, and these homes were built close together, but Bertram doubted the neighbours could hear.

He searched the wardrobe and concluded there was nothing of note in this bedroom aside from its neatness and the absence of a masculine presence. Not one trace of Vincent or John. Bertram would ponder the significance later.

Marguerite might have hidden documents in the kitchen, but if anyone had died for incriminating papers, it was Clarence, a man with his own set of principles. Bertram padded to the home's second bedroom, in the back of the house. The dog trailed him. The single bed was stripped of sheets, the dresser emptied of contents. Marguerite had been busy disposing of the vestiges of the men in this home. The dog sniffed the large bookcase, which overflowed with books. Histories. Nature studies. Charles Dickens. A slim volume titled *Fingerprinting Decoded* caught Bertram's eye. Clarence had mentioned his reading on the subject.

Bertram pulled out the fingerprinting book and flipped through the pages. No sheet of paper fell out. It would take time to go through every book. If he were Clarence, he'd hide a document in the book someone was least likely to look at. Bertram's gaze lit on the widest tome titled *The Underground Ancient World*. He picked it up.

The corner of a sheet of paper stuck out from the side of the book. He opened it and found a dozen sheets hidden between the pages. Columns of letters and numbers interspersed. No words that made sense.

The dog barked and bounded into the hall. Was someone at the front door? Bertram stuffed the papers into his inside coat pocket and darted to the hall to escape out the back. The dog blocked the route through the kitchen. *Damn.* Bertram tried to slip past the barking mutt, tripped over it, and crashed into the bathroom door.

Footsteps from the front of the house.

Marguerite marched toward him. "You."

He regained his balance. The dog guarded the kitchen entrance, its teeth bared.

"Why are you here?"

Bertram rubbed his sore shoulder. "Why are *you* here?"

"It's my house." Marguerite crossed her arms.

She leaned into the wall, enough for him to squeeze past her. The dog barked and chased him to the front door.

"What do you want here?" Marguerite screamed behind him.

He slammed the door in the dog's face and hurtled down the stairs. In the middle of the street, he stopped to catch his breath. He looked back at the house.

Marguerite stared out the living room window, the drapes drawn to frame her face. She looked directly at him and didn't move or close the curtains. Bold of her. A challenge, but he'd got what he needed—if he could decipher the papers.

* * *

When Katharine arrived home from work, the children were playing fort with the next-door neighbours. She dodged snowballs all the way up to the porch.

John came outside holding a pot of soup for his dinner with Marguerite, who had closed the drug store early. "She handled the chicken broth so well at lunch that she asked me to add potatoes."

"I'm glad her stomach is settling down." If Marguerite's condition were passing the three-month point, her baby would be due in late April.

"Your dinner is bubbling on the stove," John said. "I'll see you in the morning."

His walk down the stairs came close to a trot, and Katharine had to thank Marguerite for John's improved mood and mobility. Inside, Katharine changed out of her work clothes and finished preparing their meal of vegetables in chicken broth.

During dinner, she asked the children about their "school" day. Katharine no longer cared that it included minimal academics. Her goals for their instruction by John had dropped to making it through the day with no one dying or getting sick or hearing news of someone else's misery, like the death of Arthur Fielding.

From Mr. Fielding's talk of the boy, Katharine suspected he was his father's favourite, the smartest and most dynamic of his sons. Mr. Fielding's long-range plan had been for his eldest to manage his downtown store while Arthur would manage the Tuxedo Park branch, the largest and newest. Son number three and young Thomas would get the other two stores. The Fieldings had no daughters. Tragically for Mr. Fielding, one of his stores was now open for an outsider. This could be Marguerite if she pursued her higher education.

After dinner and cleaning up, Katharine asked the children to play the piano songs John had taught them that day. Lillian stumbled through a simple song, while Henry performed with skill for an eight-year-old beginner.

Katharine glanced at Eddie's photograph on the sideboard. The old Eddie would have scorned a son's desire for a career in music, which would offer little chance of earning a living wage. He'd have done everything to discourage Henry, who had inherited his father's stubbornness. She could see the two of them coming to blows, with her caught in the middle. But how would Eddie, changed by the war, respond? She had no clue, and she shouldn't assume life would be easier with Eddie here. Every indication pointed to the troops returning by next spring.

Henry bolted from the piano stool, bringing the concert to a close. Katharine hustled him and Lillian through their bedtime ritual. When they were finally tucked in, she made herself tea, put a classical recording on the Victrola, and took out her mask-making kit. With most patients now cooperative about wearing the masks and some taking extras home for family use, the supply at the office was running low.

The front door clicked. She recognized John's shuffle into the house. Why was he back? *Please not more miserable news.* She met him at the entrance.

He dumped his coat on the hall chair. "We have to talk."

Her body tense, she led him into the living room and sat on the davenport.

He took the armchair, his expression grim. "Marguerite's leaving tomorrow morning."

"For where?"

"We'll decide at the train station."

"We?" Too shrill. "You're going with her?"

"She tried to discourage me, but I can't let her run off alone to who knows where."

"Why this sudden need? I spoke to her this morning at the store. She didn't mention this at all."

John crossed his left leg over the right. "This afternoon she went home from work to check on the dog and encountered Detective Bertram in her house. Did he tell you this?"

"No." She forced her voice calmer. "Bertram? In Tuxedo Park today? Why would he go in her house when she wasn't there?"

"Good question," John said. "He purposely picked a time when she'd be away. Marguerite is convinced his motive was to plant evidence against her and set her up for murder or selling liquor under the table through the drug store."

"That's nonsense." Katharine folded her arms.

"Is it? My manager at the club says the cops planted booze in his house so they could charge him with illegal sales. Fortunately, his lawyer got him off."

"Was he selling illegally?"

"Probably." John rocked his top leg up and down. "Marguerite can't afford a sharp lawyer. She's terrified Bertram is out to frame her, lock her in jail, and hang her for a murder she didn't commit."

"He'd never do that intentionally."

"How can we know that for sure?" John said. "After Bertram scurried out of her house, Marguerite returned to the drug store, called police headquarters, and spoke to the chief, who seemed unaware of Bertram's intrusion. He's acting on his own."

"I know he is but not to frame Marguerite. Did she find the 'evidence' she thinks he hid?"

"She searched everywhere but says he'd hide it where only he would 'find it' to prove his cleverness."

"John, her house isn't huge. There's no clutter for concealing things. Her theory makes no sense. Why would Bertram want to frame her?"

"To emerge the hero who outshines the chief and takes his place. A common ambition." John uncrossed his leg. "Though she does tend to be dramatic."

"I've noticed that." Katharine might find the story plausible if she believed that Bertram had an immoral character. "Can you do anything to change her mind?"

John snickered. "You try doing that once her mind is set. My only choice is to go with her to help where I can."

She wanted to stop John but had to concede it would be wrong to let Marguerite run off alone in her mental and physical state. This situation was worse than Katharine could have imagined.

John rose. "I've got to pack. We leave early tomorrow. It'll be easier if I stay over at Marguerite's, so we won't disturb you in the morning."

Katharine followed him to the hall. "You won't disturb me. I'll stay home from work."

"No need," he said. "Before coming here, I went to Pina's apartment. She's agreed to look after the children tomorrow and promised to be here before nine. Mornings aren't her favourite time of day, but she moved to Tuxedo Park to help Marguerite."

His plan was set. "Running away won't help her, John."

"Nor will facing a conspiracy against her. You're part of it too. She knows you've been out to get her from the start."

The truth in that stabbed, but she'd only wanted to get Marguerite if she were guilty.

"I almost forgot," he said. "Marguerite asks that you look after the dog, give it food, gradually train it to eat at our place. Henry and Lillian will love having a feral pet."

"I won't."

He chuckled. "Curious the dog returned today. It scratched on her door during lunch, returned from the wilds no worse for wear. We let it in, fed it."

Forget the cursed dog. This might be the last time Katharine saw John for weeks, months, years. "How will I know where you are?"

"I'll write or call if I can."

"No, you won't. Marguerite won't want me to know where she is for fear I'll tell Bertram."

"You might do that," he said. "She thinks you two are lovers, but don't worry. I defended your honour by saying you wouldn't romp in my vacated bed with the children in the next room."

She scowled but would miss his teasing.

John disappeared into his bedroom. To avoid spending these precious moments arguing, Katharine stifled her hostility to the hasty plan and collected his shaver, toothbrush, cream for his chafed leg, saxophone, some cookies for the trip, and the cash she'd kept in the kitchen jar. It wouldn't even cover train tickets, hotels, and meals for the first few nights. Had Marguerite withdrawn enough money from her bank before it closed earlier this week? This wasn't Katharine's concern. John and Marguerite were out of her hands. If Katharine called Bertram to let him know, would that prove her involvement in the so-called conspiracy?

His suitcase packed, John went to kiss the sleeping children goodbye. He and Katharine hugged farewell at the front door.

"Be careful," she said.

"I'll try to find a way to make contact that doesn't expose her whereabouts."

Cold air blew in as he opened the door. This was all so impossible. The door closed and he was gone.

Conspirator or not, Katharine picked up the phone and asked the operator to connect her to Bertram's home. He answered within a minute.

"Were you in Marguerite's house?"

"Yes," he said with a touch of amusement in his voice. "Did she tell you she caught me in the act? I found papers written in a code that I've partially figured out."

She explained about Marguerite and John's planned departure in the morning.

"I was thinking I'd see you about this tomorrow but given the situation, it would be best for me to come now, if it's not too late for you."

"It's not." No point in going to bed when she wouldn't sleep.

They signed off. She went to the kitchen to make tea to settle herself down. As she filled the kettle, she heard sounds at the front door.

John stood in the entrance. "Marguerite isn't home." His voice filled with alarm. "Her door was locked, but I know where she hides the key out front. I went into every room twice and the basement. Her suitcase was gone. She tricked me, never bloody intended for me to join her. Has she gone downtown to a hotel or to catch a night train?"

Katharine felt his despair, but this was better than the original plan. "Either way, what can you do?"

"Go downtown and check the station first and then nearby hotels." He gripped the handles of his suitcase and saxophone case.

"John, if this is what she wants—"

"I'll grab a taxicab if one happens by Centre Street, or the streetcar."

A second plan set. "You'll come home if you don't find her?"

"I'll see. No, I'll stay downtown in case she's somewhere other than a hotel, like with a friend, and check the station in the morning. I've got to go. This is wasting time."

He gave her a quick hug and was gone again.

Bertram lived downtown. He might be able to waylay Marguerite at the train station. Katharine called him again. She tapped her foot, impatient.

The operator reported no reply. He'd left already. Katharine hung up. What could she do? She paced the hall and went into the kitchen to make herself tea and wait for his arrival.

Chapter Twenty

Warmed by the fireplace, Bertram sat on the davenport across from Katharine. She picked up the teapot from the coffee table.

"None for me, thank you," he said. "I don't want to spill on the papers." He took them from the inside pocket of his suit jacket while she poured herself a cup. "Curious they're written in code. Clarence said that when Vincent was overseas, he applied for a job in code-breaking intelligence but was turned down."

"John told me this too. Are you certain it's Vincent's handwriting and not Marguerite's? I've seen both in connection with my work."

He passed her a sheet of paper.

She scrutinized the page. "Yes, this is all his." She handed it back.

"Mr. Fielding described Vincent as the meticulous manager who handled detailed accounts while Marguerite, his assistant, came up with the innovative ideas. One idea might have been to use the drug store for illegal alcohol sales." Bertram fluttered the papers. "Essentially, they list the dates of the import and distribution of specified amounts of whisky, rum, and other liquors that qualify for a doctor's prescription. Not so different from the store's legal accounts—but why record these ones in code and keep the documents at home rather than at the office?"

"The obvious reason would be that these orders are outside the legal business."

He nodded. "The Tuxedo Park branch has a large storage room that backs to a lane, where delivery vans might slip in at night unnoticed."

"And then deliver the products to ... do the papers list the recipients?"

"Yes, in code within code." He smiled at her puzzled expression and glanced at the pages he held. "The vendors are double coded as well. The base code is fairly simple. Numbers are letters in numerical and alphabetical order and vice versa, aside from the letters of Marguerite's name and the numbers one, five, and seven. Would her birthday—or possibly Vincent's—be July 15 or May 17?"

"I don't know but could find out from their files at my office."

"Presumably, Vincent used the double code to protect the vendors and recipients. Your call interrupted my deciphering."

"Sorry." Her eyes twinkled over her teacup.

He loved her interest in the deductive aspects of the case. Quite likely, he'd have cracked the double code if the chief hadn't wasted an hour of his day reprimanding him for illegally searching Marguerite's house.

Bertram had instinctively lied. "If any evidence of wrongdoing was there, she destroyed it," he'd told the chief and humbled himself with an apology. "You were right. I latched on to the case for personal reasons. This failure has convinced me to let it go and focus on my real work."

Evidently the chief had believed him, otherwise he'd have been sacked.

Katharine sipped her tea. "Marguerite's urgent departure strikes me as an overreaction, even for her." She elaborated on John's account of the evening's events.

Bertram tried to maintain a neutral expression while he wondered about Marguerite's call to headquarters after he had searched her house. Had the chief accepted her call because the two were in cahoots? Had he threatened her in a way that frightened her? If she knew he was involved in illegal activities, she might have attempted blackmail—perhaps it had backfired.

Katharine described John's departure to find Marguerite and set her teacup on the coffee table. "The question is, what do we do now?"

We? A pleasing notion. "I'll continue working on the code," Bertram said. "The key is to think like Vincent. I've played with the letters of his whisky brand. No luck."

"John knew him better than I. He'd have suggestions."

The doorbell rang.

"John?" Bertram said.

"He wouldn't ring." Katharine hurried to the front door.

Bertram heard her voice at the entrance and then another voice he couldn't make out. He was tempted toward the hall, but this wasn't his business.

He set the papers beside him and poured himself a cup of tea. Katharine's husband, dressed in his military cap, stared from his portrait on the sideboard. Every day, the newspapers reported on the Great War's imminent end. Germany was beaten and suing for peace, but the battles weren't over yet. In the coming months, Katharine's husband could die of wounds or disease. He might be dead already, given communication delays. If the man survived relatively unscathed, Bertram hoped he appreciated the blessings of a wonderful wife and home.

Katharine re-entered the room. "That was Pina. She wanted to know what's going on. First, John showed up and asked her to mind the children with no explanation. I gave her the gist, and she'll still come here tomorrow." Katharine resettled on the rocker by the fireplace. "About an hour later, Marguerite appeared at her door asking to stay the night because she was afraid to be alone with two ghosts in her house. Pina offered her the sofa-bed in the living room. Marguerite undid her coat buttons then muttered something in French and left. Pina found it odd."

"I dare say, and I don't suppose Pina could repeat any of those French words?"

"She doesn't understand French, but she found Marguerite agitated. When she didn't return, Pina grew concerned and went to her house. She'd locked the doors, which Pina said was unusual for Marguerite. The house was dark, and no one answered the doorbell. Then Pina came here to see what we knew. John hadn't told her about Marguerite and him leaving Calgary. I advised her to go home and let me know right away if either one reappears." The doorbell rang again. Katharine jumped. "Pina?"

This time, Bertram followed her to the hall since it might be his business. Dr. Upton stood on the front porch dressed in a cape and fur hat. Cold air blew into the house.

"Marguerite telephoned me," he said. "She asked if she could spend the night at my house, said she was worried about being alone in her home, where two people had recently died. Naturally so. We agreed I'd pick her up outside of Fieldings' store, after she attended to some matters there." He paused for a breath.

"What matters?" Katharine asked.

"She didn't say." Dr. Upton looked over her shoulder. "Detective Tanner? Why are you here? Is there a problem? Is Marguerite in trouble? An accident!"

"Not as far as we know," Bertram said. "Did you meet her outside the store?"

"She wasn't there," Dr. Upton said. "I searched the whole area, and the building was dark. No response to my doorbell ring. My first thought was she'd changed her mind and gone home. But I drove to her house, and it too seems unoccupied. I saw the light in your window and thought ..." He looked down then up. "She often turns to your brother for help." His voice trembled.

"John isn't here," Katharine said. "I don't know where Marguerite is. Perhaps a streetcar came by while she was waiting? Maybe she was cold and hopped a ride to your house. She can be impulsive."

He tapped his hat. "Why didn't I think of that? It would be something she'd do. If I drive quickly, I might catch her before she reaches my door."

"Please phone me if she's there," Katharine said. "I'm concerned about her too."

He nodded, said goodbye, and left.

Katharine closed the door. "Do you think she went to his house?"

"Your suggestion makes sense," Bertram said. "Or she impulsively continued on the streetcar to a downtown hotel."

"Did she want him to pick her up at the drug store so John wouldn't see his car on our street? Or did she go to the store for another reason? To clear out the safe?"

Katharine's eyes widened and narrowed. "That's cruel of me."

"It might be true. She'd need money for her travels. While you wait for the doctor's call, I'll walk to the store to check things out."

"Good idea."

"I'll be back in less than twenty minutes."

Bertram threw on his coat and went out to the cold and dark. As he passed the house next to hers, he realized he'd left Vincent's papers on Katharine's davenport. But he trusted her with them, and he doubted John or Marguerite would return tonight.

At the last house before the lane, he recalled his picnic lunch behind Fieldings' store and slipped into the lane to check for a light in the office window. The room was dark, but a motorcar was parked in the lane. He lit a match to see the licence plate and colour and make of the vehicle. *Blue, Packard.* He blew out the match, grabbed his notebook and pen from his jacket pocket, and blindly jotted the five digits, then heard footsteps behind him.

Crack

Something struck the back of his head. Through piercing pain, he twisted around.

Crack

A blow to his forehead.

The assailant's face blurred. Bertram collapsed to the ground.

* * *

Katharine's telephone rang. She dropped the papers on the davenport and ran to answer.

"She's not here," Dr. Upton said. "I'll wait—" His voice broke. He coughed to clear it. "I'll wait up for her awhile and leave a light on after I go to bed."

She shared his disappointment. "It's possible she thought of another errand and will arrive later."

"How many errands can one do in the middle of the night?"

"Try to sleep. We'll know more tomorrow."

"I have my doubts."

She did too. "If she does come, I want you to call me even if it wakes me up."

He paused. "Is your brother with her?"

"I don't know." *True.*

"Naturally, you're worried. I will call, but I don't hold out hope."

She silently agreed and was almost certain Marguerite was downtown or on a train to an unknown destination with or without John.

Katharine hung up and glanced at the front door. What was keeping Bertram? Had he found something of interest at the drug store? If it weren't for the children, she'd go look for him, rather than wait uselessly here. The children tied her to home, but the leash extended the length of her yard.

She put on her coat, went out to the sidewalk, and peered down the street. Any second the lamplight might illuminate his silhouette.

It didn't. Had something gone wrong?

Unlikely. Bertram was a police officer, trained to handle unexpected situations. But he was alone. She hadn't noticed him carrying a gun. The case was no longer official. He'd visited her tonight as a civilian. His decoding of Vincent's papers had convinced Bertram the store was engaged in the trade of illegal liquor. Men who operated outside the law were dangerous. Gangsters.

She shivered. Was she overreacting as much as Marguerite?

"Katharine," a voice called.

She turned toward Irene's house.

Gladys stood on the front porch. "I saw you outside and wondered ... not another death on the street, I hope?"

"Nothing like that." Katharine edged closer and noticed Gladys wore her nightgown. "John's out and I want to go somewhere, but the children ... there's a long explanation."

"Save it for later. I'll tell Irene and be over in a jiffy."

"I didn't intend—"

Gladys retreated into the house.

No sign of Bertram down the street. Why not accept her neighbour's offer? Katharine went inside, stashed Vincent's papers in a sideboard cupboard, and returned to the porch. Minutes later, Gladys crossed from her yard. She wore a coat over her nightgown.

"Take as long as you need," she said.

"Thank you for this. I owe you a favour."

Gladys smiled. "I'll make certain to collect."

Katharine headed for the city sidewalk. No Bertram all the way to the corner. The windows of the drug store were dark. She pressed the doorbell. No answer. She touched the doorknob, gave it a turn, and pushed the door. To her surprise, it opened. She looked in, her heart beating faster. Someone stood between the window to her left and the rear counter.

"Bertram?" She stepped inside.

The man who approached her was around Bertram's size but moved differently.

She stopped two feet from him. "Mr. Fielding?"

"Katharine?" He halted. "Why are you here? I thought ..."

She remembered his son had died. "I'm sorry for your loss. Marguerite told me."

Light from the street flowed in from the front and side windows, turning the counters and cabinets into shadow images in the near darkness.

"My boy." Mr. Fielding stroked his forehead. "It's been a helluva day. Pardon my language."

"I understand."

"Work seemed my sole escape from the endless platitudes and outpourings of grief. I came here to take my mind off ... and discovered we were robbed."

She looked around the store. In the dim light, nothing looked out of place.

"They stole every penny in the safe," he said. "How they broke through our door lock and safe combination is beyond me."

Katharine thought of their patients' money in Dr. Upton's less secure premises. "Did they break into our place too?"

"You should go check."

She turned toward the door, which had closed automatically behind her. "I didn't bring my handbag with the key."

"It can wait until morning. The police won't send anyone before then." He sighed. "We had quadruple our normal amount of cash in the safe due to the bank closure."

"Did they steal anything else? Medicines with street value?"

"None that I could tell from my cursory check. No vandalism. A small blessing."

"You do have insurance?"

"Yes, but a break-in feels like a violation. Nothing is safe in this world."

Including his sons.

Katharine had heard no sounds in the store since arriving. Bertram couldn't be in here. It was also peculiar to be speaking to Mr. Fielding in darkness. Since she was closer to the light switch, should she turn it on? Or did this darkness suit his sad mood?

"Who is Bertram?" Mr. Fielding asked, startling her from her thoughts.

* * *

Bertram sat on the gravel lane, massaging his throbbing head. How long had he been out? He picked up the bottle that lay beside him. It was too dark to read the label, but the shape of the bottle suggested it contained whisky. He was lucky it hadn't broken from the two blows and shattered glass all over him.

Light flashed from the street. A vehicle drove into the lane. Bertram rolled to the wall to miss being mowed down. The delivery van rumbled past him, pulled up in front of the Packard, and parked. Was the van here for a liquor pickup? He prayed the driver had missed seeing him in the headlights.

A faint light illuminated a man's head behind the Packard. The van driver must be carrying a torch or flashlight. When he passed the rear of the car, Bertram would be in his sight line. He lurched for the Packard and flattened himself against the door. Was the man his assailant, returned with a van to dispose of a victim he'd left unconscious or believed dead?

The Packard was parked beside the table and chairs, where Bertram had eaten lunch three days ago. A narrow space lay between the table and the car's nose. The Packard had been there the last time, and he'd guessed it belonged to Mr. Fielding. The office window was still dark.

Bertram duckwalked backward between the car and table. The torchlight rounded the rear of the car. He slunk behind the table, which was adjacent to the delivery door. The torch lit up the table. Bertram tensed and prepared to run the other way down the lane if the man spied him between the table legs. The light shifted toward the car. The goon had missed him.

Bertram fumbled for a chair, gripped its wobbly legs, and carried it back to the space between the table and car. The man remained in his spot and moved the torchlight in an arc to scan the whole area where Bertram had fallen. If the assailant found nothing, he might give up and leave. Bertram didn't want him to get away.

The man rotated. In seconds he'd face the street, his back to Bertram.

Bertram held the chair legs. He edged forward, scurried past the car's doors, raised the chair, and whacked the burly man on the back of the head. The man cried out and turned toward him. Bertram struck his face with the chair. The man went down with another cry.

He lay on the gravel unmoving but could revive any second. Bertram squatted and felt beneath the man's jacket for a gun. He was too large to be Mr. Fielding. Bertram found a gun, plucked it from the holster, and slid it into his coat pocket.

The man still hadn't moved. Bertram pressed his fingers to the fleshy wrist and felt a pulse. What to do before he woke up? The same thing the goon had planned for Bertram. Drag him to the van, lock him in the back. Bertram rifled through the man's pockets. No keys. They must be in the van, which he hoped wasn't locked.

Bertram stood and rubbed his head; its throb diminished to an ache. Mr. Fielding's office remained dark. Since his car was here, he had to be in the store, in the main area or storage room. Once Bertram disposed of this goon, he'd steal inside. The gun might persuade the owner of the drug store to talk.

* * *

Katharine realized that when she'd entered the drug store, she said Bertram's name aloud. "He's Detective Tanner. I think he spoke with you."

Mr. Fielding glanced back at the office door. "A few days ago."

"He's looking for Marguerite. She was here earlier tonight."

"Why? She never works evenings."

The answer hit Katharine seemingly at the same time as it did Mr. Fielding.

"God Almighty," he said. "Was Marguerite the thief? Why would she do that?"

She needed money for her new life. That explanation could wait.

"This accounts for the easy entry to the door and safe. The witch." His shoulders shook under his suit jacket. He wore no overcoat. "After all I've done for her, given her employment, permitted her to work as long she wants despite ... and she steals from me?"

Evidently, Marguerite had decided to burn her Calgary bridges before disappearing.

"Good riddance to her." Mr. Fielding shook his head. "I don't understand that woman. She's erratic."

Or she had reason to be afraid.

"I've kept you long enough," he said. "Time for me to return to my sorrowful home. Let yourself out while I get my overcoat." He headed for the office.

So he hadn't been on his way out when she arrived. His startled response to her arrival had given her the impression he was expecting someone other than her. Wouldn't he wait for that person now? Was he pretending to leave to get Katharine out of the way?

Outside, a streetcar's lights lit the cabinets filled with drugs that could cure or kill. Like Vincent and Marguerite, Mr. Fielding, a pharmacist, understood how these medicines worked. As a regular visitor to Vincent and Marguerite's home, he'd have known about Vincent's evening whisky habit and might have learned about Clarence's health condition, which Marguerite treated with a Chinese herb that reacted like opiates.

Mr. Fielding owned this store. If he wanted to run an illegal liquor business, it would make sense to do it from the Tuxedo Park property, which had the largest storage room of his four drug stores. And unlike Vincent and Marguerite, Mr. Fielding was a prominent local businessman with connections to city hall and the police. Both might close their eyes to his crimes for sufficient reward.

Had Vincent been involved in the operation? Or found out about it and blackmailed his boss as he'd blackmailed Pina about her abortion? Katharine would bet on the latter—Vincent was a petty operator. Easy to see that Mr. Fielding would seize an opportunity to get rid of him.

Was Marguerite involved in any of these activities? Or was she ignorant of them until Clarence decoded Vincent's papers and told her what he'd discovered?

Mr. Fielding strode out of the back office, a large shape in his overcoat. He was over twenty years Katharine's senior, but physically her equal or more. He stopped a few feet away. "You're still here?"

She planted her shaking legs apart. "Tell me what happened to Bertram."

"How would I know? I had no idea he was anywhere near here until you mentioned him." He brushed past her, bumping her sideways.

She steadied herself and rotated toward him. "Why are you in a rush to leave?"

He stopped at the door. "I told you I have to get home. My wife needs me at this difficult time."

His sympathy ploy touched her heart, but not enough for her to abandon Bertram. "I'm not going until you tell me the truth."

He turned around. "There's no truth to tell."

"Did you kill him, like you did Vincent and Clarence?" The thought of Bertram dead made her arms weak. She folded them to her chest.

"Why would you say that? You're as mad as she is."

Marguerite's sudden flight now seemed reasonable. Katharine stared at Mr. Fielding through the darkness. His bulk blocked the door, her only exit.

"Fine," he said. "If you must know, when I went to my car earlier, before you arrived, I found a man lurking in the lane. Was he Detective Tanner?"

"I don't know." Katharine forced her voice not to waver.

"I was carrying a bottle of whisky to drown my grief in at home and thought the man pulled a gun. Instinctively, I hit him with the bottle. He fell down. I stooped to attend him and realized he'd aimed a pen at me. A foolish response on my part. He panicked, too, and ran down the lane. That's the last I saw of him."

Panic didn't sound like Bertram. And if he had taken a roundabout route to her house, he'd have discovered she wasn't there and deduced she'd come to the drug store to look for him. He'd be here by now.

"Why did you return to the store rather than continue home?"

"This is my store," Mr. Fielding said. "I can come and go as I please. Moreover, I resent your accusation that I murdered Vincent and Clarence. To my knowledge, the police and medical experts declared both died of natural causes. Who are you to question them?"

Mr. Fielding's stores offered the choice of numerous medicines that in large doses would destroy Clarence's weakened gastrointestinal system. Easy to slip into Marguerite's home while she and Clarence were at work and douse Clarence's food. She wasn't eating, and if she had eaten and died, that would be another troublesome person out of the way, just as Mr. Fielding hadn't cared if she drank from Vincent's poisoned whisky bottle.

Mr. Fielding snorted. "My advice is, stay away from things that don't concern you and look forward to your husband's return. You're one of the lucky ones whose beloved didn't die overseas."

"Like your son?"

His body shook.

Her stab was cruel, but it was her only weapon. She took a guess. "And Vincent was a nasty blackmailer who deserved life less than your son."

Mr. Fielding moaned. "The world is unjust." He slumped against the door.

She hated herself for turning the knife blade. "And Clarence?"

"The sickly survive while the strong go to war and die."

"Did he want money from you, too, after Vincent's death?"

Mr. Fielding reeled forward. She jumped to the side so he wouldn't knock her down and struck the camera counter. He tottered back and into Bertram, who had pushed the door open. Mr. Fielding regained his balance.

"I have a gun to his back," Bertram said. "Katharine, are you all right?"

"Extremely all right." Although her hip throbbed, and she leaned into the counter to support her quivering legs. "Are you all right? Mr. Fielding says he struck you with a whisky bottle."

"Then called his man to take care of me," Bertram said. "Now, Fielding, let's pay a visit to your storage room. I'll lock you in there with the liquor until my colleagues arrive to make an arrest."

"You're bluffing," Mr. Fielding said. "The chief—"

"Prefers kickbacks to doing his job right, I know," Bertram said. "But he answers to city council. I have key pieces now to put you in jail, including a goon locked in a van who might talk in exchange for clemency."

"Can your colleagues pick up Marguerite before she leaves town?" Katharine asked.

"That will be my first phone call. I suspect she'll provide additional pieces of information for a couple of murder charges."

"Who'll believe a thief and liar?" Mr. Fielding spat on the floor.

Bertram prodded him with the gun. "Katharine, I can take it from here. You're free to go home."

She longed to hug her children but wanted to see this through. "I'll stay."

"Are you sure?"

She pulled away from the counter and steadied her legs. "I wouldn't miss it."

Chapter Twenty-One
November 11, 1918

Katharine tucked the children into bed, gave them extra hugs, and kissed them goodnight.

"The party concert was fun," Lillian said. "Can we do it again?"

"Whenever you want."

"I liked playing the drums best," Henry called from his bed across the room.

"Me too," Katharine said.

The three of them had taken turns on the piano, pots and pans, and banjo, and there had been more laughter than tuneful harmonies.

The children's celebration complete, Katharine strode down the hall to prepare for the adults' arrival. She partly regretted not marking the historic occasion at today's spontaneous downtown parade, but, as Dr. Upton had said, while the Great War was over, the influenza continued its killing spree. He wouldn't attend her celebration tonight, purportedly to limit his social contact. She suspected his real reason was to avoid John and Marguerite, who were now sharing Marguerite's home.

The circular sitting arrangement in the living room looked perfect for a friendly gathering. She and Henry had moved the sewing machine to John's former bedroom to make space for the davenport along its vacated wall. The rocker and armchair now backed against the fireplace, the coffee table between them and the davenport, and two kitchen chairs stood against the sideboard. She'd sit on the piano stool and John would use the third kitchen chair, beside her, when he wasn't standing to play the saxophone. He'd promised to come, with or without Marguerite.

The doorbell rang. Katharine went to greet her first guests. Gladys and Irene both wore masks. Katharine put hers on to respect her own rule for the party. Influenza cases in Calgary were decreasing, but they shouldn't be complacent, and today's mass gatherings could spur a rise in numbers.

"I'm glad your friend could mind your children." Katharine directed them to the davenport. "Everyone agreed to no drinks or food, but I've put glasses of water on the coffee table."

Pina arrived next. She took a mask from the basket on the telephone table.

"How was the parade?" Katharine asked.

"Swell. Despite the news only arriving this morning, people packed the sidewalks. I couldn't hear for horns and cheering."

"That makes me glad I stayed home."

"Do you still want me tomorrow for child-minding?"

Katharine nodded at their code for *rendezvous in Pina's apartment.* During the past two weeks, Katharine and Bertram had met there thrice. Henry and Lillian adored playing games and making up stories with Pina, who slept in John's bedroom those nights. Katharine always left the apartment by 4:00 a.m. so the children wouldn't question her absence in the mornings. Sometimes she hated the secrecy and stealing home through the dark—other times she found it exciting despite her guilt at being unfaithful to Eddie. Pina's comment that he'd probably bedded women in Europe was irrelevant. That wasn't the marriage they'd had or the one Katharine wanted for the future.

She told Pina to choose a chair.

"After my day outside, I could use some warmth from the fireplace." Pina settled on the rocker and chatted with Gladys and Irene about the war, the flu, and the drug store's illegal liquor operation.

"Marguerite told me the police captured her at the Palliser Hotel," Irene said. "Is that true?"

"It was the train station," Pina said, "after she'd spent the night at the less majestic Alberta Hotel."

The police had apprehended Marguerite and John early on the Friday morning as they boarded a train to Toronto. They threw

Marguerite in jail for theft, questioned her intensely for a week, and ultimately agreed to drop the theft charges if she'd talk. In the end, she convinced the police she'd been unaware of the store's illegal activities until Clarence decoded Vincent's papers and discovered Mr. Fielding's name repeatedly in the double-coded column of liquor buyers. Clarence had confronted him and offered to remain silent if Mr. Fielding let Marguerite work as long as her condition allowed.

"It cost Clarence his life," Pina said to Gladys and Irene.

When he and Marguerite first became aware of the store's illegal activities, they still believed Vincent had died a natural death. Marguerite gradually became uncertain. After she discovered Bertram in her house and talked to the chief, she phoned Mr. Fielding from the drug store. He was at home mourning the loss of his son. Mr. Fielding told her not to worry, that the chief was in his pocket. As long as she played her role as the ignorant, grieving widow, she'd escape Vincent's and Clarence's fates. He hadn't used those precise words, but she interpreted his meaning and grew desperate to leave Calgary and go where Mr. Fielding wouldn't find her. If Toronto didn't feel far enough, she'd head for the United States.

"Marguerite also told me she plans to apply to pharmaceutical college," Irene said.

Katharine rested a hand on the sideboard. She admired Marguerite for overcoming her fears of academic learning and embracing the difficulties of combining studies with parenting. "That's right, but she first has to apprentice two more years."

"John will go with her, help look after the child, and contribute income from music jobs," Pina said. "By then, the clubs will be booming. This flu can't last forever."

"We said that about the war," Irene noted.

Gladys patted her hand. "Even our never-ending war ended today. Do you think we've learned from that experience?"

The front door clicked.

John burst in carrying his saxophone case. Marguerite followed despite her threat to boycott the event if Bertram attended. She blamed him for her week in jail. Understandable, but Katharine would choose him over her any day.

"I'm glad you came," Katharine told Marguerite, and meant it. "This is a masked gathering."

Marguerite plucked one from the basket. The drug store had closed for the week following Mr. Fielding's arrest and reopened after Marguerite was released from jail and Mr. Fielding hired a manager. The fact he'd done that from his jail cell suggested he still worked his connections from prison. Mr. Fielding had retained Calgary's best defence lawyer. The police were building a solid case regarding the trade of illegal whisky but slim cases for murder, mainly thanks to the chief's orders not to investigate and to destroy the prime evidence—the bottle of whisky.

Katharine and Bertram agreed they wouldn't mind if Mr. Fielding eluded the hangman. The war that had taken his son had inflicted a greater punishment.

Pina, Gladys, and Irene welcomed Marguerite and John into the living room. John walked to the music stand in the far corner. He was steadier on his leg these days and didn't complain of chafing or pain. Katharine sometimes forgot which leg was artificial. Dr. Upton predicted that post war, medical researchers would produce improved prostheses to help the war's thousands of amputees.

Marguerite took the armchair. Her condition was still too early to show. John had told Katharine that, while he'd been attracted to Marguerite from the start, their relations began after her husband's death and Vincent was the child's father.

Gladys looked at the vacant chairs in front of the sideboard. "Who's left to arrive?"

"Bertram, the detective," Katharine said.

Marguerite sniffed. "He was promoted to chief after harassing me."

Katharine was sure that Bertram's decision to remain on the Calgary police force was right for him. "He's bringing Julia, the receptionist at police headquarters."

"Are they dating?" Gladys asked.

"Not that I know." Katharine caught Pina's glance.

Bertram was helping Julia get through the stress of her father's dismissal from the police force and the charges laid against him, as well as her discovery of his criminal character. Bertram had encouraged her to continue on the job and did his best to squash colleagues' criticisms and jokes about the former chief. He thought she might benefit from this evening away from her family and the case. Had he purposely planned to arrive just in time for the music to protect Julia from the inevitable questions?

Katharine stood in front of the sideboard and kitchen chairs. She clapped her hands until the room was silent. "Bertram and Julia have spent the past two-and-a-half weeks at work hearing about nothing but bootleg whisky and murder. Let's give them a holiday and wrap up our talk about this before they arrive."

"I'm tired of hearing about them too." Marguerite scowled.

"Here's to moving forward to cheerier things." Gladys raised her glass of water. "Since you're up there, Katharine, how about a speech?"

"That was my speech," Katharine said, prompting a ripple of polite laughs. She scanned her circle of family and friends. "Except, I want to put this war behind me but remember it so there will be no more wars, and our sons won't be called to fight when they're grown to young men."

The others muttered agreements.

Katharine's throat clammed shut. She pictured Henry in his twenties dressed in a soldier's uniform and carrying a real gun, not a child's toy.

"Ready for music?" John said.

She blinked the image away. "You start. I'll wait in the hall for Bertram."

"John, play for them the song you wrote," Marguerite said.

He raised his hands in protest. "It's not ready for the public."

Marguerite and the others urged him on. The doorbell rang. Katharine ushered in Bertram and Julia.

He apologized for their late arrival. "I was playing catch with Julia's boys and lost track of time."

"Could I use your bathroom?" Julia asked. "It was a long streetcar ride, with the crowds."

Katharine directed her to the end of the hall. Evidently, they'd come from Julia's home in southwest Calgary. To her surprise, Katharine wasn't bothered by Bertram's spending time with Julia, an attractive widow.

He thanked her for inviting Julia. "She needs people on her side."

"She's fortunate to have you."

"It's the right thing."

She mentally finished his sentence: *Nellie would want me to do this.* He mentioned his late wife a little too frequently for Katharine's taste. It made her think he wasn't ready to move forward with her. She also found herself annoyed with his tendency to reason through everything. *What are the pros and cons of our rendezvous arrangement?*

Irrational as it was, she preferred Eddie's instinct to leap into situations, including the misadventure of war. She wanted to give Eddie a chance. Not the Eddie before the war, but the Eddie changed and grown by the profound experience. She loved her nights with Bertram but suspected they were meant to be a bridge to the right person for each of them.

Julia returned from the bathroom as John's saxophone melody drew to a close. "That's a beautiful song," she said. "It makes me want to cry."

All the other pairs of eyes in the living room were damp.

"That's enough mellow," John said. "Katharine, how about a rousing 'Alexander's Ragtime Band'?"

"What fun," Pina said. "I might get up and dance."

Katharine sat on the piano stool and found the sheet music for the song she'd forever associate with the evening of Vincent's death; that night, John had been on the sax, Henry on the pots and pans, and

Lillian on the banjo, before Clarence rang their doorbell.

"One, two, three," John began.

Katharine touched the keys and remembered Vincent and Clarence, whose lives had been cut short. She thought of the millions lost or maimed in the Great War and the millions more who would die from this vicious influenza.

Behind her, Pina's dance steps tapped the living room floor while others sang along, and John blasted his saxophone. Katharine played for her family and friends. *Let them find joy where they can.* She played for herself in this moment and for a future of boundless possibilities.

The End

Selected Bibliography

Cameron, Donald M., Editor-in-Chief. *The History of Pharmacy in Alberta: the First One Hundred Years (from leeches to lasers)*. Edmonton: The Alberta Pharmaceutical Association, 1993.

Davis, Kenneth C. *More Deadly Than War: The Hidden History of the Spanish Flu and the First World War*. New York: Henry Holt and Company, 2018.

Eaton, Winnifred AKA Otono Watanna. *Cattle*. Halifax & Toronto: Invisible Publishing, 2023. First published Toronto: Musson, 1923.

Foran, Max and Foran, Heather MacEwan. *Calgary: Canada's Frontier*. Calgary: Windsor Publications (Canada) Ltd, 1982.

Montgomery, L. M. *Rilla of Ingleside*. New York: Aladdin (Simon & Shuster), 2015. First published 1921.

Paterson, Isabel. *The Shadow Riders*. New York: John Lane Company, 1916.

Sheffield, Gary. *A Short History of the First World War*. London: One World Publications, 2014.

Stead, Robert J.C. *The Cow Puncher*. Toronto: Musson, 1918.

Susan Calder books also published by BWL Publishing Inc.
A Deadly Fall
Ten Days in Summer
To Catch a Fox
Winter's Rage
Spring Into Danger

Susan Calder is a Calgary writer who grew up in Montreal. *A Killer Whisky* is her sixth published book and her first historical mystery novel. Susan's short stories and poems have won contests and appeared in numerous magazines and anthologies. She is a member of the Alexandra Writers' Centre Society, Crime Writers of Canada, Sisters in Crime, and the Writers' Guild of Alberta. Her non-writing passions include travel, biking, and hiking in the beautiful mountains near Calgary.

Website: www.susancalder.com
Facebook: Susan Calder Author
X: @SusanCalder20
BWL Author Page: Calder, Susan - BWL Publishing Inc. (bookswelove.net)